Hooves & Horns

The Enchanted Alehouse, Volume 2

Gemma Perfect

Published by PERFECT INK PUBLISHING, 2025.

PERFECT INK PUBLISHING

PERFECT INK PUBLISHING
www.gemmaperfect.com

Copyright © Gemma Perfect 2025

The right of Gemma Perfect to be identified as the author of this work has been asserted in accordance with Copyright, Designs and Patents Act 1998

All rights reserved. No part of this publication may be reproduced, stored in or transmitted into any retrieval system, in any from, or by any means without the prior written permission of the author.

This is a work of fiction. Names, characters, businesses, places, events and incidents are either the product of the author's imagination or used in a fictitious manner. Any resemblance to actual persons, living or dead, or actual events is purely coincidental.

The authorised representative in the EEA is NH, 111 Riverchapel View, Courtown, Wexford, Y25 HF60

HOOVES & HORNS

Thank you for so much kindness & support!

gemma x

Chapter 1

The enchanted alehouse seems to shift and then settle, like an old man trying to find a comfy position in bed so he can sleep soundly through the night.

If it could speak, it would have let out a contented sigh.

The fire burns a little brighter, and Graily's room magically empties – she won't be needing it for a while, and the alehouse quietly makes a few other changes, while the guardians sleep soundly in their beds. Or in their swamp.

The alehouse and its inhabitants have settled into a gentle, domestic routine in the few days since Graily was magicked away by Professor Parfait.

They still haven't tackled the old building next door; it seems like too big a job, but they while their days away quite happily, making grand plans for the place, and eating too much magical food.

Ettie is always up earliest, and today is no exception. She pads down to the den to curl up in front of the fire and read. She magics up a cup of tea to sip on and tucks a blanket all around her. She smiles.

When she left the magical academy. Well, when she was thrown out of the magical academy, she thought she'd never be happy again, but she's happier than ever. She feels comfortable in her own skin, and with her abilities. She smiles over at her certificate – the proof that she finally passed her exams. She's propped it up on one of the bookshelves, next to Sticks' new certificates – one for his healing and one to show he's allowed to peddle magical creatures. His certificates will go in the shop once it's ready.

'Morning,' Dayne says, her voice bright as usual. 'Any plans for today?'

'Not a one,' Ettie says, and they both grin.

'I'm enjoying the peace,' Dayne says, sitting down on her pixie-sized chair, and tucking her feet under her.

'We need it. The fires, the foxes...' Ettie trails off when she sees the hurt on Dayne's face. She sends some magic her way, just a small nudge of peace, happiness, hope.

Losing her childhood home in a deliberately set fire was heart breaking for Dayne, her father and her brothers. Losing the place her mum had lived was harsh, and Ettie knows it will sting for a long time. She sends another small dose of magic across the room to Dayne.

'Tea?' Ettie asks, and Dayne nods.

Tea in hand, she sighs.

'I didn't think I'd ever be happy after my mum died. I hated losing her. I hated what my dad was doing...'

'But your instinct to help others never faltered,' Ettie reminds her.

Dayne nods. 'I've always been a fixer. It makes me happy to make other people happy.'

'That's rare,' Ettie says.

Dayne shrugs and sips more tea.

'Hey – you look different.'

Ettie grins and smooths down her hair.

'Wait! Your ears!'

Ettie giggles. 'I'd been keeping them as a reminder of my failure.'

Dayne makes a sympathetic face.

'But now I'm a fully qualified witch. Now that I'm proper, I magicked them away.'

Dayne shrugs. 'I liked them.'

'So did I,' Ettie says, 'but I like losing what they stood for.'

'Me too. Though I always just thought they were cute.'

'Hungry?' Ettie asks her, changing the subject.

Dayne grins. 'Always.'

Ettie magics up some croissants and some crispy bacon.

Dayne takes a big bite of the bacon.

'Delicious.'

Ettie grins. Graily's food was divine, and the smell of it cooking or baking always seemed to make it taste better, but her magic food is pretty tasty too.

'I wonder how she's getting on,' Dayne says, and Ettie smiles that they were both thinking about Graily at the same time.

'I was just thinking about her too. About how good everything smelled when she was making it.'

Dayne nods appreciatively.

'I might try to cook or bake something this week,' Ettie says. 'I've got time to practice. And if it goes wrong, I can just magic up something else.'

'Good idea,' Dayne says. 'I want to get cracking on the new pet shop. Sticks is dragging his feet and I don't know why.'

Ettie cocks her head, not sure why either.

'I think he wants to do it and get it done, but it's a big job I suppose.'

'Not once we get going,' Dayne says. 'I'm a whizz with my tools.'

Her face falls, but Ettie holds up her hand.

'I forgot! I need to make you your own tools. Pixie sized everything.' She shrugs. 'I should really make everything super sized for Sticks too.'

'Who are you calling super sized?' Sticks asks, walking into the room, scratching his belly, his green skin tinged ever so slightly with mud.

'Did you shower?' Dayne asks him, raising an eyebrow.

'Of course,' he says, but he turns around and leaves the room.

The two girls giggle, and head through to the kitchen to wait for Sticks to get showered and dressed.

Chapter 2

Sticks is bashful when he joins them.

'I showered this time,' he says, hands up.

'Why not the first time?' Dayne asks. 'I know a smelly boy when I see one.'

Sticks readjusts his top. 'I'm all damp now,' he complains.

'Aren't you damp when you get dressed after being in your swamp?' Ettie asks him, wrinkling her nose. One time she's been in Sticks' swamp and one time was enough. More than enough.

'If it wasn't for you moany women who want everybody to be clean,' he says, taking a seat on the bench and resting his elbows on the table. 'I'd sleep in my swamp. Then I'd have a wee nap at the side of the river while the mud dried.'

'A wee nap? After you wake up?' Dayne's eyes are wide. She's enjoying some lie-ins since she moved to the alehouse, but she's always been an early riser.

When her mum was alive, she woke up to help her with the chores. With eight of them in the tree house there was always something to do. When her mum was ill, she woke early because she wanted to spend as much time with her as she possibly could. And, of course, it wasn't long enough. After her mum passed away, she was looking after herself, her dad, her five brothers, working up at the posh houses to make money to give to the people that her family were menacing for money.

She blows out her cheeks. No wonder she's exhausted.

'So you'd dry in the sun, baking all the mud right in?' Dayne asks, and this time she's the one wrinkling her nose.

'Don't knock it until you've tried it,' Sticks says, rubbing his hands together, and then smoothing the skin on his arm. 'It's why my skin's so baby soft. Now stop whingeing and tell me what's for breakfast.'

Ettie and Dayne smile at each other and then at him; they can't be mad at him for long. This is the early stage of their friendship, and while they're all being themselves, they're not at the point where they want to get too critical with each other. Not quite.

Ettie holds up a hand, waggling her fingers and her eyebrows at the same time. 'What's your pleasure, fine Sir?'

Sticks grins. 'Custard tap,' he whispers and Ettie shakes her head. Dayne breaks into peals of giggles.

'Are you going to let that go?' Ettie asks him. She cannot think of anything more ridiculous than a custard tap.

'Why would I?' Sticks shrugs. 'I cannot think of anything more delightful than a custard tap. It's custard. On tap.'

'It would be easy to do,' Dayne says, cocking her head. 'With your magic and my mechanics...'

Ettie grins. 'Let's get some breakfast in us first, then we need to look at the shop. It won't get done by itself... though it could get done by magic.'

'No!' Sticks holds up a meaty hand. 'No magic. Just good old fashioned hard work.'

'Seconded!' Dayne says. 'I cannot wait. Ettie's going to make me tools. Pixie sized.'

'And I was talking about making super-sized ones for you,' Ettie says. 'I saw that you broke a few of the garden tools too.'

Sticks looks bashful. 'I'm not as delicate as I could be, I suppose.'

'We don't care. But if you have ogre sized stuff, they'll be sturdier, right?'

He shrugs, but then nods.

'So is the plan to start the shop today?'

'Might as well,' Dayne says, while Ettie conjures up some croissants, toast and piping hot tea.

'I suppose we don't have anything else to do,' Sticks says. 'Hey, do you think we'll hear anything from Graily. I'd love to know how she's getting on.'

'Me too,' Dayne says, eyes shining. 'I bet she's having the best time.'

'I bet she is too,' Ettie says, hoping they're right, and that Graily's okay. She knows it was the right thing for her to go; she thought so, and then the magic scroll confirmed it. She knows they all have the freedom to leave if they want to, but why would they?

But for Graily? She'd been a prisoner for so long, forced to work long hours, and sleep in a tiny cubby hole that was so small she couldn't even stand up. She needed freedom, choice and also, Ettie thinks, to prove herself. Despite making the best damn food she'd ever tasted, Graily felt like something was missing, felt like she could do better, and who were any of them to hold her back or stop her fulfilling her potential and following her dreams?

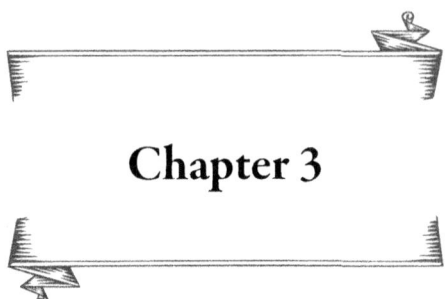

Chapter 3

They are smiling, thinking about their friend Graily, when there's a tap on the window.

Sticks grins; it's a red-crested, bobble headed pigeon.

He opens the window and holds out a hand.

The pigeon struts into the room, head bobbing almost comically.

Ettie and Dayne coo over him, but the pigeon drops a small rolled up piece of parchment, and then flies out of the window.

'Not very friendly, was he?' Ettie says, picking up the little scroll.

'They are too professional to be friendly,' Sticks says. 'Bobble heads pride themselves on getting the job done, one hundred percent accuracy, and faster than you'd ever believe. Under promise and over deliver, is their motto.'

'Really?' The girls say at the same time, both trying to hold in their giggles; Sticks looks so serious.

'Really. Takes a lot of training to join the bobble head squad.'

'The bobble head squad?' Dayne asks, her voice dangerously squeaky.

Ettie smothers a snort of laughter with a cough.

'Yeah.' Sticks nods his head, sagely. 'They train for years. They have to be fast. Good sense of direction. If their bobble heads are too bobbly – and they can't always help it – they get dizzy and fall down.'

'Dizzy?' Ettie asks, because this time it's Dayne who's covering her giggles with a cough.

'Yeah, dizzy. And once they're down, their heads are too heavy for them to get back up.'

'What? So they never get back up?'

'Not without help. Bobble heads sleep standing up. Lying down could be catastrophic.'

'Catastrophic!'

This time the two girls can't hide their giggles and Sticks rolls his eyes. 'Nothing funny about bobble heads, let me tell you, if you'd ever been to their training camp, you'd know it.'

The two of them bite down on their lips, so they don't let out any further giggles.

Animals and magical creatures are serious business for Sticks, and they don't want to offend him.

'Now stop messing and open the scroll,' Sticks says, folding his arms across his chest, a frown on his face. An indignant croak from Dumpling, squashed in his pocket, has him quickly taking the frog out of his shirt pocket and tucking him in his trouser pocket instead. 'Sorry buddy,' he says, folding his arms once again.

'Sorry, Sticks,' Ettie says, un-scrolling the parchment. She'd almost forgotten why the bobble-headed pigeon was there in the first place.

Her eyes scan ahead to the bottom of the letter.

'It's from Graily!' she says, and Dayne squeals and Sticks claps his hands, animosity forgotten.

'To my dearest friends,' Ettie reads aloud, touching her hand to her heart. 'France is wonderful. I think you'd like it.'

'We should go one day,' Dayne says, and Ettie and Sticks nod their agreement. Ettie isn't sure she ever wants to leave the alehouse, not really, but Sticks would happily go anywhere. Though he wouldn't take Dumpling; he knows the French are partial to frogs as a delicacy instead of as a pet.

'The first day at the cookery school, Professor Parfait told us all that cooking is magic, and I agree with him. Ingredients you would eat on their own might taste disgusting, but when you cook with them or bake them, they turn into something delicious. I really like it here, and I'm so glad you all helped me take this opportunity. And my reading and writing have come on leaps and bounds. I miss you all. Graily.'

Dayne claps her hands. 'I love that. She sounds so happy.'

'No mention of Smudge,' Ettie says, eyebrows raised. 'I bet she's off somewhere causing trouble. Thinking she's all chic.'

Dayne giggles. 'I think a talking ladybug is chic, in any country.'

Ettie shrugs and Sticks scratches his head. 'I'm happy if she's happy. Now what shall we do first? Pet shop or custard tap?'

Ettie groans and throws a croissant at him.

He laughs, catching it, and stuffing it in his mouth, crumbs everywhere.

'Shop.' Dayne stands up and shakes out her wings. 'When I came downstairs this morning, I could smell your animals,' she says, pointing a finger at Sticks. 'They're very welcome here. But very smelly too.'

Sticks tries to look offended but then he lets out a deep rumble of a laugh.

'Oh, I can't even say it isn't true. Those bog headed beetle bugs absolutely stink. Bet they're a delicacy somewhere though.'

They are laughing as they head out to the dilapidated building next door.

Chapter 4

The three of them stand on the road, outside the old building that is going to be the new home of Hooves and Horns.

Ettie sighs deeply. 'I could do the whole thing in about ten minutes,' she says, cracking the knuckles on both hands.

Dayne tuts. 'And where's the fun in that?' she asks, hands on her hips, beautiful wings fluttering.

Sticks grins. 'We've got to get our hands dirty, Ettie,' he says.

'Do we though? Really?'

Sticks and Dayne laugh and lead the way along the stone path to the front door.

'You should go first,' Dayne says to Sticks. 'It's your shop.'

He grins, scratches his belly and pushes the door open. It creaks inwards, unlocked. He coughs; the place is dusty and smells of mould.

Dayne flies past him, flitting all the way to the roof, which has several holes in it.

'It's huge,' she says, coughing as some dust catches the back of her throat. She swoops down and hovers between Ettie and Sticks.

Ettie wrinkles her nose and holds out her hands.

'Seriously!' she says, wiggling her fingers, sparks of magic shooting out.

Sticks shakes his head. 'We have to build it, fix it, put our blood, sweat and tears into it.'

Ettie sighs and rolls her eyes.

'Okay, but at least let me clear the dust, fix the roof and get some light in here. We can't fix what we can't see.'

'Fine,' Sticks says, folding his meaty arms across his enormous chest.

Within minutes the space is clear of dust, debris and too many spider webs to count. The roof is fixed, and there are bright lanterns hung everywhere, helping them to see how big the space really is.

Dayne whistles. 'It's enormous. Five times as big as the old shop.'

Sticks nods, his expression sad, like it always is whenever he remembers Hooves and Horns burning down because of Philomena the fox.

'That place was perfect,' he grumbles, kicking at the wall.

'Careful,' Ettie says. 'The whole place might fall down.'

Dayne laughs. 'It's not that bad. We need stone, wood...' she trails off, because looking around there really is so much to do. The building is huge, but empty. They need to make rooms, and they need to make windows, and they'll need an awful lot of help to do it.

'We need a crew,' Sticks says, scratching his chin. 'I wonder what those orcs are doing.' He looks at Dayne. 'You know the ones your dad had to help us.'

Dayne shakes her head. 'They've gone, back over the sea,' she says.

'I'm glad,' Ettie says. 'They were wild.'

'Orcs are,' Sticks says, shrugging. 'Okay, a crew...?'

'My dad might know some other people who could help,' Dayne says, chewing on her lip, her wings fluttering even though she's still.

'Or magic,' Ettie says, offering for a final time. She can understand why he wants to build it with his own hands, to put in the work, and to see it all come together, but she's so used to using magic to make her life easier, just looking at how much needs to be done here is making her stressed.

'I know some giants,' Dayne says, thinking of Derek and the other giants who live in the retirement village.

'Giants might be too big,' Sticks says, scratching his belly. The thought of all this work is making him hungry, and there's a tiny bit of him that wishes he wasn't so proud, that he'd just accepted Ettie's offer of magical help.

Chapter 5

'Does it need an upstairs?' Dayne asks, flying up to the roof again.

'No, all on one level is easier,' Sticks says, giving his knees a little rub. 'I'm older than I used to be.'

'And you need the space outside too?' Dayne asks, and Sticks nods.

The three of them head out to the back of the building, and it's lovely and grassy with loads of trees to provide cover. The river runs through it too.

'They'll love this,' Sticks says, wiping a stray tear and then grinning bashfully.

Ettie hugs him, and Dayne lands on his shoulder.

'It was really awful what happened to your shop. I'm so glad Amma and Blast got all the animals out. This will be great for them, Sticks. Look at this.'

She gestures at the outside space, taking in the beauty of it.

'It is good,' he says. 'Better than good. Shall we have a sit down and a cuppa while we think about what to do?'

Ettie nods and conjures up a picnic rug for them, and some tea, pasties, sandwiches and cakes.

She really could complete the whole project by the end of the morning, but non magical people love to get their hands dirty. She can see that Dayne is desperate to help out.

'I can't do the heavy lifting,' Dayne says, picking up a cake that's twice the size of her, and then licking the icing off the top. 'But I'm really quick with painting, and I've got an eye for design.'

'I know what I need,' Sticks says. 'Everything I had before, but bigger, and better, and...' He trails off again, and Ettie clocks it. He's up to something, but she can't figure out what it might be.

'My dad will know suppliers,' Dayne says. 'He knows everyone.'

'Great,' Sticks says, refilling his mug with tea. 'I've got a good feeling. With the shop and my swamp, and all my animals, this will be better than before.'

'And with Amma still helping and Lox locked up, you don't have to worry about anything,' Ettie says, glad that the King listened to them, and arrested Philomena, the other foxes, the sheriff and Lox.

'With friends like that, eh?' Sticks says, picking up a pasty and taking a huge bite.

'You have friends like us, now,' Dayne says, grinning. 'And I have friends like you – friends who won't desert me because they're scared of my dad.'

'I am a little bit scared of your dad,' Ettie says, taking a sip of tea.

Dayne laughs. 'I know. How can someone so small be so deadly, right?'

'Exactly,' Ettie and Sticks say at the same time.

They all laugh.

'But I think getting him a job with the King was a genius move,' Dayne says. 'He'll have to stay on the straight and narrow and so will my brothers.'

'You think they'll find it easy?'

Dayne cocks her head, a thoughtful expression on her face.

'I don't know that it'll be easy... but I think they can do it. I've told them all to come here on Sunday, if that's okay?'

'Of course it is,' Ettie says.

'Absolutely,' Sticks says. 'I can pick his brains about who to use to supply the stuff I need for the shop.'

'I can also keep an eye on him and my brothers,' Dayne says. 'I don't think they'd risk annoying the King, especially now they've all got a job and somewhere to live.'

'What will your dad do with the barber shop?' Ettie asks.

'He's sold it,' Dayne says. 'To one of the other pixies. One that actually likes to cut hair.'

Ettie conjures up another pot of tea and pours them all a cup.

'I like it when everything works out,' Ettie says, sipping her tea. 'You know, Graily is off in France. Smudge is happy being chic. Your dad and brothers have new jobs and a new home. And we have this place,' she says, gesturing with her hand.

Dayne finishes her tea and sighs. 'If it's an alehouse, or was an alehouse, does that mean we might get customers?'

Ettie sits up, tiny sandwich paused halfway to her mouth.

'I never thought of that, but of course, the scrolls said something about feeding people and fixing people and healing people... that will be strange, after it just being the three of us.'

'It might be fun?' Dayne says, although it comes out as a question.

The three of them are quiet, looking at each other. It feels exciting that they might get customers at the alehouse, but also scary.

Chapter 6

Sticks rubs his belly, and lets out a massive burp, before scratching his chin, finding a bit of jam and licking his fingers.

'Let's go inside,' he says. 'We can't do anything until we see Bugsy. Until then, I might like a snooze in front of the fire.'

'He's not coming until Sunday,' Dayne says. 'You can't just snooze until then.'

'I could,' Sticks says, and then he grins at Ettie. 'Or we could go to the bar room, figure out the best place to put this custard tap...'

'You're not going to be happy until you get it are you?'

Sticks sighs. 'I am happy. I never thought I'd be happy again after the shop burnt down. When I thought all the animals were dead.' He swallows down a sob. 'But I am happy. The custard tap would just be the icing on the cake.'

'Or the custard on the tart,' Dayne adds with a giggle.

Sticks points at her, a massive grin on his face.

Ettie smiles at Sticks. How can she deny him something that is so easy for her to do and would mean so much to him? And if he's got his custard tap, then he'll stop nagging.

'Come on, then.'

The three of them traipse through to the bar room and then pause.

'The alehouse is making changes,' Dayne says, and she's right.

The bar room was pretty nondescript when they all arrived at the alehouse. Big, with a rugged flagstone floor, candles in sconces dotted along the walls. The tables were long and solid, with benches and some chairs. And the actual bar, with room behind it for whoever was serving the customers.

But today, it's changed. There are windows for a start, three of them, arched in shape and letting the light stream in through them. And there's a door.

Sticks opens it, steps outside, then comes back in.

'Definitely gearing up for customers,' he says. 'I wonder if people might like my custard tap. I'm not sure I want to share it.'

Ettie bites her lip.

'If we get any customers, we just won't tell them it's here.'

Sticks grins and points at her.

'I like it.'

The long, rectangular tables have vanished and, in their place, are round tables made of solid wood – not as bashed up with age and use as the long tables were. Each table has six chairs dotted around it. There are flowers in the centre of each table, as decoration, and over the fireplace there's a shelf full of pretty ornaments. Around the edges of the room are little booths, with chunky tables and heavy benches.

'This is weird,' Ettie says, trailing a finger along the table, and then lifting the flowers to smell them. 'It certainly looks like the alehouse is getting ready for customers.'

Sticks lifts up a mug from behind the bar. 'There are new mugs too.'

'How many?' Dayne asks, flying over to take a look.

'Fifty,' he counts.

'Fifty,' Ettie repeats, then she shrugs. 'I guess it is an alehouse. It makes sense that we might have customers. Really, it's an alehouse with rooms, which means we could even get guests who want to stay the night... or longer.'

'That will be weird,' Dayne says, wrinkling her tiny little nose.

Ettie nods. 'I mean, we've already had your animals.' She nods at Sticks. 'But that didn't feel scary because they're yours. And your family.' She nods at Dayne. 'That felt familiar too.'

'I wonder who it'll be,' Dayne says, eyes shining. 'I love meeting new people.'

Ettie sucks on her teeth. She really doesn't like meeting new people. It always makes her feel uncomfortable, less than. She sighs; she'll just have to get over her insecurities and be welcoming.

'Do we have to look after them? The customers? The guests?' Sticks asks.

'I suppose so,' Dayne says, rubbing her hands together.

'We'll make them welcome,' Ettie says, nodding.

The three of them stand, just looking at the room, at the changes the alehouse has made, and then they turn together, and run up the stairs.

Graily's room is empty, Sticks' room still has his healing stuff in it, even though he sleeps in the swamp, Ettie and Dayne use their rooms to sleep in, and spend time in, but now the small corridor that led to each of those rooms has grown longer.

Beyond the last door it stretches down, and there are extra doors, one on each side. Sticks throws one open. Inside are two beds, two wardrobes, two chests of drawers and two little tables next to the beds.

Ettie blows out her cheeks.

'We're definitely expecting guests.'

'And it seems like the alehouse knows,' Dayne says, eyes shining. 'It's so clever.'

'So clever,' Ettie repeats, her stomach churning.

Her world was very small when she lived at the magical academy. She had her best friend Liss, and others who would speak to her, or chat about mundane things, but she didn't have friends. She was older than most of them, after failing her exams so many times, for a start, but she also found making friends hard. She never knew how to start a conversation, what to say without sounding or looking silly, so most of the time she said nothing at all.

Being thrown out of the academy forced her to be more sociable than she ever had been. She went from the familiar and comfortable to living with strangers, and building a new life.

She's so happy that Sticks and Dayne are at the alehouse with her, but after the trouble with the sheriff, and the fires, and the orcs, and the drama, she really was hoping for a quiet time. Time to adjust to her new home, her new surroundings, her new friends.

She smiles and touches the wall. She should have known that the alehouse would have other plans.

She looks at Sticks. He's shifting from side to side, and she just knows he's worrying about his custard tap.

'I'll have it done by the end of the day,' she says, and Sticks punches a fist into the air, and Dayne claps her hands.

Chapter 7

'So we just wait?' Dayne asks, flying behind Ettie, heading through to the kitchen. 'For customers or guests. They could come any minute.'

'Or they could come next week,' Sticks says, lifting his arms.

'I think we get on with our days,' Ettie says. 'We'll know soon enough if anyone turns up. In the meantime, we'll just go about our business.'

'I want to visit all the people I used to take money to,' Dayne says. 'I want them to know that they're safe, and that my dad won't hurt them anymore. I also want to keep helping them.'

'Keep helping them?' Sticks asks, moving Dumpling back to his shirt pocket. 'What else did you do other than give them money?'

Dayne cocks her head, a slight blush covering her freckly little cheeks.

'I used to fix things for them. So Derek, one of the giants who lives up at the Dewberries, he had a terrible gambling problem, and he was a bit of a hoarder. Stuff would be broken and need fixing, things would be messy and need cleaning, so I would help.'

'That's amazing, Dayne. You didn't need to do that,' Ettie says, conjuring up a teapot full of tea.

'I like helping. And fixing. And I'm good at it. I'm handy, and my pixie dust always helps smooth the way.'

'I never understood pixie dust,' Sticks says, pouring tea for all of them.

'You never understood it?' Dayne asks, sipping her tea and looking at Ettie with her eyebrows raised. 'How about a little biscuit to dunk?'

Ettie obliges and Dayne grins, dipping a chocolatey biscuit into her tea, and then sucking the melted chocolate off.

'Yeah, like it's magic,' Sticks says, eating a biscuit and spitting out some crumbs as he talks. 'But it's not magic.'

Dayne giggles. 'It's pixie magic.' She gestures at Ettie. 'I can't do what you do. Conjure anything up, but pixie dust adds a little something that only pixies have.'

Sticks still looks confused. And covered in chocolate.

'So Ettie's magic – and the magic your mum did would have a specific outcome – conjure up biscuits, put out a fire, start a fire, make someone able to read. Whatever.'

'Right...' Sticks says, another biscuit in hand.

'But pixie dust can't do anything on its own. It's special but not particularly powerful. So if I was helping Derek to fix a bunch of stuff he'd wrecked, I'd just sprinkle a little pixie dust around and it would all be better, go smoother, be easier.' She shrugs, wrinkling her tiny nose. 'That sounds rubbish, but I know what I mean. I just use it and everything feels better,' she says. 'I've never questioned it before.'

She takes another biscuit, seemingly deep in thought. Ettie sends some peace her way. They learned about pixie dust in the academy, and it's a sweet, gentle kind of magic, but definitely not powerful or potent. She's pretty sure that the main reason everything went right for Dayne was nothing to do with pixie dust and everything to do with how clever and competent and kind she was, choosing to help people, when she really didn't need to.

'I reckon I'll have a look round the garden see what else I need to do, and then a little poke around in the new shop,' Sticks says. 'Just take a proper gander, have a shufti, you know?'

'I'll go and visit some people,' Dayne says. 'It'll be quicker now that I can fly.'

'I'll potter around,' Ettie says, thinking that she might curl up with some ale and the book she's reading. 'And I'll get lunch ready for one. And shall I write back to Graily?'

'Good idea,' Dayne says. 'Tell her we love her and we miss her.'

Sticks grins. 'Tell her we can't wait for her to come home and make even better food than she did before.'

They are all happy with their plans for the day and finish their tea in a peaceful silence.

Chapter 8

S<u>omewhere else</u>
 Posey, a freckle faced, flat nosed, red skinned troll snuggles back under the covers.

She can hear her mum and her stepdad – a goblin, not a troll – yelling at her, but she's not getting up.

She's sick of them, she's sick of working at this place, she's sick of being a troll, and all she wants to do is hide.

Eat worms and hide.

She burrows deeper under the covers, pretending to sleep, but knowing that any minute her mum, all grumpy and annoyed, or her stepdad, all mean and shouty or her brother, all smelly and stupid will burst into her bedroom, rip the covers off her body and demand that she get up and help because she's a no-good, lazy, waster, good for nothing, leaching, waste of space...

The insults will rage on and on, and she'll ignore them, tune them out, pretend she can't hear them while she showers and gets dressed, even though they'll laugh at her and ask her why she bothers. Nobody expects trolls to be clean and tidy. Nobody cares what you look like. Are you chasing after some bloke, eh, Posey? Dressing up and getting all fancy. Getting too big for your boots, girl, getting too fancy for the likes of us hey, with your fancy education and your clean hair.

She'll shower and dress and ignore them while she eats her breakfast and then she'll go to work in the tavern, while her mum sits around complaining about her, her stepdad marches around watching her work and complaining about her, and her brother picks the dirt out of his toenails and flicks it across the room while complaining about her.

Every single day is the same, every single day is awful, and every single day she wonders why she didn't stay away after she finished her training.

She knows why her mother came to visit her and acted so sweet, and said that she needed her help, because only she could do it, and only she was capable, and only she could get them out of the hole they were in. And once she'd done that, she could go, she could live her life, she could be free.

Now Posey knows that was a lie. She knows that her mum and stepdad and her brother have screwed everything up so badly, spending money they didn't have, borrowing money they couldn't pay back, alienating customers so not enough people come through the door, that she'll be here forever, being picked on, being made fun of, being made to do all the work, to desperately try to pull them out of the hole they're in.

And if she succeeds, she won't get any thanks, and if she fails, she won't get any thanks.

She pulls off the covers and stands up.

She cannot bear it.

When her mum bursts into the room, she's already showered and dressed, and eating worms, her bright purple hair tied neatly into plaits, that stand vertically off her head in long points,

'Morning,' her mum says, clearly put out because Posey is up and ready to work without being pestered for a change. She looks almost disappointed, and Posey bites her lip, so she doesn't smile.

'There's some cleaning to do before we open,' her mum says, not asking her nicely if she'll do it, never saying please or thank you for anything she does – and she does everything.

She's the only one who serves the customers. She's the only one who cleans and clears the mugs and dishes. She's the only one who makes pasties and pies. She's the only one who wipes the tables, sweeps the floors, lugs the rubbish outside to the fire pit.

If she wasn't here, this whole place would fall apart.

But she's stuck. She knows it and they know it.

Trolls aren't looked at favourably in the magical community – similar to ogres and orcs, they have a bad rep, and it's difficult to get past.

She wishes the professors in her school had warned her that she could be the most qualified troll in the whole world, and she probably still wouldn't get a job, because nobody likes trolls, and nobody trusts trolls. Maybe she wouldn't have wasted three years training – but then, those three years away from home were the best three years of her life.

She traipses out of her room and down to the bar.

Her mother was right – there's a load of mess that needs clearing up, which means that once again, after she had done all the work yesterday and fallen exhausted into her bed, her mum or stepdad or brother, or all three for all she knows, had enjoyed themselves a little after-hours party. No doubt eating and drinking the stuff they can hardly afford to pay for, and then not having any left if any paying customers did wander in.

She's sick of them all, and she's sick of the place.

Chapter 9

Posey is fuming as she clears and cleans the bar. There's mess everywhere, rubbish just strewn on the floor, drinks spilled and not cleaned up, smears of food on the tables, with flies buzzing around it.

It was spotless when she finished up and went to bed. She hates her family, and she hates how selfish they are.

She blames her stepdad. She can't really remember because he's been in her life since she was five, but she's sure things were better before he came along.

He's just loathsome. All three of them are.

She throws open the doors when it's time to open and contemplates running straight out of them and never looking back.

Maybe in a book that could happen, maybe in a book you get a second chance, but she knows she won't.

She wishes and prays every night that something might change, but every morning she wakes up in the same bed and does the same thing; she works all day with no help and no thanks.

There are no customers, so she sits on a stool at the bar, a dirty stool which has seen better days. All the furniture needs sanding down and cleaning up, but she doesn't have the time to do it, and she knows nobody else will ever bother.

'Girl, what are you sitting around for?' her stepdad asks, marching into the room, his little goblin eyes all squished up and beady.

She gestures around the room, once again spotless, thanks to her, and completely empty.

'There's always something to do,' he says, and she sighs.

'There's always something you could do,' she says, and then wishes she hadn't. He can never let anything go, and he won't let her cheekiness pass by either.

'What did you say, young lady?' he asks, his voice high pitched and singsong. He shouts less than her mum and brother. They're trolls; quick to anger and quick to placate, usually, but he's a goblin. He's sly and quiet and snake like. She hates him so much; she wishes he would just disappear.

'You heard me,' she says, standing up, wondering why she's being so bold, and what he might do to stop her.

She never pushes it, she never answers back. She wants to, but never does, same as she wants to not work or not clean up or not do everything, but she always ends up doing it.

Anything for a quiet life. Or maybe she's just as worthless as they say she is. Maybe she's a waster, a loser, a useless troll that nobody likes, and nobody wants. Maybe that's why she keeps her head down and gets on with it, because what other choice does she have?

He stands in front of her, sneering. 'I heard you. And I didn't like what I heard,' he says, voice low, menacing.

She stands her ground, for once, meeting his eyes, and refusing to look away. Her legs are shaking and her butt is sweating, but she doesn't falter and she doesn't blink.

'I look after you,' he says, through gritted teeth. 'I took your mother in, even with you two kids shackled to her. I took her in, and made her happy. I gave you all a roof over your head and worms in your bellies. And this is the way you speak to me?'

His voice is dangerous now, low and silky. A shudder runs through her whole body.

Just say sorry, a little voice in her head urges her. Say sorry and get on with the day, sweep or dust, even though it's clean. Just show willing.

He takes a small step towards her, closing the gap between her, standing closer than is comfortable.

'What do you have to say for yourself girl?'

'What's going on here?'

Posey's mum comes into the room, and rushes to her husband's side. She places her hand on his arm and glares at Posey.

'What did you do?'

'What did you say?' her brother asks, barging into the room, and taking in the scene with unconcealed delight. 'What did you do now Posey?'

Chapter 10

Posey feels like time is standing still. She knows if anyone walks in, it will go a different way. Her stepdad will take a step back, and her mother will smile to cover it all up, her brother will be disappointed but he'll bring it up another time, hoping to stir it all up again.

She looks at her stepdad, lips curled, beady eyes flashing with something – joy or power or something. He's enjoying this.

Her mother is glaring at her, furious that she's rocked the boat, and assuming it's Posey's fault when, really, she doesn't know that; she doesn't know what's actually going on, because she'd never ask, and she doesn't care. As long as Posey does everything and she has a quiet life, she really doesn't care.

Her brother is grinning, itching for it all to blow up, itching for Posey to get a telling off, or for a real shouting match to kick off between them all. He'd love to see her get walloped, that's what he's really hoping for.

Posey takes a step back, and her stepdad grins; he thinks he's getting to her.

'No,' she says. Just one word. One tiny word, and she feels a huge surge of power flood through her.

'No?' her stepdad, mum and brother all say at the same time.

'No,' she says, untying her pinny and placing it on the counter. 'No.'

'No what?' her stepdad says, confusion making his expression even uglier than usual.

'I'm done,' Posey says. 'I'm done with you.' She points at her stepdad. 'You're the most lazy, nasty, useless sack of crap I've ever met.'

'Posey!' her mother says, sounding shocked and also scared.

'And you,' Posey says, ignoring the fact that she can almost see steam coming out of her stepdad's nose, he's so angry. 'You're the worst mother in the history of the world. You don't love me or look after me, and you never stick up for me. You make me do everything.'

Her mum opens her mouth to argue but Posey holds up a hand. 'Everything! And you,' she turns to her brother. 'You're so useless and pathetic and stupid, I can't even be bothered to look at you. I do everything, but not anymore. I'm done.'

'Done!' her stepdad's voice is higher than usual and spit flies out of his mouth. 'Done!' He picks up her pinny and throws it at her. Posey lets it drop to the floor. He steps closer and takes hold of one of her plaits, pulling her along to get her back behind the bar. She screams at him to let her go, but he ignores her. 'You're done when I say you're done,' he says, and throws her to the ground. He leans over and slaps her hard, right across her face. The sound is too loud for the small room, and the silence after is deafening. The air is thick with ill will.

Her stepdad gets his breath back, still looming over her.

Her mum rushes to his side and takes his arm.

Her brother climbs on a stool, so he can see her on the floor, humiliated and low.

Posey holds a hand to her cheek. It stings so much, and she wants to cry, but she won't. She digs her nails into her palms to stop herself. They will not see her cry. They will not see her fall apart.

'Now get back to work,' her stepdad spits at her, 'and don't you dare put a foot out of line again.'

He storms off, pleased with himself.

Posey meets her mum's eyes, but she looks away, without saying a word and then follows after her husband.

Her brother lets out a hoot. 'You've done it now, sis,' he says, laughing. 'Damn, he told you.'

Posey ignores him. She stands up and straightens her clothes, tidies her plait, and picks up her pinny.

'Yeah, he told you,' her brother says, leaving the room.

Posey looks around the bar room where she spends all her waking hours. She has no hobbies, no friends, no fun. She's not a prisoner, exactly. She's allowed to go for a walk, she's allowed to sit in the sun, but her life is small, and so is her happiness.

She places the pinny back on the counter and walks out of the open door.

There's nobody outside, except a bird, a dark blue feathered blue bear, she thinks. The bird pecks at a worm, and then fluffs out its wings before flying away.

She watches it with longing in her eyes.

She has nowhere to go and nothing to do, but she knows she cannot go back inside her house. She cannot face her mother again, who didn't lift a finger to help her, or utter a single word to stick up for her. She didn't expect anything better from her stepdad; he's always been a pig, and her brother is a waste of space.

But her mum? The way her mum looked at her, the way her mum chose her husband over her, her own daughter. Posey feels sick. The tears finally come and they're hot, stinging her face, making her feel small and stupid.

She takes a step away from the house, the tavern, her home, and another one. She doesn't turn around and she doesn't slow down.

Chapter 11

Eventually she stops, under the shade of a tree, her back against the hard, sharp trunk.

What has she done? Is it too late to turn around and go back? She's tired, and lonely and afraid.

She's a troll, alone in the world. Maybe three or four hours from home, but not so far that she couldn't turn back.

She sinks to the floor. She can't go back. She wouldn't dare.

Her stepdad isn't a very nice man, but he's never laid a hand on her before. He's crossed the line today, and nobody stopped him, nobody told him off, her own mother watched, saying nothing, condoning it, and forgiving him. Letting him know there was nothing to forgive him for, really.

She feels sick, but she cannot go back. The only way now is forward, unknown, frightening and... free.

She smiles softly, crying again.

She's free. She can leave and find somewhere else, somewhere better. Who knows, maybe she'll get to do her dream job, the one she trained so hard to get qualified in, maybe she'll make friends, fall in love...

She stands up, brushing the mud from her clothes and heading off again.

It wouldn't be quite so scary if she had a plan, somewhere to go, someone who could help her.

She could go back to her school and ask them for help, maybe ask if they knew of any jobs going. She shakes her head. She knows they wouldn't help her, and not because they're mean or unkind, just because they've all got a million other things to do.

People are busy, and the troubles of one little troll aren't anything they'll want to be bothered with.

She trudges along, one step at a time, trying not to think about where she'll sleep, or what she'll eat, just trying to get as far away as she can from her old life.

A piece of paper flies across her path, buffered by the wind. She thinks of picking it up; it's what she's trained to do. Tidy up, pick things up, move things out of the way. She'd never leave a mess for anyone else to tidy. Now she smiles. She's free; she doesn't have to clean up other people's mess. Not anymore.

She keeps walking, head down.

There's another piece of paper, dancing ahead of her this time, falling to the ground, then gently lifting in the wind, skimming along the floor, like a stone skims along the water.

She laughs. There must be some very messy people around here.

She reaches down and picks it up.

It's a little bit muddy and a little bit scuffed, but she can read the words easily enough. They fill the whole page.

HELP WANTED. Experienced bar staff for an enchanted alehouse. Mustn't be small minded or rude. Must treat all creatures equally.

She shakes her head, looking around to see if there's anyone near, someone who might have dropped this, someone who it might belong to.

There's nobody in sight.

She reads it again.

It's describing her.

She laughs. This feels weird.

'Okay, this is me,' she says out loud, feeling more than a little bit silly. 'But how do I get from here to there, wherever that might be?'

The loud neigh of a horse behind her, has her laughing again.

'Really? Hey buddy? Are you here for me?'

The horse neighs again, and Posey takes hold of its reigns. There must be someone here, an owner, concerned that their horse has run off.

She pats its nose and the horse snorts softly.

The piece of paper in her hands gives a little tug, then jumps up and flutters to the East.

'You're showing me the way?' she asks it, and it turns in a circle, before flying back into her hands.

Posey closes her eyes. Trolls don't have any magic, though she's seen it in many other creatures. She's seen it used for good and bad. This has to be magic.

She climbs onto the horse, leading it around slowly to see if she can see who it belongs to.

The horse neighs.

'I suppose you're taking me wherever it is I'm supposed to go?'

The horse neighs and the piece of paper tugs again.

Posey nods. The day couldn't get any stranger. After the showdown with her stepdad, the way she walked away and didn't look back, and now some magic she doesn't understand helping her out, she's ready to just go with it.

'Come on then, lovely, take me away,' she whispers, putting her faith in the horse and the random piece of paper.

Chapter 12

Ettie waves Dayne off at the front door, sees Sticks out of the back door, and then snuggles up in the den next to the fire. It's burning as bright as ever, and the heat is just right.

She writes the letter to Graily, making sure to add what the others asked her to. She rolls the parchment into a scroll, and places it on the table.

Once she's read for a bit, she's going to cook dinner. Not magic it up, cook it.

She loved how good the alehouse always smelled when Graily was there, always something delicious baking or cooking, and always smells that made her mouth water.

They are all happy that Graily is happy, but she misses the home cooking, and she knows they'd never complain, but she's sure the others miss it too.

Cooking is like magic, and if she can rustle up a potion to make someone invisible, then she should – in theory – be able to rustle up a decent meal. And there are still a bunch of recipe books in the kitchen, so she should be able to make something lovely.

Ettie cocks her head. Someone's coming to the door. Is it a customer or a guest?

She waits for the knock, and then takes a deep breath. Typical that anyone would show up when she's alone.

She opens the doors, plastering a smile on her face and trying to remember that she was chosen for this role, chosen to be a guardian for this place, and if she was chosen it was for a reason. The reason being that she can do it.

Standing in the doorway is a nervous troll, with bright red skin and absolutely fabulous hair. Her hair is gravity defying, twisted into two long plaits that stand up vertically, three feet long and bright purple. It's hard to age a troll, but she looks young. Ettie smiles wider, not wanting to be rude. Trolls are notoriously grumpy and petty but this one looks… nice. She remembers Sticks admonishing her, ever so gently, that she shouldn't be judgemental.

'I'm Ettie,' she says. 'Welcome to the alehouse.'

She steps back, letting the troll come inside. She's a guardian, not a gatekeeper.

The troll hesitates, but then follows her inside. She's clutching a piece of paper. 'My name is Posey,' she says, and Ettie wonders what her accent is; she's not local. 'I think you need some help.' She pauses and takes a deep breath. 'And so do I.'

Ettie ushers her through to the den. If this troll is in trouble, then Ettie will help her, no matter how scary trolls might be.

'You need help?' Ettie says, gesturing for her to sit. She does, but then she holds up the piece of paper.

'Bar staff,' Posey says, though it sounds like a question. 'I found this.'

Again, not a question, though it sounds like one.

Ettie reads the parchment.

HELP WANTED. Experienced bar staff for an enchanted alehouse. Mustn't be small minded or rude. Must treat all creatures equally.

Ettie shakes her head. She didn't write this, and she knows Dayne couldn't have because of the size of it, and she knows Sticks couldn't because of the number of words on it.

She thinks about the feathers, the scrolls, the way each of her new friends made their way here, how each of them was supposed to find their way here.

She nods. She can accept this. She has always had a funny feeling that the alehouse knows more than it would if it were just an alehouse. Even for an enchanted alehouse, it has a magical aura about it. She feels like it knows stuff, and that's weird.

'I'd love to work here,' Posey says, again with that inflection at the end of her sentence that makes it sound like a question.

'And we'd love to have you,' Ettie says, knowing that the others won't mind her saying yes. After all, this isn't her taking over or giving Posey permission to stay. Some magic brought her here. Some magic wrote the advert. And something about her feels familiar. She's clearly meant to be here. Same as her. Same as Sticks. Same as Dayne. Same as Graily. Maybe for a little bit of time – maybe for a long time. But only time will tell.

Ettie resigns herself to always being a little bit on the back foot where the alehouse is concerned.

'So you've done this kind of work before?'

Posey nods. 'Yeah. I'm good.'

'You'll need accommodation?'

'Yes please. But I don't need much.'

'You'd want paying?'

Posey shrugs. 'We can talk about that.'

Ettie nods.

'I'll show you around.'

'Thanks. Oh, and I'm a troll. I hope that's okay.'

Ettie nods. Everyone is welcome here.

Chapter 13

Sticks sits down on a rock and pulls his little bag of sweets out of his pocket. His supply is never ending now he has Ettie to conjure them up for him, and he's tried a new flavour which has quickly become his favourite – butterscotch. Sweet and creamy; he can't get enough of them. They're just about keeping him happy while he waits for his custard tap.

He rubs his hands together; he's so excited for his tap. There are benefits to the way his life has turned out. He misses Lox, but his animals are all safe, and Amma is working even harder than usual to help him. She's also learning loads, and clearly paying attention to the books she took from the shop.

He needs to get another stock of books for the new shop. Apart from the ones Amma took home, all the others were burned in the fire. Ettie will be able to help him.

He bites his lip. He's sad and angry about the fire, about the foxes, about Philomena, but the biggest sting of all is Lox.

But, he's always one to look for the silver lining, and the new swamp is brewing nicely, and might be better than the last one. He's so close to the river, now, he can swap between the two quite nicely. He scratches his belly.

Having a witch on hand to feed him constantly reminds him of being home with his mum. She was a witch and his dad was human, although of course his parents were both ogres. Toady-loo and Dave are his real parents now; they adopted him when he was three. And Toady was just like Ettie; she made magic look easy.

He was never hungry then, and it looks like he won't be hungry now. When he lived alone, there were days when food was a little harder to come by. It's easy if you're an ogre who eats animals, but if you don't, it's not always easy to be satisfied with berries.

Here, he gets pies and croissants and a hundred other food things that are delicious and satisfying.

He stands up with a groan, rubbing his lower back and stretching out this way and that. Ettie could magic them a kitchen garden in seconds, but although he's aching, he still wants to do the work himself.

It gives him something to do.

He loves that perfect balance of doing nothing – lazing in his swamp, eating his sweets, napping – and then doing so much, he has to do the first few things again just to recover.

The garden looks good and he's proud of what he's achieved. Instead of the messy scramble of bushes and brambles and weeds, and rotten wood and rubbish, there are clearly defined raised beds, ready to plant seeds in. That'll be Ettie's job because he doesn't have any seeds.

She can magic them up, and he can plant them, and Dayne will enjoy helping. She's a handy little pixie, and her only limits come from her size; she's strong and capable, and he's glad the three of them are friends.

He grins. He's very happy to be at the alehouse, to have his new swamp, and to have his new shop.

'Hello!'

He turns and beams at Amma.

'Morning Amma. Sweet?'

She shakes her head, no.

'No thanks. Ettie let me in, I've seen all the animals. They're looking good.'

'They are. They'll be happier once they're in the new shop, but until then, it'll do, won't it?'

He looks to her for reassurance. He loves having his animals close, but he hopes it's not blinding him to their welfare.

'It'll do,' she says, eager to reassure him.

'Do you want to see it?'

'I thought you'd never ask!'

Sticks grins and scratches his chin, laying down his trowel in the mud.

'Follow me, then,' he says, and she does.

He throws open the door, smiling at how much better it looks now it's clean and dust free. And now there aren't any leaks coming in through the dodgy roof.

'Wow, Sticks, it's huge!' Amma says, her eyes shining.

'I know. Much better than the last one. Come and see out the back.'

He proudly shows her the river as though he made it himself, and Amma beams.

She touches his arm lightly. 'Sticks, this is going to be just wonderful.'

'I know,' he says. 'In fact, I think I should do a little bit of work right now – get started on it, you know?'

Amma makes a, I'm not sure that's a good idea, kind of face, but Sticks is already marching back to the old building, with purpose in each step.

Chapter 14

Dayne spins through the air, letting the breeze carry her, and then flying up when she drops. She wishes she'd had her wings fixed years ago; she's not even sure why she ever objected.

Sure, there's nothing wrong with broken wings, but there's also nothing wrong with taking help when it's offered.

It also means she can get from one place to another in a jiffy. She flies straight to the Dewberries – the retirement village for giants, where Derek lives.

He beams when he opens the door, and she flies up so she's face to face with him, well body to face, because he's so massive.

'Look at you!' he says, voice booming, huge grin on his face. 'I always wondered why you didn't fix them wings sooner.'

She shrugs. 'I suppose it felt like cheating,' she says.

'Cheating! Do you know the old giant Edgar?'

She shakes her head, no.

'Edgar lost a leg to a flesh eating porcupine.'

Dayne makes a face. 'Nasty.'

'Nasty indeed. Well, he got a false leg, and he was able to get about. He was always a bit wobbly after, and he'd get splinters by the handful, but there's nothing wrong with fixing things. Isn't it you that tells me to never throw anything out? I can fix it, you always tell me.'

She smiles. She's so glad she can fly, but it sometimes feels strange, like she's betrayed herself by not accepting herself the way she was.

'Funny girl,' Derek says, opening the door wider.

Dayne looks around the room, and then up at Derek, who is bursting with pride.

'Derek!'

She flies right up to his face and then leans against his rough skin.

'Look how tidy it is, how clean.'

He beams. 'I took your advice.' He looks down at the floor, scratches his ear. 'I got help, and I'm seeing my kids again.'

Dayne squeals and flies in a loop. 'Oh, Derek, I'm so proud of you. Well done.'

'And I don't owe your dad any more money, so there's no need to get your coins out for me. I stopped gambling.'

She grins. 'Derek, I don't have any coins. My dad isn't doing that anymore. He's not lending money or beating up the people who don't pay it back quick enough.'

Derek drops onto his chair, and Dayne flies over and hovers in front of him.

'He stopped?'

'He did. He found out what I was doing for you, and for everyone else, and... he works for the King now.'

'The King!'

If Derek is annoyed that the man who used to terrorise him now has a cushty job working for the King, he doesn't show it.

But then his face falls. 'Does that mean I won't see you anymore?'

Dayne grins and flutters her wings and her eyelashes. 'You don't get rid of me that easy, Derek! Who's going to fix all the things you keep breaking if I'm not here?'

He grins and holds out a finger. She high fives him.

'I'll still visit, for as long as you want me to,' she says, and he grins.

'I'll always want you to. You've helped me so many times I can't even count. And you got me back on the straight and narrow. I'll never be able to thank you enough.'

'No need for thanks, but a cuppa would be nice.'

Derek grins and heads out to his kitchen to make a cuppa. She flies after him.

'Cake?' she asks, spying what looks like a carrot cake on the side.

He nods, laughing. 'Can't hide stuff from you now you can fly, can I?'

She shakes her head. 'You wouldn't want to hide cake, though, would you?'

He shakes his head and cuts a small sliver for her. It's still almost as big as she is, but she happily tucks in, sitting on the counter top and scooping the cake into her mouth.

'So anything need fixing while I'm here?'

He shakes his head, but then frowns.

'Will you visit, even if I don't need anything fixing?'

She grins and nods. 'We're friends me and you, you can't get rid of me that easily.'

'Good. You're a good girl.'

Dayne grins. She's twenty five, but he always calls her a girl. She guesses when you're the size Derek is, everyone else looks smaller and younger.

'If there's no jobs need doing,' she says, 'I reckon I'll just have another cuppa and then I'll head off.'

They drink their tea, eat their cake, and Dayne fills him in on everything that happened after her last visit to him.

He cries when she gets to the bit where her house burned down, but he's laughing by the end, and she's happy too.

Seeing the house burn down had really felt like the end of her world, but she's happier than she's been since her mum passed away, and she knows that she'll only get happier.

Chapter 15

Sticks flings open the door to the new shop from the garden, and marvels once more at how clean and light it is since Ettie fixed the roof and sorted the lighting out.

'Here,' he says, pointing at the wall next to the door they just came through. 'I want a hatch for the animals, so they can go in and out as they please. Over to the right I'll put the consulting room, and the rooms for the animals who need treatment. I thought we could have... what are you grinning about?'

Amma laughs. 'I just like seeing you so excited. After what happened with the fire...' She shakes her head. 'I hate that I didn't save the shop, Sticks. I feel so guilty.'

Sticks crosses the floor quickly and, as gently as he can, touches her shoulders.

'No, Amma, you mustn't feel guilty. None of it was your fault.' He wipes a tear. 'If it wasn't for you and Blast, all the animals would be dead. You've nothing to feel guilty about. You saved them.'

'But we lost the shop, the books, the medicine...'

'We. I like it when you say we. But we only lost things that can be replaced.'

She smiles. 'The shop is really important to me, Sticks. The shop, the animals, you.'

He grins and holds out a meaty fist for a fist bump. Amma laughs and sighs.

'So, I thought we-' He puts a huge emphasis on the word, and then laughs, his grin huge. 'We could have some space for...' he trails off, frowning and biting his lip. He coughs. 'Anyway, we can talk more about the plans. Dayne is going to help me get something drawn up. I'll show you though; I'd love to have your input.'

She smiles. 'I'd be happy to help.'

'So here,' he says, frowning at a pile of bricks he hadn't noticed before. 'I'll move these now, but here, I thought it would be good to have some feeding bowls out for snacks and drinks, so the animals that roam freely can help themselves. What do you think?'

'I think it all sounds marvellous,' she says. 'I can't wait to see it all come together.'

He beams and scratches his belly, just as Dayne flies through the open door.

'Amma!' she flies over to the tall, thin, orange elf and high fives her. Amma just holds her hand still so she doesn't hurt Dayne.

'Isn't it great?' Dayne asks, gesturing around at the big empty building.

Amma nods. 'I can't wait to see what you guys do with it.' She turns to Sticks. 'I have to go, but I'll be back later to help.'

He nods, and Dayne waves at her.

'She's so nice,' Dayne says, and Sticks nods, but he's already walked over to the pile of bricks, and he's moving them to make a tower.

'That's dangerous,' Dayne says. 'If they fall, you'll hurt yourself. Stack them in a block.'

Sticks grins, but keeps building the bricks into a tower.

Dayne rolls her eyes, and flies around the building again, right up into every corner.

'It's going to be so good,' she says.

'It's going to be amazing,' Sticks agrees with her, beaming.

He steadies the tower of bricks, and then spots a weed growing out of the wall.

'Look at that,' he says. 'This place is such a mess.'

'It's better than it was,' Dayne says, flying over to the back wall.

Sticks shrugs. Better, but still a mess. Cleaner, but still dirty. He rearranges the bricks quickly. He wants to climb up and grab the weed. It's really not that high.

He climbs the bricks stairs; they're wobbly but he steadies himself on the wall.

Just a little higher. He makes a lunge, grabs at the weed; the weed comes away in his hand, and he falls to the floor with a loud 'oof!'

'Sticks!' Dayne flies over and hovers helplessly.

'I'm okay.'

'You're not. You're bleeding.'

Sticks puts his hands up to his face. He is bleeding from his nose and a graze on his cheek.

Damn it.

'Come on, Ettie will help you.'

'I can help myself,' he grumbles and Dayne hovers closer, patting his arm.

He winces.

'Sorry, and I know you can heal, but it'll be quicker if Ettie helps you. Come on.'

She can't help him to his feet and she just wants to hug him, as he stumbles up, wincing and rubbing his knees, the trickle of blood rolling down his face.

Chapter 16

Ettie shows Posey around and then leaves her in the bar room, getting acquainted with the different ales and brews they serve. Well, that they stock. They've only had the pixies and orcs here, and they weren't really customers. Not in the literal sense.

She's not sure what Sticks and Dayne will think of her offering this stranger a job; she wouldn't mind if one of them had done it instead of her. They won't be cross. She thinks. She hopes.

She'll cook – it'll give her something to do, and it'll stop her worrying about Posey.

The pantry has food and ingredients, but also a long shelf of cook books and recipes written out on parchment.

She grabs a hefty looking book, the kind of book that looks like it means business, knows what's what; that's what she needs. She doesn't know how to cook because she never learned because she never had to.

Her family are all witches and magic was always used to produce food out of thin air. Nobody would bother toiling over a hot stove, if they could just wriggle their fingers and magic the food onto plates, but she knows how happy cooking made Graily, and she knows how wonderful the smell of cooking and baking is, and so she's going to try.

She opens the book.

'Hello, dear!'

She slams it shut, and looks back at the shelf, contemplating choosing a book that won't answer back.

'I'm the best there is,' the books says, and Ettie opens it again. 'Hello again!' the book says, and Ettie takes a deep breath.

This will be a learning curve, but now that she's left the academy and doesn't take lessons anymore, she finds she's missing the structure and rhythm of the day, when she had a jammed timetable full of lessons and lectures, practical skills to hone and theory to learn.

This will be fun.

'Hello!' she says, trying to sound brighter than she feels.

'Novice or expert?' the book asks, and Ettie grins.

'Novice. I mean I don't even know where to start.'

'You start with me,' the book says, 'lovingly written to guide and nurture your culinary skills.'

Ettie beams. This might actually be fun.

SHE SLAMS THE RECIPE book shut, and the recipe book cries out with indignation.

'You can shush!' Ettie says, running her hands through her hair, and then wiping a tear of frustration from her face.

It turns out listening to a bossy book and trying to cook with unfamiliar ingredients, when she'd usually just swish her fingers to magic up whatever she might need, isn't actually any fun at all.

She looks around the kitchen, always so spick and span when Graily was running it, and now, just days after she leaves, a disaster.

There are blobs of wet dough everywhere – including the ceiling. There are clouds of flour dotted around – including her nose, and there's a nasty burn on her finger, which she's magically healed, but is still sure she can feel hurting her.

She slumps onto the bench and rests her head on the heavy wooden table.

'I'm done,' she says, her head still down.

'I can help,' the sing song, far too cheerful voice from the recipe book calls out.

'You're not helping,' Ettie says, lifting her head and scowling at the book. 'You're condescending. And you're patronising.'

'Aren't they the same thing, dear?'

'Argh!' Ettie picks up a wooden spoon and bashes the book with it.

'Ow!' the book cries out, and Ettie hits it again and again and again.

'Ettie,' Dayne's voice is small, unsure.

'Has she gone mad?' Sticks asks Dayne, and Ettie spins around to see the two of them staring at her, concern and amusement in equal measure in both of their expressions. And blood all over Sticks' face.

She jumps up, her kitchen failure forgotten.

'What happened?'

'The shop,' Sticks says, his tone and expression bashful.

'He made some stairs out of bricks and climbed them. And fell. Ettie why are you... you know...'

Ettie's shoulders sag, and she ties her hair up off her face with a flourish of her fingers.

'Well, I'm not mad, though I might end up there,' Ettie says, hitting the book one more time with the spoon. 'You need to be careful Sticks. That place is a hazard, an accident waiting to happen.' She punctuates her words with another slap to the book with the spoon.

The book cries out and Dayne flies over, alarmed.

She flitters near Ettie's shoulder.

'Ettie. You're hitting a book.'

'Not just any book,' the sing song voice calls out again.

Ettie hits it again, and this time the book stays silent.

Ettie sighs, looking around at the mess she's made in the kitchen. She cleans it up with a swish of her magic.

'I wanted to bake something nice. So we wouldn't miss Graily so much,' she says. 'Sit.'

Sticks does as he's told, and with quick magic, Ettie cleans the blood off his face. None of the injuries are so bad that they need anything else. She sends some healing his way, some pain relief, some embarrassment relief.

She conjures up a cup of sweet tea for him. And then conjures some for her and Dayne too.

'That's so sweet,' Dayne says, and kisses her cheek. 'To think about cooking for us, but…'

'I know.' Ettie sighs again. 'But someone told me that sometimes the magic is in the doing. And I wanted to do it, instead of just magic it. I wanted you to smell the food baking, and think about Graily, and then I thought we could all be sad and miss her together, you know.'

'I miss her,' Dayne says, 'but I don't feel sad. She's doing exactly what she wants to be doing. And she's doing it in France.'

'I suppose.'

'I miss her too,' Sticks says, scratching his chin. 'But I'm happy she's happy.'

'Did you write back to her?' Dayne asks. 'We'll get that sent off – that will make you feel better. But you don't have to cook. And if you do want to, then maybe a different recipe book would be more helpful.'

'Hey!' the book cries out with indignation.

Chapter 17

'It's not just the book,' Ettie says with a big sigh. 'It's me. I'm in a grumpy mood, and then I gave Posey a job, and I thought you might be angry with me.'

Dayne holds up a hand. 'You gave someone a job?'

Ettie sighs. 'Yes, well, I actually think the alehouse gave her a job.'

'Huh?' Sticks says, scooping a bit of floury goop up with a finger and licking it. He makes a face, but then tries a bit more to be sure.

'Gross,' he says and Ettie laughs.

She conjures up a pile of cookies.

'It is gross. I just couldn't think straight with the book barking orders at me. It was like being in an exam all over again. Her voice is so high pitched too.' Ettie shudders. 'It went right through me.'

'It's okay,' Dayne croons. 'No more cookbooks. Now tell us about Posey.'

'Yeah, how did the alehouse give her a job?' Sticks says, eating a cookie but still eying up the uncooked flour gloop.

'Sticks!' Ettie says, and he looks up, sheepish.

'Sorry. I don't like it, but I'm not sure that I don't like it, if you know what I mean. I just need to check.'

'You don't like it. It's not cooked,' Dayne says, a little sharper than she planned. 'Sorry,' she says, 'but this morning it was just the three of us, and now there's someone else. Is she going to live here?'

Ettie shrugs and nods and wishes she hadn't even answered the door.

'She had a job advert with her, she's done the job before...'

'What job?' Dayne asks, wings fluttering with annoyance.

'The bar tending job.'

'We don't have any customers,' Dayne says. 'We certainly don't need staff.'

She flies out of the kitchen, and Sticks follows her. Ettie reluctantly traipses out after them. She didn't think they'd be mad at her.

It feels unfair.

Sticks is standing in the doorway to the bar room, Dayne hovering at his shoulder.

The bar room is packed. Well, packed might be exaggerating slightly, but there are customers. Customers none of the three of them want to serve.

Sticks shuffles backwards.

'Let's go in the den,' he says, and the three of them sit down. Ettie lowers the fire to a simmer; she's already hot and bothered.

'So, we do have customers,' Dayne says, smiling at Ettie. 'Sorry.'

'It's fine. I didn't think we'd have customers, or guests,' she says gesturing at the ceiling, thinking about the extra bedrooms the alehouse had magicked up. 'But we do. and I don't want to stand around all day serving them.'

'Nor me,' Dayne says. 'I like fixing and helping, but not all the time.'

'And I'll have the shop,' Sticks says.

'Which we'll both help you with,' Ettie adds.

'So...?'

'Her name is Posey. She's a troll. But she seems friendly.'

'And she had a job advert?'

Ettie nods. 'Yes – a piece of paper, something about having experience and not being mean, or being kind, or being accepting... something like that.'

The three of them are quiet, and Dayne clears her throat.

'How about you magic us up something to eat? I'm certainly peckish.'

'Me too,' Sticks says, and just then his tummy grumbles.

They all laugh, and Ettie magics them up some tiny sandwiches and cakes, a nice mid morning snack.

'Do you know what I miss?' Sticks says. 'Those little puffy, sweet, jammy, sugary things Graily made.'

Ettie conjures them up and they all dig in.

'Let's just fill our bellies,' Dayne says. 'I suppose if the alehouse can bring all of us here, it's stupid to think it would stop at that.'

'Not stupid,' Ettie says, 'just what we thought it would be without Graily. It's nice with just the three of us.'

'We should go and introduce ourselves to Posey,' Sticks says. 'Trolls can be tricky.'

'Tricky?' Dayne asks. 'I don't think I've ever met a troll. What makes them tricky?'

Sticks shrugs. 'Same as ogres really. We've always had a bad rep.'

'Really?' Dayne shrugs. 'I've never really given them much thought.'

Ettie nods. 'There's the troll under the bridge.'

'What bridge?' Dayne asks, and Ettie and Sticks smile.

'Not an actual bridge,' Ettie explains. 'Just a bridge in a story. The troll wouldn't let the goats pass.'

Sticks snorts. 'Trolls don't let anyone pass. Notoriously mean, petty, spiteful... Like I said tricky.'

'Um.'

They all turn to see Posey standing there, her expression difficult to read.

'Sorry to interrupt,' she says, and Ettie notices that the drawl she spoke with earlier sounds different. More clipped. 'There's a hedgehog looking for a pixie in the bar room. I figured you might know.' She turns on her heel and marches out of the room.

Sticks rubs his meaty hand over his face. 'That's not good,' he says.

'We'll talk to her,' Ettie says, her stomach twisting. Posey seemed so nice, and now they've upset her. 'But I'm assuming the hedgehog is looking for you?' She looks at Dayne.

Dayne nods, miserable. 'I feel sick.'

'We'll explain it to her,' Sticks says. 'I wasn't talking about her… just trolls in general.'

'I know,' Ettie says, rubbing his arm. 'But I'm afraid she doesn't know that.'

Chapter 18

The three of them traipse into the bar room, feeling uncomfortable.

Posey doesn't look at them; she's busy serving even more customers. It seems like the alehouse is doing a roaring trade. Sitting at the crossroads of four villages, close to the academy and the palace, apparently there are lots of people who need a little drink to wet their whistles as they go about their business.

Posey seems to have a system going already. She has a sink full of hot water behind her, and tankards washed and draining on the counter next to that.

They watch her serve a customer, chatting and smiling as she does.

Ettie gives Sticks and Dayne a serious look. They have some apologising to do.

Then they all spot the hedgehog at the same time. Absolutely tiny, but dressed in the smartest outfit and carrying a handbag almost as big as her.

'Mrs. Dinklepants,' Dayne says, flying down so she's closer to the tiny, talking hedgehog.

Mrs Dinklepants blinks up at Ettie and Sticks, and Sticks takes a step backwards, so he doesn't scare her. The bar room is full of customers but Sticks still stands out as the largest. And, if you didn't know him, the scariest.

Ettie smiles her warmest smile.

'What's wrong, Mrs. D?' Dayne asks, landing on her feet beside her.

Mrs Dinklepants bursts out crying, and Ettie crouches down. 'Is it okay if I carry you through?'

They won't hear themselves think in the bar room, and they all want to get out of Posey's way.

Mrs Dinklepants nods, and Ettie gently scoops her up. Sticks lumbers back to the den and clears space on the table, moving some books and some empty teacups.

Ettie lays her hand on the table, letting Mrs. Dinklepants scuttle off.

'What's wrong?' Dayne asks, and Ettie and Sticks take a seat. Dayne turns to them. 'Mrs. Dinklepants was one of the people I used to help. One of the people who my dad and brothers...' she trails off because Mrs. Dinklepants is wailing.

'Hey,' Dayne turns to her, wiping at her tears with her finger. 'What's wrong?'

Mrs. Dinklepants takes a shuddery breath.

'Frank. Frank is what's wrong.'

Dayne shakes her head and then grins. 'Oh, Mrs Dinklepants, you don't know? My dad and my brothers won't be bothering you anymore. I was going to head over to see you today. You won't believe the stuff that's gone on the last few days.'

Mrs Dinklepants looks sombre. 'I heard. I heard about the fire. And I'm sorry.'

Dayne shrugs. 'We're all okay, which is the main thing, right?'

Mrs Dinklepants shakes her head.

'I was so worried when you didn't show up to my house...'

Dayne squeezes her hands and then turns to Ettie and Sticks. 'I was supposed to go to Mrs. Dinklepants' house after I went to see Philomena.'

Ettie and Sticks make a face; they can't help it.

'I'm sorry,' Dayne says. 'I got kidnapped.'

'I heard about that too,' Mrs Dinklepants says, and Dayne chuckles.

'Everyone is so gossipy,' Dayne says, still chuckling, but then she looks at Mrs. Dinklepants. 'If you know that I was kidnapped, and you know our house was set on fire, then surely you know the ending of the story?'

Mrs Dinklepants shrugs.

'Yeah, my dad and my brothers work for the King now. They're not doing what they used to do anymore. So you don't need to worry about Frank or any of them.' She shoots another glance at Ettie and Sticks. 'I knew he was the worst one.'

Mrs Dinklepants bursts out crying again, her tiny hedgehog paws up to her tiny hedgehog face.

Ettie sends some comfort her way, and Sticks aches to dry her little tears.

'Frank came to my house this morning,' Mrs Dinklepants says, her voice trembling.

Dayne shakes her head, her little freckled nose creased into a frown.

'Why? To say sorry?'

Ettie and Sticks both know that's not why and exchange a sympathetic glance.

'No, Dayne. He came to my house and threatened me. Told me that I still owed thirty seven gold coins, and that if I don't pay up by Friday, he'll...' She can't speak because she's crying too much.

'He'll what?' Dayne's voice is a whisper.

'He'll snap off every one of my quills,' she says, her voice shaky, her tears dripping onto the table.

Ettie and Sticks gasp, and Dayne shakes her head. 'Oh, no, no.' She looks at Ettie and Sticks her expression aghast. 'Why? Why would he...'

Ettie clears her throat. 'We'll sort it out, Dayne. Whatever he's doing and why, we'll figure it out. Mrs. Dinklepants, Dayne will get to the bottom of this – we'll help her. We won't let him hurt you.'

Mrs. Dinklepants is sobbing and Dayne takes her in her arms, gingerly, for a hug. It's strange to see someone small enough that Dayne can hug them.

'I won't let him hurt you,' Dayne says softly to Mrs. Dinklepants. Then she turns to Ettie and Sticks. 'But I'll kill my brother. I'll bloody kill him.'

It takes twenty minutes of sweet tea, tiny biscuits and some meal worms before Mrs. Dinklepants is calm enough to scuttle away.

Dayne lets out an angry scream of frustration.

'I can't believe him. I saved his backside, got him a cushty job with the King, and he's still going round threatening little old hedgehogs. I'm going to kill him, I'll rip his wings off, I'll-'

'Let's go to see your dad,' Ettie says, sending some calmness toward Dayne, who's so irate that her wings are blurry because they're fluttering so quickly.

'Your dad will sort him out.'

'I'll sort him out,' she says. 'Lairy piece of crap.'

Sticks raises an eyebrow at Ettie, who smiles gently and sends more calming magic towards Dayne. It seems like she needs it.

Chapter 19

'I was going to see her this afternoon,' Dayne says, 'just to fill her in on what's been going on, and to tell her she needn't worry anymore, but that I'd still visit. If she wants me to.'

'I know she would,' Sticks says, scratching his chin, and finding another bit of dried jam. He peels if off and eats it.

Ettie wrinkles her nose. Sticks is so wonderful, but also sometimes so wonderfully gross.

She shakes her head. 'She'd love to see you; I'm sure all the people you helped would still like to see you. But we can worry about that later. Let's head up to the palace and see your dad.'

'Shouldn't we talk to Posey first. Sort things out with her?'

'I think she's run off her feet at the moment, and she won't appreciate us getting in the way. We should go. We won't be long.'

'Ooh, we might see Flump too,' Sticks says, rooting around in his pocket, pulling out an indignant Dumpling, before finding what he was looking for. He holds up a dead, squashed, gnarly looking bug.

'Found this,' he says, looking chuffed to bits.

Ettie and Dayne wrinkle their noses.

Sticks tuts. 'It's a cappywally.'

'Of course,' Dayne says, grinning. 'We knew that.'

'Huh?' Sticks looks confused.

Ettie laughs. 'We didn't know. She's pulling your leg.'

'I'll pull your leg one of these days,' he says darkly, causing Dayne to burst out into peals of laughter.

'Right, no more leg pulling required. I'm assuming Flump will appreciate this little snack?' Ettie asks.

Sticks grins, placing the bug reverently back in his pocket and warning Dumpling not to touch it. 'Flump will love it,' Sticks says, proud of himself.

'Well, that's sorted. I'll take us there,' Ettie says, and they step outside of the front door, shutting it carefully behind them. Ettie sends some peace Posey's way before she leaves.

They arrive with the magical swish that Sticks and Dayne are getting more accustomed to, and stroll up to the palace doors. They know they won't get thrown in the dungeon now like they did the first time they showed up. Most everyone knows their faces and they count Briella, the princess, as a friend.

And it's Briella they see first, strolling down the steps of the enormous and fancy stairway with a man they all assume to be Nathaniel – her true love.

'Hello,' she calls out, delight clear on her face. She's used to being polite to people she doesn't like, but she really likes the three of them, and it shows.

Dayne flies up so she's level with her face.

'Oh, Dayne!' Briella squeals. 'You can fly!'

Dayne can't help but look bashful; she made such a fuss about not wanting to fly for so long, and didn't realise how much she longed to be able to flutter her wings and soar. She only wishes she'd done it while her mum was alive; she would have loved to fly around with her. They would have had so much fun.

But she wasn't ready.

It took Ettie and Sticks to show her that there wasn't anything wrong with 'fixing' herself with magic.

Briella gives them all a stern look.

'Are you here to see me or Flump?'

They all laugh, and Sticks looks particularly shifty.

'You of course,' Ettie says.

And this is...?' Dayne asks, raising her eyebrows, a cheeky look on her face.

'You know!' Briella says, laughing. 'This is Nathaniel. Who I would have married with or without the say of a fluffy penguin or my father.'

Nathaniel kisses her cheek, and smiles at the three of them, really craning his neck to look up at Sticks.

'I've heard all about you. It's a pleasure to meet you.'

He kisses Briella again. 'I must head off. I'll leave you with your friends.'

Briella watches him go, a dreamy expression on her face.

'We're getting married soon,' she says. 'And I'd love you all to come.'

Ettie and Sticks nod, and Dayne lets out a squeal.

'We wouldn't miss it for the world,' she says.

'We wouldn't,' Ettie adds, enjoying the look of joy on Briella's face. 'How's your sister, Alaysia, getting on? She wasn't quite so happy with her love match, was she?'

Briella has the grace to look concerned and beckons them all to follow her to the library. She asks for tea and biscuits and then shuts the door.

They all sit, and Briella leans forward.

'She won't come out of her room. She's fuming.'

Chapter 20

'Why?' Ettie says, alarmed. 'Your dad won't force her to marry anyone she doesn't want to.'

Flump, the fortune telling penguin of love had foreseen Briella's love match with Nathaniel, but had declared that her sister, Alaysia would marry a gnome called Pietter. Alaysia wasn't happy.

Sticks scratches his belly looking distressed.

'Flump wouldn't want anyone to be unhappy,' he says. 'He knows the love match, but the heart might have other ideas.'

'Her heart does,' Briella says, her voice low. 'She won't listen to me or talk to father. She just clams up. She's upset.'

'Would it help if we spoke to her?' Ettie asks.

'We brought him here after all,' Dayne adds. 'We'll feel responsible if she's sad.'

Briella sighs. 'I thought it was funny at first. It really knocked her off her high horse. All she wanted was a title and to leave this place for good. But Flump naming Pietter as her match rattled her.'

'It's not set in stone,' Sticks says, and Ettie sighs.

'This is why I hate fortune telling magic. We feel obliged to do things we don't want to just to align with the future we think is written out for us. We have the ability to change, to make another choice, and anything is better than marrying someone you don't love.' She nods pointedly at Briella. 'You know that.'

Briella nods. 'I was so happy that she was miserable – she can be a cow-bag you know – that I forgot how painful it would be to marry for duty and not love.'

'We should talk to her,' Ettie says. 'And you should talk to your dad. He'd reassure her, same as he did with you.'

Briella makes a face. 'He's away for a few days – official business.'

'That's a pain,' Sticks said. 'But Ettie will talk sense into her.'

'Any one of you could,' Briella says. 'But she's refusing to come out of her room. I'll see what I can do. Maybe I'll bring her to the alehouse.'

'That would be lovely,' Dayne says, clapping her hands. 'We love visitors. Hey, is my dad around?'

'I can ask,' Briella says. 'He's doing a wonderful job.'

Dayne beams. 'Really? You're not just saying that?'

Briella shakes her head. 'I wouldn't say he was if he wasn't. It's part of the reason my father's gone. He feels so confident that Mr. Bugsy can keep everyone on the straight and narrow.'

Dayne grins, so proud of her dad.

Briella leans in. 'He's really quite terrifying, isn't he?'

Dayne laughs and Ettie and Sticks nod their agreement.

Sticks blows out his cheeks. 'I could crush him like a bug, he's so small and I'm so big, but he makes me sweat.'

Dayne turns, hands on hips. 'Really?'

Sticks nods, dead serious. 'Really. Scariest thing I've ever seen with wings. And I've seen spike nosed black bees up close.'

Dayne spins around to Ettie, who makes a, sorry, face but also nods. 'Sorry Dayne. I know he's your dad, and he was wonderfully helpful with the foxes, but he's so scary.'

'He wouldn't hurt any of you!' Dayne says, feeling sensitive.

'Oh, we know that,' Sticks says. 'Unless we crossed him. But there's still something so frightening about him.'

Dayne shrugs. 'He's just got presence, that's all.'

Ettie nods. 'That's all it is. People look up to him, look at how the King trusts him.'

Dayne is beaming again.

A smiling house goblin brings in tea and biscuits, and Briella asks her to fetch Flump and find out where Bugsy is.

Briella notices her guests looking at the happy goblin.

'We've changed a lot around here since Graily left. All out servants are happy and healthy and part of the family.'

'I love that,' Dayne says, hauling a biscuit bigger than her off the plate and dragging it over to where she's sitting.

'Me too,' Ettie says. 'Everyone deserves to be happy.'

'Even my sister?'

They all laugh, and then the servant comes back with Flump. She tells Briella that Bugsy is in the stables.

Flump flaps his sweet little wings and squeaks with excitement when he sees Sticks, and Sticks scoops him up for a big hug.

'You're getting big for a wee man,' Sticks says, and tickles Flump's fluffy belly.

'He doesn't stop eating,' Briella says, smiling at the penguin. 'Though he's moved on from books to puddings.'

'They love a pudding,' Sticks says, stroking Flump's face. He pulls the bug out of his pocket and Flump wriggles with excitement. Sticks feeds him the bug and croons to him like he's his baby.

The girls turn away, so they don't get the giggles.

They all take turns for cuddles and then reluctantly leave.

'Don't forget to bring your sister to see us,' Ettie says, as they head out of the door.

Chapter 21

A servant leads them through the palace, across the courtyard and into the stables.

Bugsy is lounging on a pixie-sized chair, barking orders to the stable hands, who are rushing around doing his bidding.

The three of them watch from the doorway.

'See,' Sticks says, gesturing at him. 'Every single goblin here could kill him in an instant.'

'Why would they want to kill him?' Dayne asks, affronted.

'He is quite bossy,' Sticks says.

'We don't kill people because they're bossy. He's not doing anything wrong. They obviously like him, respect him and want to work hard for him.'

They watch for a little longer and Sticks nods his head. 'Fair enough. They look happy.'

'They are happy. You can't always judge a person on what they used to be like. We all change.'

'True,' Sticks says, his cheeks turning a little pink.

Ettie pats his shoulder. 'Come on,' she says. 'Let's say hello.'

Dayne's face falls and she blows out her cheeks. With the joy of seeing Briella and Flump, she'd completely forgotten about Frank, and the real reason they'd come to the palace in the first place.

'Bella, bella, bella,' her dad calls out to Dayne when he spots her. He flies over and gives her a huge hug.

'Dad,' she says, staying in his arms for longer, savouring being a child again, being with her dad.

'Everything okay?' he asks, sensing that it isn't, drawing back and watching her expression.

She shakes her head, gutted that she has to bring this to him, gutted that after everything they'd been through as a family, and still ended up with this wonderful opportunity for her dad and her brothers, that Frank couldn't keep his nasty habits to himself and just be normal for once.

'What's up?' Bugsy glares at Ettie and Sticks, who shrink back, even though they've got nothing to do with the reason Dayne is feeling sad.

'It's Frank,' she says, letting out the words and a big sigh at the same time.

Bugsy makes an annoyed sound, and throws back his head.

'Bane of my life! What's he done now?'

Dayne swallows back tears. 'Can we go outside?'

Bugsy leads the way, and Ettie and Sticks stay in the stables, giving them some privacy.

Sticks pets each of the horses in turn. Ettie sits on a weathered stool, and watches him. He really is in his element when he's with animals, creatures, any living thing that he can look after really.

'You want to try?' he asks, brushing one of the foal's manes.

She shakes her head. 'I'm okay,' she says. She doesn't want to tell him that horses freak her out with their big teeth and tails that look weirdly like human ponytails. She knows he'd be sad, and think she was missing out on some horsey kind of fun, but she'd rather keep her distance. She knows they kick if you get too close, and maybe spit too – or is that camels?

'We'll get a wriggle on with the shop,' she says to him, when he's in front of her again, having made his way around every single horse in the barn, patting them, stroking them, brushing their manes and tails and singing to them. He really is the most gentle of giants.

'I'd like that,' he says, pausing long enough to get a headbutt from a horse so he'll keep petting him.

'Lovely creatures,' Sticks says. 'Sure, you don't want to pet one, or have a ride?'

Ettie scoots back on her stool, and almost falls off it. 'No, I'm good, thanks Sticks.'

'Are you scared, Ettie?'

'No.' She holds up a hand. And then another one. 'Not scared, just sensible. I know horses can be skittish, and anxious and so can I. Not a good mix.'

'You're not skittish, you're lovely,' he says, and Ettie smiles.

'Thanks Sticks.' She gestures to the open door with her thumb. 'Do you think it's safe to go out now?'

'I'd give them a little longer,' Sticks says. 'No point in getting too close when he's angry. He might bop us.'

'I think so too,' Ettie says, wondering how she's ended up between a pack of scary horses and a furious Italian mobster.

Chapter 22

Dayne takes a deep breath. She hates this. She thought all the drama and stress was over. She thought her dad and her brothers were over all the criminal stuff and on the straight and narrow. Going from what they were doing to working for the King is such a huge step up, and a massive opportunity. It's not criminal. It's responsible and it's respectable. But Frank just had to ruin it. If the King finds out that her brother is still menacing people for money, then he won't allow Frank to work for him. He might throw the whole lot of them out, and then they'll be homeless and jobless. Which means they'll want to stay at the alehouse with her again.

She shudders.

'I had a visitor today at the alehouse,' she says.

Bugsy nods, and sits on a rock. 'Go on.'

'Mrs Dinklepants.'

He frowns.

'Cute little hedgehog?'

He nods. 'I know. Terrible drinking habit, always borrowed more and more money. I never hurt her, Dayne.'

'Well, the boys did, she told me all about it when I'd go to help her. And Frank...' She sighs. 'Frank went to see her this week and threatened to break all her quills if she didn't give him the money she still owed.'

Bugsy's expression darkens, his eyes turning black.

'Little-'

'Dad!' Dayne interrupts him before he can let loose a foul mouthed rant. 'What are you going to do?'

'I'll sort it,' Bugsy says, flying up and spinning around. 'Little shit! I made them all promise me it was over. All the bullshit, all the criminal shit. Damn him.'

'Damn him indeed,' Dayne says, relief flooding her. 'So you'll fix it?'

Bugsy nods. 'I'll fix it all right.'

'And I don't have to do anything?'

'You don't have to do anything.'

Dayne grins, and Bugsy pulls her in for a hug.

'Sorry, love. I've caused you no end of trouble.'

'It's fine dad. Look at where you are now, and what you're doing. The princess Briella told me how highly the King thinks of you. It's why he's gone away. Because he trusts you.'

His face darkens again. 'I thought I could trust your bloody brother. He's always been a thorn in my side that one. Too full of himself, and too fond of using his fists.'

Dayne sighs. 'Dad, you have to sort him out. If the King finds out...'

Bugsy flies closer to her. 'You don't say a word.'

'I never would. Only to you.'

He nods. 'Damn Frank.'

Dayne sees Ettie and Sticks lurking at the open stable door and beckons them over, a big smile on her face.

'Sorted,' she says. 'Let's go.'

'Am I still all right to come on Sunday?' Bugsy asks. 'With your brothers?'

Dayne nods. 'Only if they want to. But yeah, Ettie will do a lovely Sunday roast.'

'Ooh will you?' Sticks asks, scratching his belly.

'Reckon you've had enough roasts,' Bugsy says.

Dayne shoots him a glance. 'Dad!'

'What?' Bugsy says, patting his own tiny belly.

Sticks busies himself rooting through his pockets for a sweet, too embarrassed to remind Dayne to ask her dad about suppliers for the shop. He might say something mean again.

Ettie pats his arm.

'Let's go,' she says, brightly. 'We've got a load of stuff to do.'

'Bye dad.' Dayne hugs her dad, whispering in his ear to not make fun of Sticks.

Sticks gives a half hearted wave, and Ettie smiles brightly at the tiny but very scary pixie. She loves Dayne so much, and her dad has been nothing but helpful to them, but she can see why Dayne found it hard to keep friends when she was young.

Chapter 23

Back at the alehouse, the three of them stand outside the bar room.

They need to face Posey. Sticks needs to apologise, and him and Dayne need to meet her properly, but they all feel sick.

'I know what it's like more than both of you,' Sticks says, scowling. 'Having people judge you for something you can't help.'

Ettie sighs and pats his arm. 'I know. I still remember you telling me to be more open minded, when I was nervous about the orcs.'

Sticks nods. 'I've been judged harshly my whole life. And I'm the sweetest pea you'll ever meet.'

Ettie and Dayne exchange a smile.

'Sticks you are.'

'And I think Posey is,' Ettie says. 'I know she had the advert with her, but she also had a lovely energy. She seems kind and friendly, but sad too. And I've heard the stories about trolls too. I was a little bit nervous.'

'We need to talk to her,' Sticks says, and pushes open the door. The girls follow him reluctantly into the bar room, and it's quietened down significantly.

There are just two customers, both cloaked, sitting at a booth, full tankards of ale in front of them, and three men sat around one of the round tables, playing stones.

Posey freezes when they walk in, and then quickly busies herself at the sink.

Ettie walks over to her, sending magic her way, magic that might make her feel less hostile, less attacked, less sad. She gently touches her elbow.

'Hey, Posey. Would you have a moment to sit with us? I'd like to introduce you to the others.'

'I'd say I've seen enough of them to say no,' Posey says, turning and wiping her hands on her apron.

Ettie briefly wonders where she found an apron. Then smiles softly; the alehouse would have provided it.

'Posey please. What you heard was awful, but it wasn't about you.'

'No? Just trolls in general? Like I said, I've heard enough.'

Sticks lumbers over. 'Posey. I'm sorry. I was being rude about trolls when you overheard me. And it's unforgivable. I know more than anyone what it's like to be judged.'

He smiles his most gentle, kind smile, but Posey is still scowling.

Dayne flies over, hovering in the air between Sticks and Posey.

'Posey, please. The alehouse brought you here, we'd love to meet you properly.'

Posey sighs, and then nods slightly.

'Fine, but you've got five minutes. I want to clean this place up before I leave.'

'Leave?' the three of them say in unison, and Posey nods.

'I won't stay where I'm not welcome.'

As soon as they sit in a booth, which definitely shifts in size to accommodate Sticks, Ettie magics up a pot of tea and teacups.

'Tea?' she asks, and Posey nods, unable, or unwilling, to meet any of their eyes.

'You've worked really hard today,' Ettie says, gesturing around the room. 'It's the first time we've ever had customers.'

'It was fine,' Posey says, quietly, then clears her throat. 'I like being busy. And I feel at home in a bar room.'

'You've worked in one before?' Dayne asks, fluttering her wings, smiling softly, and aching for Posey to like her, like them. She hates upsetting people. Unless they deserve it. 'I'm Dayne, by the way.'

Posey nods at the introduction. 'I grew up in a tavern,' she says. 'My family own one.'

'We could really use that kind of experience,' Ettie says. 'We've never done it, or anything like it.'

'I'm Sticks,' Sticks says, blushing ever so slightly. 'I run a shop,' Sticks says. 'Or I will once it's fixed up, you know…' he trails off, still mortified that she overheard him.

Posey is quiet.

'Posey,' Sticks says, his voice catching. 'I couldn't be more sorry. I feel sick. I might be an ogre, but I'm not a mean one. I try to be kind and gentle and helpful. I work really hard to show people that ogres can be the good guy.'

Posey looks up at him, her expression hurt. 'That's not what I heard,' she says.

'I know,' he says. 'And I could cry. I was explaining to Dayne about trolls. And I used all the mean, spiteful, unfounded stereotypes, and I'm sorry.'

'Ettie told us you were lovely,' Dayne says. 'She said you were friendly.'

Posey closes her eyes. When the piece of paper blew her way, and the horse turned up out of the blue, she really felt like something beautiful and magical was heading her way. Now she just feels sick. Why isn't anybody ever nice to her? Is she really that bad of a person that she doesn't deserve kindness?

'I've had a bad day,' she says, and the three of them beam at her. She bristles.

Ettie shakes her head and touches her arm. 'No, Posey, we all had really bad days the day we came here too. It's like the alehouse knows who needs help and it steps in. It must have sent the advert your way.'

Posey nods. 'And a stray horse to bring me here. It disappeared the minute I climbed off it.'

'Please give us a chance,' Dayne says.

They all smile at her, softly, willing her to forgive them. Willing her to stay.

'I feel like I was meant to come here,' Posey says, already feeling like the argument this morning happened in another life.

The others nod. They all know that feeling.

'We were brought here in a similar way,' Dayne says. 'You're meant to be here.'

'But you have free will to leave,' Ettie says, anxious that Posey doesn't feel trapped.

'But we want you to stay,' Sticks adds, wanting her to know that she's welcome.

Posey sighs.

'I wanted to leave. And now I'm not sure.'

'Give us a chance,' Ettie says. 'We haven't been here long ourselves. We were all brought here. And when you're ready you can tell us where you came from, and we can help you, if you need us to.'

Posey pours herself another tea, and sips it, thoughtfully.

Chapter 24

She nods. 'I'll give it a week,' she says. 'Now if you can show me to my room?'

Ettie stands up. 'The rooms are all upstairs,' she says, and Posey falters.

'I don't like being upstairs,' she says. 'I feel hemmed in if I'm not on the ground floor, or below.'

Ettie closes her eyes for only a second and sends a silent plea to the alehouse to give them what they need. She's sure it will.

'Okay,' Ettie says. 'Let's take a look.'

Sticks and Dayne stay in the booth, and Ettie leads Posey out of the bar room.

Where there were only three rooms downstairs when she got here, the den, the kitchen and the bar room, the alehouse made space for Sticks' animals when they needed it, and she grins when she sees a new doorway right next to that one.

'Here,' she says, and pushes open the door.

Posey heads inside the room and then turns to Ettie, a smile on her face for the first time since she overheard Sticks.

'This is great. Exactly like my room at home,' she says. 'Down to the colour on the walls.'

Ettie pokes her head in and smiles. The room looks nothing like her room, or Dayne's room or what had been Sticks' bedroom. She knows the alehouse has given Posey something that suits her. She places a hand on the wall, and whispers, 'thank you.'

'I'll leave you to get yourself settled.'

'My bag's in the bar room,' Posey says.

'I'll grab it for you,' Ettie says, happy to help.

Once she's taken the bag to Posey and told her that she'll see to the bar room with the others, Ettie slides back into the booth, resting her head on her hands.

'What a day!' she says.

Sticks frowns. 'Is she okay? Will she stay?'

'I think so,' Ettie says. 'There's a bedroom for her, right next to the room your animals are in.'

'Ooh, I hope the smell doesn't bother her,' Dayne says, and Sticks sighs.

'We need to get on with the shop.'

'We do,' Ettie says. 'But without any more accidents.

Sticks nods, his expression very serious. 'Absolutely. First thing tomorrow,' he says.

'Today,' Ettie says, and they all look up as Posey comes back into the bar room.

She pulls a seat from one of the round tables rather than joining them in the booth.

'Maybe I jumped to conclusions,' she says, but Sticks shakes his head.

'It doesn't matter. I said what I said, and even though it wasn't about you specifically, it was about trolls, and that was uncalled for.'

Posey nods. 'Thank you. I like my room, and I'm happy to stay. But I'm not promising anything.'

'No – that's fine,' Ettie says, just relieved that they have some help, because the bar room door has swung open and three cloaked goblins have just walked in.

'Do you want help?'

'No,' Posey says, tucking the chair under the table, and getting back to work.

'But if you need help, yell,' Ettie says. 'Ooh,' she says, a smile breaking out over her face. 'I know what'll work even better than yelling.'

She faces the blank wall just to the side of the bar, on the left of the door to the rest of the alehouse and wiggles her fingers.

A giant pewter bell appears, fastened securely to the wall.

'Just give it a ring,' she says, 'and I'll be through to help you.'

Posey grins, and nods. 'All right. I don't think I'll need you, but you never know. Thank you.'

Sticks hovers for a second, and Ettie knows he still feels bad, and still feels like he hasn't apologised enough, and feels like he should do something else to make it up to Posey.

Ettie touches his arm and nods her head towards the alehouse.

He follows her and Dayne through to the kitchen.

'I know,' Dayne says. 'But you need to give her a minute. Remember how discombobulated we all were when we got here.'

'Discombobulated?' Sticks asks.

'Yeah, it means-'

'I know what it means. I just don't hear it often.'

Dayne giggles. 'I love it. It's one of my favourite words. It sounds so funny.'

'Lunch?' Ettie asks.

Sticks plonks down onto the bench. 'I thought you'd never ask. Now tell me, how do I make it up to Posey?'

'By staying calm,' Ettie says. 'We're strangers to her.'

'True,' he says, scratching his belly. 'Maybe she'd like to borrow Dumpling. Pets make people happy.'

Dumpling gives an indignant croak from his pocket, and Sticks gives his pocket a pat.

'Just go easy on her,' Dayne says. 'It's a lot to come here, and find us, and suddenly she's working her butt off, and then you're rude about her-'

'I wasn't rude about her,' Sticks says, grumbling.

'I know. And she knows that now. But I bet it still stings,' Dayne says.

'I sent some healing magic her way,' Ettie says. 'That might help her feel better. And her room is lovely. She said it has the same coloured walls as her room at home.'

Dayne shakes her head. 'This place is so flipping clever.'

The three of them are grinning.

'Just take it easy,' Ettie says to Sticks. 'This place is looking after all of us; we just have to let it.'

Chapter 25

Ettie magics them up a feast of pie and mash. Two different types of pie, and some mash with cheese in, and some without.

'We've got a lot to do next door,' she says.

'And here,' Dayne adds, pulling apart a giant crust of pastry and plopping crumbs into her mouth. 'I mean if we're going to have customers, and guests and a pet shop next door.'

'I can't wait though,' Sticks says. 'I couldn't sleep last night for thinking about the shop. I kept running it over and over in my head. Making the shop a bit bigger, making the back part bigger, making the outside area bigger and...' he trails off, suddenly looking shifty.

Ettie looks at Dayne, but she doesn't seem to have noticed, but Ettie caught it. Something, again. A look. A furtive look.

'Sticks...' she says, stretching his name out, a warning note in her tone.

'What?' he looks at her, eyes wide, grin wide too.

She shakes her head. She'll let it go; but she'll keep an eye on him.

She flourishes her hand and her magic easily whips up some of the puffy, sweet, jammy, sugary things that Graily made when she was here.

Sticks wipes the jam from his chin and sucks it off his finger.

There's a load of it still there that he's missed, but Ettie and Dayne don't have the heart to tell him; they just exchange a quick smile.

'It's really strange,' Ettie says, chewing on a piece of pie crust, and then taking a sip of ale. 'Being here with you, I feel like I've known you for ages. Meeting Briella, and meeting Amma, and then rescuing Graily, and meeting the King. And then meeting all your family Dayne, and then the big party with the pixies and orcs. Everyone we've met at the palace...'

She trails off, and Sticks exchanges a glance with Dayne, and a shrug.

'Strange?' Dayne asks, sipping sweet tea.

'Yeah. Strange,' Ettie says. 'I don't think I realised how isolated I was at the magical academy.' She pauses, eyes closed. It feels strange speaking so frankly to her new friends. But they're more than friends now. She shares a house with Dayne, and Sticks is their neighbour in his swamp.

She opens her eyes. 'Okay, this is embarrassing.'

'Ettie...' Dayne's voice is soft and she flies over to be closer to her friend.

'I didn't have a lot of friends in the academy. Only Liss really. And some of that is down to me; I find it really difficult to make friends. I never know what to say. I feel small and stupid.' She takes a small sip of ale, then tops up her mug with magic. 'And then every year I failed at the academy that feeling got bigger, and I had less in common with the new students and I found it even harder to make friends. I've seen more people, spoken to more people, been around more people here than I have for such a long time...'

Dayne tuts and makes a sad face. Sticks struggles up from the sofa and moves to the chair next to her. The chair gets bigger to accommodate him.

'Poor Ettie. You've been really brave, then. And we all feel a bit like that,' Dayne says, knowing that she finds it super easy to talk to anyone and never runs out of things to say.

'In the end nobody would pair up with me; I was the failure whose only friend was a teacher. Everyone thought I was a loser, and nobody would give me the time of day. Nobody went out of their way to be mean, but nobody went out of their way to talk to me either.' She swallows down her embarrassment. 'It was like I was invisible.'

'Poor Ettie,' Sticks says, and gently leans over to hug her. Ettie rests her head on his huge shoulder, and Dayne flies over to land on his arm. It's as close to a hug as they can all get without squashing Dayne.

'I guess I just feel happy here. And more like myself than I have for a long time. And I just want to say thank you. And I think it's important that we make guests, customers, Posey, feel happy too. It's hard to make friends sometimes.'

'I would never have known that about you,' Sticks says, chewing thoughtfully on some pie crust. 'If you feel anxious around people, you hide it really well.'

'I do,' Ettie says. 'And it's exhausting.'

'Well you don't have to hide anything with us,' Dayne says, fluttering her wings. 'You're our friend and if you need help, time alone, whatever, then just let us know.'

'We're a team,' Sticks says.

The three of them smile, the fire warm, and their bellies full.

Chapter 26

'A team with a lot to do next door,' Ettie says, finally standing up and stretching. 'The shop is really important to Sticks and we need to get it done.'

'But we still need a crew,' Dayne says.

'I think I've got an idea,' Ettie says, a smile pulling at her lips.

'Go on,' Sticks says.

Ettie grins and sits back down.

'We need people we can trust. People who get the job done.'

Sticks and Dayne lean forward.

'People like pixies,' Ettie grins.

Dayne scoffs. 'Good idea. But pixies are a little bit too little.'

'Not with my magic, they're not,' Ettie says, with another grin. 'I've been mulling. Dayne with your dad as project manager, your brothers as his crew, and anyone else they could drag along to help, it would be done in no time.'

Dayne flies up in the air, turning slow somersaults, as she ponders this idea.

'Frank too?'

Sticks sighs. 'If your dad has sorted him out.' He turns to Ettie, his expression thoughtful. 'This might work.'

'There's no way it won't work,' Ettie says, clapping her hands. 'Come on you guys. You know I can do magic.'

'She can,' Dayne agrees, nodding at Sticks.

'She can,' Sticks says, grinning.

'So what do you think?'

'I think it's brilliant,' Dayne says, clapping her hands together. 'But one condition.'

'Go on.'

'You make me big too.'

Ettie grins. 'You're on. So we need plans. If we have a crew, we can't be vague. They have to know exactly what they're doing.'

There's a small cough from the doorway, and they turn to see Posey standing there.

Ettie smiles widely, and stands up to usher her in.

'Hey, come on in. This is the den. You're always welcome in here.'

Posey smiles softly, taking in the ogre-sized furniture, and the pixie-sized furniture.

'Your magic?' Posey asks, and Ettie shakes her head.

'The alehouse.'

Posey raises her eyebrows. 'Really?'

'This place is magic,' Dayne says, eyes shining, half about the magic of the place she now calls home, and half about the thought of being big – if only for a little while.

'It is,' Sticks says, blushing slightly when he remembers how rude he was about trolls, and how Posey overheard him. 'It's why we know you're meant to be here,' he adds.

'We're all meant to be here,' Ettie says. 'Sorry, did you need help?'

Posey smiles and shakes her head, her vertical plaits wobbling, but never drooping. 'No, everybody left, so I closed for a minute – I hope you don't mind, but I needed the loo. And a drink. And some lunch.'

'Absolutely,' Ettie says, smiling too wide because she knows she's trying too hard. 'Did you find the loo?'

'I did.'

'Well, I can handle the other stuff you're after,' Ettie says. 'What would you like?'

Posey shrugs. 'What have you got?'

Sticks and Dayne grin at her, and Dayne flies over and sits close to her. 'Anything,' she says, smiling. 'Absolutely anything.'

Ettie nods and Posey bites her bottom lip.

'I feel cheeky.'

'It's not cheeky,' Sticks says. 'She loves it. She can rustle up anything.'

'Okay, um, chicken wings.'

Ettie flourishes her hands, and a plate of glistening chicken wings lands on the table in front of her.

Posey grins. 'Okay – that's cool.'

'Right?' Dayne says, waggling her eyebrows. 'But don't be shy. If you're hungry, eat. We do!'

Posey picks up some chicken and bites into it, grease dribbling down her chin. She closes her eyes. 'This is delicious.'

Ettie beams.

'Speaking of food,' Posey says, 'a few customers asked about food. If we'd be serving it alongside the ale?'

Ettie frowns. 'I hadn't thought of that. To be honest, we hadn't thought we'd have customers at all.'

She turns to the others, then back to Posey. 'Should we feed them?'

Posey shrugs.

'It would be easy enough to do. You're a witch.'

Ettie nods. 'But I don't want to be stuck serving customers all day.' She frowns, shaking her head. 'Not that there's anything wrong with serving customers.' She runs her hands through her hair. 'Sorry Posey. We're really nice, all three of us, honestly, but... we keep putting our feet in our mouths.'

'It's fine,' Posey says, with the most genuine smile she's had since she arrived.

Ettie meets her eyes. 'Are you sure? You don't hate us all and think we're ridiculous.'

'Not at all, though it does seem like you haven't given much thought to the fact that you live in an alehouse.'

Ettie smiles and Sticks and Dayne laugh.

'We'll tell you our story one day, and then you might realise that we're still playing catch up.'

'You're on,' Posey says. 'In the meantime, can I have some fish tacos?'

'Sure.' Ettie magics them up in seconds and Posey devours them.

'Anyway,' she says, 'I overheard you talking when I came to the door. I'm used to bar work, and I'm more than happy to be doing it, but lots of people won't give a troll a chance, so I don't get to use my qualifications.'

The three of them lean in closer.

She grins. 'I'm an architect.'

Ettie laughs and Sticks and Dayne both let out a whoop at the same time.

Ettie looks at the fire and shakes her head.

'This is you, isn't it?' she asks the fire, the alehouse, Anya.

The fire burns a little brighter in reply.

Chapter 27

Posey stands up. 'I'll get back to work, but if you want my help...'

'Want it?' Sticks splutters. 'We desperately want it and need it and couldn't do this without you.'

Posey beams.

Ettie touches her arm. 'We'll come and help you. It should make the afternoon fly by. And I need to do some work behind the bar.'

Sticks' ears prick up and his eyes widen.

He mouths the words, custard tap, and Ettie nods.

Dayne giggles as Sticks punches the air, and then she flies over to Posey.

'Sticks has been nagging Ettie for a custard tap in the bar room.'

'A custard tap?'

Sticks heads out of the room after them. 'Yeah, not for customers, though, or guests. This would be just for me. Right Ettie? Right Dayne?'

The girls giggle and then Posey opens the door. A small trickle of customers pours in, and Ettie takes Posey's lead, taking their orders, pouring the drinks, and taking the coins in exchange.

'You didn't have any money in the tills,' Posey says. 'I thought it was easier to make everything one gold coin.'

Ettie nods her agreement. Nothing they are serving costs them any money; it's all just filled up with magic. Not Ettie's magic, but some magic the alehouse owns. It really is the most peculiar of places.

Ettie uses her magic to wash the mugs and tankards, and hands Sticks a cloth to clean the tables. He grumbles a bit but she gives him a look and he gets on with the job.

Dayne can't do anything much; she's too small, but she keeps up the chatter with the customers while Ettie and Posey make the drinks.

'Be lovely to get something to eat,' a cloaked giant blue crested frog says, causing them to jump when he adds a huge 'ribbit' at the end of his sentence.

Ettie bites her lip to keep a straight face. As guardian of the alehouse and now hostess, she supposes, she has to make customers and guests feel welcome. Even giant blue crested frogs.

Using her magic, Ettie conjures up a big pile of sandwiches, and tells the frog to help himself. It won't be hard to make food for customers, even if they each ordered what they wanted, she could magic it up in seconds.

She pats the wall, a movement she's increasingly doing, as she realises how much the alehouse is up to. It's pulling her firmly out of her comfort zone, for sure. Making her meet new people, help others, talk to strangers. It's a lot, but she's doing it, and she's proud of herself.

The frog eats the whole lot of sandwiches, and so she conjures up some other snacks on big platters and dots them around the bar room.

Posey gives her a thumbs up.

Then she comes back around to the bar, where the mugs and tankards and ale are all stored.

There's room for a custard tap, and she won't even need Dayne's skills. Magic will do the trick.

Sticks is watching her so she makes a bit of a show, standing back and looking at the space where the tap might go, making a face – first worried, then doubtful, then bending down to get a closer look.

Dayne flutters over. 'Too hard?'

Ettie grins. 'I can do it in a second, I'm just making him sweat.'

'Mean!' Dayne says, but she's giggling.

'Everything okay?' Sticks lumbers over, a worried expression on his kind green face.

Ettie shrugs and tuts, and then laughs.

'I'm only pulling your leg. Here.'

With a flourish and a few magic words for the theatre of it all, Ettie conjures up the custard tap.

'This isn't for customers,' Sticks says, not daring to give his warning directly to Posey lest he offend her again but speaking more to the air in front of him and hoping everyone hears.

'Just for you,' Ettie says, and Sticks positions his mouth directly under the tap and pulls the lever.

It takes a second for the magic to kick in, and then a just warm enough, sticky gooey stream of custard runs into his mouth.

The girls giggle because they can hear him gurgling with delight as he drinks it down. Posey watches with her eyes wide.

'Never seen anything like it,' she says, shaking her head.

Sticks stands up and wipes his mouth with his sleeve. He gives Ettie a massive hug squeezing her so tight that she squeals.

'Sorry. But this is the best day of my life.'

'And it's for customers, too, right?' Posey asks him, a smile playing on her lips.

'Well, um, you see, um-' Sticks stutters and mumbles, again too afraid to offend Posey.

The three girls burst out laughing. 'Sorry, Sticks,' Posey says. 'I'm just teasing you. It's only for you.'

Sticks beams and pokes his head under the tap for another go.

Chapter 28

Once the last customer heads out of the door, Posey locks up, and Ettie magically cleans up all the mess, including the tables and the floor.

Sticks is still under his tap.

'You're going to make yourself sick,' Ettie says, arms folded over her chest.

'I'm not cleaning up if he pukes,' Posey says.

Dayne just makes a face, wrinkling her tiny nose, and shaking her head so much her blue hair flies everywhere.

'Ready?' Ettie asks Posey.

'Ready.'

The four of them head over to the big empty building next door and Posey whistles when she walks in. 'This is great. Do you have a crew? It'll take a lot of work.'

Ettie nods, thinking about Bugsy, and Dayne's brothers. 'We do now.'

'And suppliers? For all the stuff we'll need?'

Ettie clears her throat.

'Sticks, I know you don't want to magic the whole thing – which I could do in less than five minutes by the way.' She turns to Posey. 'These two think you need to put blood, sweat and tears into something to make it worthwhile.'

Sticks and Dayne nod their heads, and Posey does too.

'Yeah. I agree,' she says. 'The satisfaction is in the doing.'

'Fine,' Ettie says, miffed to be outnumbered. 'I won't interfere with my perfectly marvellous magic that could get your animals all happy and cosy in their new shop in a minute, but what if I magic up the supplies?'

The other three are silent.

Ettie ploughs on. 'So instead of asking your dad,' she looks at Dayne, 'to find suppliers, and take the time and effort to pick them up and buy them, I magic up wood, or glass, or nails, or whatever it is a place like this needs?'

Posey nods. 'That would be great. If you've got a crew, and you can magic up everything we need, as we need it, that would save a lot of time.'

She looks at Sticks, who nods, reluctantly.

'I was looking forward to shopping,' he says.

'Me too,' Dayne says, jutting out her bottom lip.

Ettie rolls her eyes. 'You two are like babies. Let me help you. This will make it quicker and easier, and if you talk to your dad and brothers, we could start tomorrow. Right?'

She looks at Posey she doesn't actually know how long it might take an architect to plan and design a building like this.

Poesy nods. 'If I can get some parchment and ink, I can get this all drawn out tonight. Sticks, you can tell me what you want and what you need, and I can make changes as we go along. And if Ettie is helping with her magic, it will be easier. We won't have to down tools if we've forgotten one little thing.'

Ettie beams and makes a face at Sticks.

He rolls his eyes, and then smiles. 'I built my first shop,' he says. 'Brick by brick, shelf by shelf. I feel like I should do the same with this one.'

'And you will,' Ettie says, 'but if any customers moan about the smell of your animals, you'll have to deal with them.'

Sticks nods and laughs.

Posey wrinkles her nose. 'Is that what I can smell from my room?'

Sticks nods. 'Sorry.'

'No, I actually don't mind. Smells like home. The tavern I was living in before I left was right next to a farm.'

Sticks beams, and they all laugh.

Sticks shows Posey what he wants, and Ettie conjures up a chair. Dayne flutters over.

'You don't really mind not using your magic, do you?'

Ettie laughs and shakes her head quickly. 'No, not at all. For a long time, I was so rubbish, I didn't use to as much as I should have or could have. But now, it's second nature. Sometimes I think it would be nice to do something, to go to the effort of it all, to feel proud of achieving it. But then I just think...' She wriggles her fingers, shooting magical sparks of blue and green and pink into the air.

Dayne laughs. 'As long as you're not offended.'

Ettie shakes her head. 'No, definitely not offended.'

'Good. Posey's nice, isn't she?' Dayne says, nodding at her. Her and Sticks are huddled together, which looks funny because she's stretching up and he's leaning down, but they're obviously going over all the little details.

'I think Sticks is up to something, with this place,' she says, remembering the couple of times he's been a bit shifty when talking about it.

'What do you mean?'

'When he talks about this place. He gets excited, then he starts blabbering, then he freezes, like he almost let something slip.'

'Ooh,' Dayne says, cocking her head. 'What do you think?'

Ettie shrugs. 'He told me once that his mum and dad are away hunting monsters...'

Dayne is open mouthed with shock. 'No! You don't think he'd try anything like that?'

'He loves animals, creatures, weird and wonderful things. His license is for anything with hooves and horns.'

'But he got in trouble when they thought he was peddling dangerous creatures. Surely monsters are dangerous?'

'I don't know enough about them, and I could be wrong,' Ettie says, though she has a very real feeling that she might be right.

'Monsters!' Dayne says. 'We've got enough going on without adding monsters to the mix.'

Ettie laughs. 'I know. A busy alehouse, extra bedrooms appearing upstairs, and a shop to build, and monsters?'

'Let's hope you're wrong,' Dayne says.

'Let's hope,' Ettie says, watching Sticks gesturing wildly to Posey, pointing at this and that.

Chapter 29

Back in the warmth of the alehouse, Ettie conjures up everything Posey needs to draw out the plans.

'I'll go to my room,' Posey says, 'if you don't mind. I need to concentrate. Sticks, I'll come and get you once I've made a start.'

'Do you want to eat first?' Ettie offers, but Posey shakes her head. 'Nah, I'm too excited.'

'Come through when you're hungry. You don't have to eat with us – though we'd love you to – but I can magic up anything you fancy.'

Posey nods her thanks and leaves the three of them alone.

'Do you think she's forgiven me?' Sticks asks, plonking down onto his oversized sofa, and putting his feet up on the footstool.

'Yes,' Dayne says. 'I think she's lovely. And I don't think she'd hold a grudge.'

'I think the same,' Ettie says. 'She's great – and once again, the alehouse knew what we needed before we did.'

'So clever,' Dayne says. 'I'll go to my dad tomorrow and ask for help. I don't think he'll say no, but what if the King can't spare them?'

'I'm sure he won't mind.'

'He's away, remember?'

'We'll ask Briella. It won't be all day, every day. If I'm magicking up the stuff you need to build it with, and I can keep everyone fed and watered...' she trails off, wondering if she could even perform a spell to slow down time, so if they were helping for a whole day, only an hour of real time would have passed.

'What?' Dayne asks, watching Ettie.

'Nothing, just wondering if I can help with my magic in some other way...'

'That I won't say no to,' Sticks says. 'You're not mad at me, are you? For wanting to do it without your help?'

Ettie shakes her head.

'You guys are too sweet. I really don't mind. I promise you. But I like that you're checking on me. Nobody ever bothered doing that at home, or when I was at the academy.'

'Tell us about the academy,' Dayne says, twirling a strand of her blue hair.

Ettie shrugs. 'What's to tell?'

'You were there a long time,' Sticks says. 'Did you always know you'd go there? Are there other schools for witches?'

'Magic us up some snacks,' Dayne says. 'And tell us all about it.'

Ettie sighs. Talking about the magical academy brings up uncomfortable feelings. She hates remembering what a failure she was, and she hates remembering the sick feeling she felt when she failed for the last time and was thrown out. She hates that Liss was so horrible to her, and she hates that she hasn't heard any more from her. She still, desperately, wants to hope that Liss is working undercover, trying to do whatever she's trying to do and prove whatever she's trying to prove against the new head, Professor Milton, but the more time that passes without hearing anything, the less she feels inclined to believe it.

'Come on,' Dayne says. 'Talking helps.'

'Snacks help,' Sticks says, swinging his legs around so he's lying on the sofa, hands crossed behind his head, his favourite position.

'Fine. I'll tell you all about it,' Ettie says. 'What do we want to eat?'

Sticks and Dayne call out half a dozen food and drink items, none of which really go with the other to make a meal, but Ettie does her thing and magics it all up.

The fire is low, the table is full of snacks and drinks, and even a pot of melted chocolate to dip stuff into, and she closes her eyes.

She doesn't want to relive her time at the academy, but maybe it will help. And it might help her new friends to understand what she's been through and what kind of person she used to be.

Chapter 30

E^{ttie} Ettie stands facing the enormous academy, a bag in one hand and her other hand resting on her case. All her other belongings and books are already here, waiting in her room, waiting for her to arrive and live out the best year of her life.

She beams, and turns to say goodbye to her parents, but the car has already left. Ettie swallows back tears. They didn't even say goodbye.

She shakes her head and plasters a fake smile on her face. This is a fresh start, a chance to show what she can do away from the witches in her own family who excel at every single thing they do, even breathing and existing.

She's been excited to come here, and now she's here, she mustn't let her parents lack of care upset her. She knows what they're like, and she knows that once she graduates, one year from today, they'll welcome her back with open arms.

She just has to prove herself to them, everyone here, and herself.

The noise around her is deafening as hundreds of students turn up with hundreds of family members. There are tears and hugs and laughter. Ettie sits on a bench, alone, her bag on her lap, her case by her feet.

Oh, she's heard stories about this place. Stories of the professors, the tests, the great food. She's ready to soak it all up and learn to be the best, from the best.

'This seat free?' a loud voice asks, and Ettie glances up to be met with giant shoes. She cranes her neck to look right up at a giant.

'I guess,' she says, knowing there's no way a giant will fit on this bench.

The giant sinks onto the floor beside the bench, and grins at Ettie.

Ettie smiles. One of the most exciting things about coming here was the prospect of meeting magical creatures. When her parents attended the magical academy at Thistle Batch, only witches and wizards were allowed to attend. Over time they opened the place up for any magical creatures with a magical disposition or a desire to learn. Ettie can't wait to meet giants and ogres and fairies, and who knows who she'll end up being besties with.

And it's the modern way, mixing all the creatures together. She kind of likes it, though this giant is making her a little wary. If she'd been a little wobbly on her way down, she'd have sat on Ettie and killed her.

'My name's Melissa,' the giant says. 'Everyone calls me Liss.'

'I'm Ettie. Etienne actually, but everyone calls me Ettie.'

Liss beams at her, and even though she's a tiny bit scared – she's heard all the old stories of the giants and how they always sided with the baddies – she's happy to have made a friend already. The first of many, she's sure.

A professor stands on the steps and claps her hands together.

'Final farewells,' she calls out. 'And then please head inside to the great hall. It's on the right as you go in, you can't miss it.'

'My parents have already gone,' Liss says. 'It's a long way to get back home.'

'Same,' Ettie says, refusing to admit that they didn't even get out of the car.

'Shall we go in?' Liss suggests and Ettie is happy to follow her. A house goblin comes to take their stuff away.

'I wonder who I'll be sharing with,' Ettie says.

'Oh, it's me,' Liss says. 'I asked one of the professors who I was sharing with, and she showed me on a long list, and then pointed you out.'

'Really? That's great,' Ettie says.

She follows Liss inside, careful to stand well back of the giant's massive feet – they're the size of cars, and then when they sit, she shifts her chair right over, so she doesn't get squashed.

Chapter 31

The students all quieten when the head teacher, a tall, elegant witch – Professor Essor stands up and clears her throat.

'Students, welcome. Look around you. These are your new friends and your peers. We will teach you everything you need to know to pass your exams in just one year here at the magical academy, but these people, they could be with you for a lifetime.'

The students all look around, grinning at each other. Ettie is solemn. She's waited so long to be here, built it up in her head to be the biggest thing ever, and now she's here she wants to soak it up and take it seriously. Reverently.

'Students have met future spouses, future employers, future employees. The majority of the faculty once sat right where you are and started their magical journey with us.'

She takes a sip of water. 'Some of you have magic in your bones.'

Ettie shivers. She should have magic in her bones; every other person in her family does, but she's always been just a little less instinctive. This place will be the making of her.

'Some of you love magic and everything about it and you want to learn it inside out. If you need a wand or if you don't, if you have magic in your blood or your heart, you're in the right place. Welcome!'

She lifts her cup in a toast and Ettie scrambles to her feet as the others around her stand and lift their glasses. She grabs her glass and knocks it, ale spilling everywhere. A witch opposite her scowls and cleans it up with a swish of her finger.

Ettie mouths her apology and lifts her empty hand to toast, feeling stupid.

'On that note,' the head continues, 'I'd like to welcome our newest member of the faculty. Professor Floella Lewis.'

Ettie cranes her neck to see, this time with a glass in hand to toast, and then sits abruptly down.

Professor Lewis is a troll. She's never met a troll before.

'Are you okay?' Liss whispers, which isn't actually a whisper, but more of a boom.

Ettie, mortified when all eyes dart to her, nods and smiles and stands back up. 'Of course. Just cramp in my leg. Cramp in my leg,' she says a little louder, just in case anyone is still wondering.

Professor Lewis lifts her drink. 'Thank you. I'm so excited to be here, to teach you, to fill your wonderful minds with even more wonderful magic.'

The food appears in front of them, and everyone digs in, laughing and chatting, but Ettie is silent, wondering how to start conversations with the other students, wondering what she can say that might be funny or interesting.

'Where are you from?' the efficient witch sitting opposite her asks.

Ettie freezes. Where is she from? 'Um, from, um, I'm-'

The witch to the left of her answers, and the two girls start chatting away, ignoring Ettie or forgetting about her or just not interested.

Ettie slowly eats her food. She couldn't even think straight when that girl asked her a simple question. Is it because she's away from home? Finally here? Or because her parents drove off without saying goodbye, without even getting out of the car to hug her or kiss her.

She takes a long drink of her ale.

Everyone around her is happy. They are eating, drinking, talking, laughing. She feels like she's in a bubble, like their voices are coming from too far away to understand, like her reactions have slowed down. Like she's drowning.

Nobody else asks her anything.

She can see friendships being forged in real time, things people have in common and exclaim over, things people find interesting or fascinating and ooh and aah over. She sits alone, as though an invisible forcefield is keeping her from interacting with anyone.

She refills her drink and magics up some more food onto her plate. Eating and drinking at least make her look busy, and make her look like less of a fool than she feels.

Chapter 32

When people start leaving the room to further fraternise, Ettie heads to her room. She's at the top of the tower of dorm rooms, and when she goes inside, she can see why. Giants need the head room, and this room goes right into the eaves.

Liss isn't there yet, but they don't have to pick a bed, Ettie can tell which one is her bed. The tiny one under the window. She kneels on it, looking out of the window. She can't see anybody because of the other buildings, but she can see the inky black sky, and the twinkling lights. She flourishes away a tear.

This is her life now, her fresh start, her place. She's heard so much about it, and how so many of her family members came here and had the time of their lives, fell in love, met new people, were challenged and had their horizons definitively broadened. She wants all of that, but she also feels a bit empty.

She's never been to a school before. She was home schooled by a governess, the cleverest witch she ever met, but a cold woman, a matter of fact, no beating around the bush, get things done kind of woman. She didn't have playmates or friends; she had her governess, and she had her cousins. She didn't have siblings.

This is her school. Where she'll make friends and have fun and get into scrapes and japes. She has been waiting for this her whole childhood, and now at seventeen, she's here. Ready to learn, ready to find her place in the magical world.

Once she graduates, she'll be allowed to join her family on their trips and she won't be alone again.

In the meantime, she'll settle in, she'll make friends, she'll find her feet.

She tries to convince herself, but as she curls up on the bed, she wonders if she's kidding herself. Will she always be ignored in the hall? Will she always freeze when anyone asks her a question? Will she spill things and break things and set things on fire like she often did at home?

She sits up. No. This can be different. It might have been a rocky start, but nobody knows her here. Nobody knows that she's quiet and awkward and a bit shy. She can be anything she wants here, anyone she wants. And she wants to be happy and popular.

The door opens, and Ettie sits up, tidying her hair and drying her tears with one magical flourish of her fingers.

Liss walks in and sits on her giant bed.

'Hey,' Ettie says.

'Hey,' Liss says. 'That was tough.'

'What was tough?' Ettie asks.

Liss wipes a tear from her face, but one plops onto the floor and makes a puddle.

'This whole thing,' Liss says. 'When my parents left I felt okay, but I can see I'm the only giant here, and I've already overheard three people say giants don't belong here.'

Ettie feels a flush of anger creep over her. Why would anyone be so unkind, especially when they're all new students together.

'I'm sure they're not trying to be mean,' she says. 'I'm sure it's just because the academy was only open to witches and wizards for so long. Other magical creatures weren't allowed.'

Liss glares at her, and Ettie shrinks back.

'And do you agree with that?' Liss asks, her voice clipped.

Ettie shakes her head; of course she doesn't agree. But before she can answer – why is she so tongue-tied here – Liss scoffs and storms out of the room, leaving the door wide open.

Ettie sighs. It's okay. Tomorrow is another day. She'll be nice to Liss. And make loads of friends. And everything will be okay.

Chapter 33

When Ettie wakes up, Liss' bed is empty, but she can see it's been slept in. The covers are pulled up but rumpled. Ettie fell asleep before she got back last night, so she hasn't seen her since their awkward conversation.

She doesn't have a problem with giants and trolls, not at all, she's just never met any before. It's quite fascinating to be around students who aren't just witches and wizards.

She dresses in a black pinafore dress, and swishes her rainbow hair into a bun.

She feels an equal mix of excitement and trepidation today. She was foolish yesterday to assume she'd just rock up and have instant friends and instant connections; life isn't like that. But she's also ready to make this the best year of her life, and that means showing up, doing her best, putting the effort in.

She's too early for breakfast so she explores the academy and the grounds, both of which are vast and impressive, and then heads to the great hall in time to eat. She chooses a different table today, noticing that people seem to be sitting wherever; there aren't assigned seats. But most people do seem to be coming into the room in groups or pairs, already laughing and joking and bonding. She swallows down a brief moment of panic. Is she too late? Have alliances been formed and friendship groups established?

She smiles at a blonde witch who nods but walks past her.

She closes her eyes. Breathe, Ettie. She's not too late. It's never too late.

Liss walks in, and glares at her. Ettie lifts her hand to wave, and then drops it, when Liss scowls and marches past her to sit where she'd sat yesterday. Ettie frowns. Now it looks like she's only moved to be away from Liss, which isn't the case. She just thought they should sit anywhere, move around, meet new people, see new faces.

She cranes her neck to gesture for Liss to join her, but the giant isn't looking her way.

People fill the seats around her, but they seem to know each other already, and although they all nod and smile at Ettie and a few say hello, she sits alone again. She eats and drinks, and watches the world go by, an observer not a partaker. She keeps a smile painted on her face.

This is just one meal. She'll start to make friends as the day goes by, as the week goes by. It's only her first day!

She finishes up her juice, and heads out of the hall, wandering the grounds again. It's a beautiful place and she feels at home. So much of it is familiar to her. Her parents, her grandparents, her governess, they all came to this magical academy. And they all thrived.

She's ready to do the same and she turns up to her first lesson before anybody else.

She slips inside and finds a seat at the front, so she can hear everything the professor says and really soak up all the knowledge.

The troll walks into the room, catching Ettie by surprise.

'Good morning,' Professor Lewis says, hefting the pile of books she's carrying under one arm onto the table, and heaving her bag onto the chair.

Ettie doesn't know what to say. She's never met a troll before, and she's nervous. She's already upset Liss without meaning to – she doesn't want to upset her teacher too.

She takes a deep breath, wanting to speak to her professor without putting her foot in it.

'Are you all right?' Professor Lewis asks, taking a step toward her.

Ettie nods, suddenly tongue-tied again.

Understanding flashes across Professor Lewis' expression and she turns away from Ettie, her posture stiff. Ettie wants to cry out, and grab her, and tell her she's not afraid of her, she just wants to be nice, but the door swings open and the other students flood in. Ettie feels shame creep over her. Now it looks like she was scared of the troll or mean, neither of which are true.

She keeps her eyes on her parchment, so she doesn't cry, and waits for someone to take the seat beside her. Then they'll start chatting throughout the lesson, getting to know each other and helping each other with their work.

But as Professor Lewis clears her throat and introduces herself, and her subject, magic in non-magical creatures, Ettie realises nobody is sitting beside her. She takes a quick look behind her, smile on her face, and sees that all the other seats are full, and the only empty seat is beside her.

She swallows down disappointment, and sadness. Making friends isn't easy.

She keeps her head down, refusing to make eye contact with anyone.

She keeps ruining everything – first with Liss, now with her professor, nobody wants to sit by her.

It's sad.

Chapter 34

Ettie pulls off her sparkly red boots and sighs. What a day. A rubbish day. A sad and lonely day.

Why is she finding it so hard to make friends? She looked for Liss in the great hall at break time and lunch time and tea time but there was no sign of her, and she could hardly miss her. She sat alone in every lesson; friendships already formed that didn't include her. In one lesson, when they had to work in pairs, and she was the odd one out, the professor put her in a group of three, with a boy and a girl, and they both talked to her, but she still felt left out. She felt like someone on the outside, someone who couldn't make herself seen or heard. The few times she put her hand up to answer, the professor picked someone else, and by the end of the day she had spoken so little, she wasn't even sure her voice would work anymore.

She rushed up to her room, hoping Liss would be there, hoping she'd have someone to talk to, but the room is empty.

She lies down and closes her eyes.

Tomorrow is another day. But tomorrow will be the same as today. She'll smile at people and they'll smile back, she'll wait for someone to sit beside her, but nobody will, she'll put her hand up when she knows the answer, but nobody will ask. And she'll probably put her foot in it with some other magical creatures – she's sure she saw a group of pixies in the great hall earlier, maybe she can find them and insult them too.

A wave of sadness hits her, and she feels like a warm blanket of misery has been laid over her, and she can't get out from under it; it's too heavy, too constricting.

This is only the first day, she thinks. 'This is only the first day,' she says out loud, relieved to hear her voice, to know that it does exist, that she does.

Why is this so difficult?

She reads some books, and then conjures up some cakes and biscuits, some ale. She could go down to the great hall – they have snacks available throughout the day, but she doesn't want to see anybody. It hurts to watch them laughing, and learning about each other. It hurts to eat her meals and watch other students click and bond.

Why isn't she a part of it? What makes her so different?

She eventually falls asleep and when she wakes the next day, Liss is nowhere to be seen. Ettie decides to be more positive today, more proactive. Instead of waiting for someone to sit by her, she will go and sit by people. She will start conversations. She will push herself forward, so she can't be ignored anymore.

She spots Liss immediately in the great hall, and there's nobody sitting near her.

She heads over.

'Morning,' she says, in an overly bright voice, craning her neck to see the giant.

'Morning,' Liss says, her voice flat.

'Settled in?' Ettie asks, feeling weird. Why is small talk so embarrassing?

'Sure,' Liss says, and Ettie knows she's lying. Is the giant finding it hard to settle in too?

'I was asleep before you got in,' Ettie says, hoping Liss will share where she was and what she was doing.

'You were,' Liss says, and picks up her giant mug. She doesn't utter another word, and Ettie sits through breakfast with nobody to talk to. The seats near her and Liss don't fill up, and she wonders if people are avoiding her because she's the loner with no friends.

'See you later,' she calls, as she heads out of the hall.

Chapter 35

Ettie sits on her bed and lets out a small scream of frustration. Hot tears spill from her eyes and she lets them. She's sick of smiling, putting her hand up, talking to people who ignore her, and being by herself. It was another day of being alone and feeling awkward.

Her stomach is a pit of butterflies, her face feels hot and she's itchy. She tried so hard today to make friends and be nice and push herself forward, and all day nobody has wanted to sit by her or talk to her. She was asked to answer one question, and she got it wrong.

She pulls off her shoes and lies down. This place sucks, everyone here sucks, and she hates it here. She wants to go home where she's safe and happy and sheltered and people talk to her.

People like her governess.

People like her parents when they're home.

She conjures up a magical feast of sugary treats and stuffs her face, reading a spell book, gutted that the only thing she got asked today she was wrong about.

She scowls. Why isn't this going the way she wanted it to? The way she thought it would? She's waited so long to come here, so long to be ready, and it's rubbish. She's on her own, with nobody to talk to or laugh with, or spend time with.

She sits up and pulls her shoes back on, grabbing her coat and heading out to the grounds.

The grounds are the only good thing here. There are rolling hills, thatches of forest, a lake… she hasn't explored all of it yet. But that's what she'll do. In between lessons when nobody wants to talk to her, she'll walk, and at least she'll be surrounded by beauty while she's so miserable.

She heads down a slope, turning her head at the sound of laughter. She doesn't want to see more students having fun and making friends while she's finding it so difficult.

There's a small pond ahead of her, so she veers off the path, seeing a flash of colour out of the corner of her eye. She pauses. Is someone following her?

She shakes her head. Who would be following her?

She hasn't been this way before. It's pretty; the light of the setting sun dancing on the water, and some ducks swimming. There are benches dotted all around the grounds and she spots one near the pond, and heads for it.

To the left of the pond are more trees, dense and teeming with birds, but she can't see what's on the other side. She needs to get closer.

The ducks are fun to watch, splashing and playing, and she sits on the bench watching them. They seem to make friends easily.

'Help!'

She cocks her head. Did she just hear that? Someone calling for help, or is she hearing things? Making up conversations because nobody will speak to her?

'Help!'

She stands up. She definitely heard that. A panicked voice calling for help.

From where?

She closes her eyes and calls out. 'Hello?'

'I need help!'

The voice is coming from the trees, and Ettie heads over at a sprint.

There is a pathway that runs through the forest, but it's very dark. She conjures up a tiny flame and it dances ahead of her, lighting the way.

'Oof!' she trips over something and lands with a thud on the floor, her flame extinguished.

She lifts her hands to conjure another one, and someone grabs hold of her arms, roughly, pinning them behind her.

'Hey! Get off!' she shouts and struggles but whoever has hold of her is stronger.

Fear floods through her. Is it the troll? Is she going to die?

Magical ties bind her hands and legs, and she's trussed up against a tree. Then someone lights the area with magic lanterns and Ettie can see what's going on.

Except she can't, there are five students, cloaked, standing around her in a semi circle, and each of them is wearing a mask.

'Who are you? Why am I tied up?' she asks, fear making her voice tremble.

'We are the school bullies,' a male voice says, stepping forward.

Ettie shakes her head. Surely school bullies would be more subtle about what they were doing.

'We don't like you,' a girl says, stepping forward, mask covering up who she is, what she looks like.

Ettie takes a deep breath. 'Please let me go, I haven't done anything wrong.'

'You have,' another masked student steps forward. 'You're the biggest loser here. We've been watching all the new students, we've been assessing everyone, and you've come up short. You don't have anything interesting to say. When you've answered in class, you've been wrong.'

'Nobody wants to sit by you.'

Ettie closes her eyes; she doesn't want to see them, and she doesn't want to hear them. Everything they're saying is what she feared. She is a loser. She hasn't made any friends. She can't even answer questions right.

'Do you know what we do to losers?' a boy asks, stepping forward, fist raised.

He punches her square in the nose, and she cries out.

'This isn't the last time you'll see us,' they say, and they vanish in a swish of cloaks and cruel laughter.

Ettie tries to use her magic to untie herself, but it doesn't work.

These students are mean, but their magic is advanced.

A tear works its way down her cheek and plops onto the ground.

Chapter 36

She wouldn't have thought it possible, but she falls asleep and when she wakes up her entire body hurts. She reaches up gingerly to touch her nose. The blood has dried and her whole face hurts.

It's dark in the forest, but she can see the sky through the trees is dark too.

Will she be out here all night? Nobody will care. Liss won't look for her. Her professors might start to worry if she doesn't turn up for any of her classes again tomorrow, but she'll be out here all night. Alone. Cold. Scared.

She tries to use magic again to untie herself, to free the shackles that bind her wrists and ankles and the ones that have bound her to the tree. They're not budging.

This isn't what she was expecting from her first week at the magical academy. She was hoping to make friends and have fun and become part of something.

Instead she's cold and hurt.

She lets herself cry.

'Hello?' the voice calling out is quiet but not a whisper. She just knows it's Liss.

'Over here!' she shouts as loud as she can.

'Keep calling,' the voice says.

And Ettie does. 'I'm here! Over here! Here I am!' She calls out for what seems like an hour, but she knows is only minutes, and then

Liss comes lumbering through the trees. She's so tall that her head is above the highest treetops, and she's so wide that she's taking whole trees out as she makes her way towards Ettie's voice.

Liss lowers her hand.

'Climb on,' she says.

'I can't,' Ettie says. 'I'm tied up to a tree, and my magic isn't working.'

Liss holds her hand out, fingers stretched.

'Tell me which tree you're on. I'll pull you up.'

Ettie's eyes widen, but she nods, even though Liss can't see her. She can't stay here, and Liss is too big to reach down and untie her.

'You're going to pull up the whole tree?'

'I can't think of anything else to do,' Liss calls through the trees.

Ettie smiles. If anyone was watching, this scene would look so ridiculous. She is tied to a tree, her magic not working for a reason she can't yet fathom, and Liss, a gigantic giant, has crashed her way through the trees. Her head is above the treeline, and her body below, and now she's holding out her hand, ready to rip a tree up by the roots.

Just to rescue Ettie.

'How did you know where to find me?' Ettie asks her.

'I didn't really,' Liss says. 'But when I didn't see you all day, and you weren't in your classes, I knew something was wrong.'

'Are any professors looking for me?'

'No, I covered for you. I didn't know why you weren't around.'

'Well, it wasn't my choice,' Ettie says.

'I can see that now,' Liss says, and then she giggles. 'Well, actually I can't see anything at all, except a load of leaves.'

Ettie laughs. 'Stop. Right a bit. There. That's the tree I'm tied to.'

Liss grabs hold of the tree and it takes a minute but then Ettie flies through the leaves and branches of all the other trees, a few of them scratching her, and then she's out of the woods. Still tied to a tree. But free.

Liss holds her aloft, and shoves her way back out of the woods, making a path of her own.

Then she sets the tree down on the grass verge and uses a knife to cut Ettie free.

Ettie gets shakily to her feet and wipes her tears away.

She hugs Liss around the ankle, not even able to get her arms the whole way around.

'Thank you.'

Liss shrugs.

'No, I mean it. I know we're not really friends yet…'

'I know,' Liss says, sitting down, her expression sad. 'Why not?'

Ettie shrugs. 'I don't know. I guess I thought being here would be fun, and I'd have a million friends, and…' She doesn't know what to say. 'I didn't mean to offend you. I think giants should be welcome here, and any other magical creature who wants to come here. It's more fun that way.'

'You think?'

Ettie nods. 'It's a little overwhelming, but only because I've had such a sheltered life.' Ettie says, and then smiles. 'You're the kindest person I've met since I've been here.'

Liss grins. 'I don't find it easy to make friends. I'm too big.'

'I've never had to try to make friends before,' Ettie says. 'I was home schooled all my life and I don't have siblings. This was my big chance, you know, to make friends and to have fun.'

'Mine too,' Liss says. 'I don't have any giants my age in my family, so I've always been on my own.'

'Making friends is hard,' Ettie says.

'It is when you're stuck up,' Liss says, frowning at her.

Ettie smiles. 'I'm sorry. I wasn't trying to be stuck up – I'm just scared and anxious and desperate for a friend. I want someone to talk to and laugh with and eat midnight feasts with.'

'Now, that I can do,' Liss says.

'Yeah?'

'Definitely. And maybe you'll realise that giants are really nice.'

'And maybe you'll realise that I was never stuck up, I was just shy. And awkward. And lonely.'

Liss nods at the academy.

'Time to go inside?'

Ettie nods, though her stomach is twisting. 'What if I see the bullies?'

Liss shrugs. 'You think they won't be afraid of me?'

Ettie shrugs. 'I felt like they weren't afraid of anything, or anyone. They were bold.'

'And horrible. We'll face them together,' Liss says. 'I want to work here, once our year is over, I want to take advanced studies so I can train as a professor, and when I do, I'll make sure nobody is ever bullied again.'

Chapter 37

They head up to their room, and Ettie uses a spell to lock the door.

'Just in case,' she says. 'I wonder why my magic didn't work earlier. They must have done something to me.'

'I don't like that. Tying you up is bad enough but taking your magic... it's sinister.'

'It is...' Ettie trails off. 'Do I tell someone?'

Liss shrugs. 'I would say yes, but then these guys weren't messing about. If I hadn't come looking for you, and your magic didn't come back, you could have become really ill. Sitting out in the cold and the damp all night, could have made you seriously unwell.'

'But who do I tell?'

'Professor Essor,' Liss says. 'She's the head of the place. She's bound to want to know what's going on here. I'm sure she'd want to stamp any nonsense out.'

'Yeah...' Ettie doesn't sound too sure.

'I'll come with you,' Liss says. 'She'll have to do something. She can't let those kids get away with it.'

'But I don't know who they are. They wore masks.'

'That's so creepy,' Liss says, her voice low.

'So creepy,' Ettie agrees with her. 'But clever. I couldn't identify them if I wanted to.'

'So maybe we wait. See if they try anything else,' Liss says, and Ettie nods. To be honest, she'd rather forget anything had ever happened. It makes her feel sad and sick that she was targeted for no good reason.

'Are you hungry?' she asks Liss. She is suddenly starving.

'Yeah,' Liss says. 'I could eat. What have you got in mind? Go down and see what snacks are available?'

Ettie grins and holds up her hand. She conjures up some chocolate cakes.

'Something like this,' Ettie says and passes one to Liss.

Liss eats it in one bite, and murmurs her appreciation.

'That was delicious.'

'Plenty more where that came from,' Ettie says. 'I might suck at making friends and my social skills might be lacking, but I can magic up the best food you ever ate. Go on, what do you really fancy?'

'Deep fried tarantulas?' Liss asks, her eyes lighting up.

Ettie can't help herself; she makes a face. 'Gross. But here you go.'

She conjures up a big bowl full of crispy, deep fried tarantulas.

Liss takes one and licks her lips.

'Jellied slugs?' she asks, and Ettie laughs. 'I don't even know what they are.'

But her magic knows, and she fills another bowl with them.

Liss wipes her mouth with her hand. 'This is fun. Can every witch do this?'

Ettie shakes her head slowly. 'Not every witch, no. But lots of them. I'm very good at it. But I've spent years practising. When you don't have many friends, it's easy to turn to food instead.'

Liss pats her substantial tummy. 'Tell me about it. We're going to need an even bigger room if you're going to keep serving these kinds of snacks.'

Ettie laughs. 'You haven't even tested me yet.'

'Garlic encrusted goat,' she calls out. 'Spicy lizard nuggets. Jam topped beetles.'

Every gross thing she asks for, Ettie magics up with ease, and with a giggle.

'I have never magicked up so much disgusting stuff,' she says, laying on her bed and laughing. 'No offence,' she adds.

'None taken,' Liss says, 'but it is a bit messy.'

With a flourish of her fingers, Ettie clears all the mess, all the empty and half empty bowls and plates and passes Liss a wet cloth to clean her fingers with.

'I'm glad I rescued you,' Liss says, pulling off her enormous shoes and lying down on her bed.

Her shoes are as big as a boat, and Ettie can't help but giggle.

'What?' Liss asks, one eyebrow raised.

Ettie holds a hand up. 'I can't. I don't want to be rude, not after you just saved me.'

'Go on,' Liss says, a smile tugging at her lips.

'Well, you really are giant, for a giant.'

'Giants usually are,' Liss says, dryly. She's smiling though. 'You've really never met one before?'

'Never even seen one in real life,' Ettie says. 'I wasn't sure if giants were even real for the longest time.'

Liss laughs. 'Ettie, you've got a lot to learn.'

Ettie shrugs. 'It's what I came here for. To learn, to grow, to make friends.'

'Friend,' Liss says, emphasising the one word.

'Friend. When you've never had friends, one is precious.'

Liss grins. 'You're a right softy.'

Ettie shrugs. 'Maybe, but it's true. I was really scared today. I didn't know what those students were going to do to me, and I really thought they were going to come back and hurt me.'

'Maybe you are soft, Ettie, but that's not a bad thing. I'm softer than most giants, according to my family. They're always telling me to toughen up, and not let people take advantage of me, but sometimes it's nice to be nice, right?'

'Right,' Ettie agrees, and then turns her head when tears spring to her eyes. She doesn't want to embarrass herself by crying in front of her new friend.

Especially if she turns out to be her only friend.

Chapter 38

'And that's how I met Liss,' Ettie says, misty eyed, remembering their friendship and how important it was to her, but also feeling a hot flash of shame at how rude she was to her when they first met. 'Do you think I was rude?' she asks, unable to look up at them, unable to meet their eyes.

'I don't,' Dayne says, flying over to be by her side. 'You were young. Hey, what happened to the bullies?'

'I was going to ask the same,' Sticks says. 'Did they get their comeuppance?'

Ettie nods. 'It took a while, but they picked on the wrong kid eventually. They tried to attack a witch, but it turned out she was a shapeshifter – she shifted into a werewolf and bit the lot of them. It was quite the scandal.'

Dayne and Sticks laugh.

'Anyway, Liss definitely helped me – being best friends with a giant meant that I couldn't judge them harshly.'

'You must be so sad that she turned out to be a bad one,' Dayne says, fluttering her wings.

Ettie sighs. 'I'm not convinced...' she says, but she still doesn't tell them about the letter Liss sent her. If Liss is working undercover to bring Professor Milton down, then Ettie would never blow it for her. And if she's not, if it was all a lie to make her feel better somehow, then Ettie's no worse off for believing it. Not really.

'And your exams?' Sticks asks.

'I hate talking about it,' Ettie says. 'When I failed that first year, I figured it was just nerves. I didn't make other friends, not really. There were people I said hello to, and people I worked with in groups, but mostly it was me and Liss.'

'Was she popular?' Dayne asks, flying back to her little seat.

'More popular than me,' Ettie says. 'And of course, she stayed on for further education, and then to teach. I struggled.'

'I don't know why,' Dayne says, running a hand through her bright turquoise hair. 'You're so sweet and kind. I think everyone would want to be your friend.'

Ettie smiles. 'You're kind, both of you, but I find it hard. I feel awkward when I meet new people, and shy, but they assume I'm stuck up and unfriendly. The opposite is true, though. I love people, and I love listening to what they have to say, but again, that makes me look like I've got nothing to say for myself. It makes me look boring.'

Sticks points a finger at her. 'We don't think you're boring, and we are the only ones that count. And if Liss turns out to be good, then good, and if she turns out to be bad, so what. You'll still be okay, and you'll always be our friend.'

'Thanks guys. I like having you as friends. Every day here seems to blot out all my time there.'

'That's good,' Dayne says. 'Can you magic up some sweets?'

Ettie does so, easily, and Sticks and Dayne pick what they want. Ettie takes what's left.

'The magical academy was sad,' Ettie says, chewing on a liquorice twist. 'Being there was sad, and being thrown out was sad, but now I'm here, I feel okay. I feel like I'm happier, and everything's a bit easier.'

'It's this place,' Dayne says, gesturing at the room. 'This place is magical.'

'Enchanted,' Sticks says. 'I feel better here too. I don't feel so sad when I think about the shop burning down, or Lox betraying me. Or my parents trying to eat me.'

'Poor Sticks,' Dayne says, passing him a toffee chew.

'Thanks,' he says, shoving it in his mouth. 'We've all been through some crap but look where we ended up.'

'Tell us,' Dayne says, fluttering her eyelashes and her wings.

Sticks laughs. 'Tell you what?'

'Your story. How did an ogre with murderous parents end up here?'

Sticks scratches his chin.

'I suppose it's an interesting story. With a happy ending.'

'More snacks?' Ettie asks, and Sticks grins.

'Always. Go on then. I'll tell you all about a fat little ogre who realised he could heal, and who with the help of his witchy mum, found a little bit of magic in his fat fingers.'

Ettie clears the table and then conjures up another feast – this time all sweet treats, tiny apple pies, jugs of custard, of course, chocolates and sweets.

'Candy floss,' Dayne says, settling onto her tiny chair, legs tucked under her.

Ettie magics up the candy floss for Dayne, and then settles in her chair. She wraps a blanket around her, and they both look at Sticks, waiting for his story.

Chapter 39

S<u>ticks</u>
Sticks was just three years old when he first rescued an animal - a frog faced, winged, volcanic lizard, which burnt the end of his nose and left little sooty flecks all over his cheeks like freckles every time it sneezed, which was often.

He nursed it back to health. He mended its tiny wing, sewing the frayed edges together with needle and gossamer, and he let drops of honey water drip from his fat fingers into the lizard's mouth until its energy came back. He found the right ingredients to heal it by foraging in the forest surrounding his house and when the lizard was gone one morning, instead of getting upset, he was incredibly proud of himself.

'We could have eaten that,' his mother growled at him, her grey eyes dark with venom.

'Maybe we'll have to eat him instead,' his dad joked.

Sticks backed himself into a corner of the cave and watched his parents.

He'd like to think his dad was joking, but the way they're both looking at him, eyeing him up, rubbing their already fat bellies, he felt unsafe.

'I thought we were going to sell him,' his mother's angry voice floated through the air.

'Eating him is quicker,' his dad says, giving him a sly look. 'There's a fair bit of meat on him.'

His mother looks at him, and he keeps his eyes on both of them.

He loves animals and he's watched enough of them in the forest around his home to know that sometimes animals eat their babies.

The first time he'd seen a mammy mouse chomp down her baby in one go, he'd been horrified, but the more he saw, the more he accepted it.

Loving creatures means loving them, foibles and all.

But now he's watching his parents watching him, eating your own baby doesn't feel quite so much a foible, as an abomination.

It feels like the minute he looks the other way, they'll eat him, or the second he falls asleep, he'll never wake up.

Three years old is too young to come to the realisation that your parents don't love you, and they'd rather get a meal or two out of you, than give you the unconditional love and guidance that every parent should give their child.

He keeps his face neutral, even though on the inside his little mind is scrambling.

He has to escape. He has to run away. He cannot stay here with his parents, who clearly have their best interests at heart and not his.

He's fairly big and cumbersome already – ogres always are – but his parents are eyeing each other up, spoiling for a fight, and he knows that he has to go now.

He takes a deep breath and runs for the door.

He doesn't know how long it will take them to notice that he's gone. They've fought so badly before, he's had to sort out his own food for days, but they've also made up so quickly, he's had to look the other way because the way they slobber all over each other is disgusting.

Outside the cave, he lumbers towards the trees; the forest is his playground, and he knows it far better than either of his parents.

If he doesn't stumble and he doesn't look back, he can make it to the river. Once he gets to the river, he can follow the water away from here, away from them.

He's never gone further than the third bend in the river. Not that anyone warned him not to – truthfully his parents never cared where he was – but he's a sensible boy as ogres go, and he never wanted to get lost or out of his depth.

Now he knows he'll have to venture past the third bend.

His life literally depends on it.

He hears a shout and a swear and he knows his parents are on the move.

He also knows they won't catch him.

He's only three but he's already smarter than they are, kinder than they are and more capable than they are.

He sloshes through the river, already tall enough that he can wade through the water, rather than swim. He doesn't know how to swim very well; he always worries that he'll get swept away, but he's not scared.

He'd rather drown than become dinner for his parents.

The river gets deeper and he paddles and then swims. He's not got a lot of technique; he's splashing and crashing and would never be described as elegant, but he's moving in the right direction, and although he swallows a bit more water than is probably healthy, he eventually passes the third bend, and finds that his feet touch the floor again.

He laughs and wades onwards.

Is he scared? Maybe a little bit.

Is he glad to be free? A lot.

Chapter 40

Eventually his toddler feet get tired and he heads to the river bank. He clambers up, using the tree roots and vines to pull himself up and when he gets to the dry land, he lies down in the afternoon sun.

He yawns and rubs his eyes. He's tired now. And achy. He scratches his belly. He's hungry too.

He flips onto his front and crawls along the ground, looking for a lizard or a newt or a frog, if he's lucky. Any sort of snack will do.

A frog!

He's quick and grabs hold of it with meaty fingers.

The frog lets out an indignant croak.

Sticks ignores it and brings the fat, wriggling body closer to his mouth.

The frog croaks again, and Sticks meets his eyes.

The frog croaks loudly – and disapprovingly – his gaze firmly on Sticks.

Sticks frowns.

It's like the frog is trying to tell him something.

Don't eat me, maybe. I'm just like you. Let's be friends.

Sticks knows his own parents classed him as food. He classes the frog as food.

They are the same. He kisses the frog on his slimy head.

'I won't eat you,' he says. 'I'll eat something else instead.'

He lets go of the frog, but the frog doesn't hop away; instead, he keeps looking at Sticks, blinking his eyes slowly.

Sticks grins and picks it up again. He shoves the frog in his pocket, and toddles through the bushes and trees trying to find food.

He finds berries and fruit, and he instinctively seems to know the things that are safe to eat. With berry juice dripping down his chin, he wanders through the woods, looking for more food or somewhere comfy to rest his head.

The frog croaks periodically, and Sticks chats back to him. He's not sure if the frog can understand him, or if they're having two completely separate conversations, but it helps to keep his mind busy.

It's sad when your parents want to eat you, and he is only three.

What started out as a brave adventure to save himself from becoming a quick snack for the two nastiest ogres in the village, who just happen to be his parents, has turned into a lonely, hungry trek through quite scary woods. And he's cold.

And tired.

And hungry.

All at once it's too much for little Sticks, and he plonks onto the floor and cries.

His blonde hair, like a tiny lion's mane gets sticky with dribble and snot as he cries and tries to wipe his face.

He really doesn't like this day.

Eventually he falls asleep, bracken under his head, an uncomfy pillow, and the frog standing guard beside him.

When the frog is sure the toddler is asleep, he croaks for the attention of a bushy tailed squirrel, the squirrel takes over sentry duty, and the frog hops back to the cabin in the middle of the woods.

He hops through an open window, and lands squarely on the open page of a spell book.

'Dumpling!'

The frog croaks and Toady-loo laughs, tickling him under the chin.

The frog refuses to move.

'What is it, little one?'

The frog hops back over to the window sill.

Toady-loo laughs. 'Okay – I'll bite. Do we need Dave, or will I do?'

The frog cocks his head, and Toady-loo does the same.

'I'll do – last I saw him Dave was washing his golf clubs. I don't want to spoil his fun. Never mind that he's never played a game in his life. Everyone needs a hobby.'

She picks up a jar of wriggling caterpillars, who all change colour intermittently and occasionally burp fire, and uses it as a paperweight to keep the spell book open.

Grabbing a patchwork coat off the hook, she pulls it on, and heads out of the front door.

She spots Dumpling waiting patiently on the path and grins.

'Come on then, old friend. What's the mystery?'

Dumpling hops along, going off the beaten path, and through the thickest part of the woods.

When he sees the squirrel ahead, he stops and turns to Toady-loo.

She frowns and moves closer. The squirrel hops away and Toady-loo exclaims when she sees the ogre nestled on the floor.

It looks like a baby ogre to her, maybe three or four years old. Already five feet tall, and two foot wide. He's bright green, with yellow hair that sticks up in a ring of fire around his head.

Sleeping he looks adorable, a bit sticky from snot and dribble, but sweet.

But ogres are bad news – irritable, prone to spitefulness. Usually murderous. Petty. Small minded. Only bad words come to her head as she looks at this little bundle of green.

She turns to Dumpling and lowers her voice.

'Really? I'm doing important work and you bring me here, for this?'

She holds out an arm, gesturing at the sleeping ogre.

Dumpling shakes his head.

'Fine, not important work, but an ogre, really? He'd eat you for breakfast, so I don't know why you've brought me here.'

Dumpling shakes his head again.

'What, you don't think he'd eat you. You're a snack to an ogre and you know it.'

Dumpling shakes his head again and hops over to Sticks.

He jumps onto his chest and croaks loudly.

Toady-loo covers her mouth with her hand, so she doesn't cry out, and hides behind a tree.

Sticks opens his eyes.

They widen when he sees the frog.

'Hi, frog.'

Dumpling jumps into his open hand.

Sticks grins at him in delight, making little cooing noises.

'I'm glad I didn't eat you,' he says, and Toady-loo stares from behind the tree.

Sticks lowers his voice.

'I tell you a secret,' he says. 'I'm never to eat a frog again.'

He beams at Dumpling and scratches his own belly.

'Sticks,' he says, pointing at himself. 'Sticks not eat animals, or frogs, or bugs, or chickens, or quack quacks, or cows, or lizards, or...'

Dumpling croaks loudly to interrupt the flow of animals the toddler won't eat.

'Another secret,' he says, leaning forward, his fat belly sitting in the way like a ball. 'I'm scared. I ran away. But I'm scared. What if someone hurts Sticks? Or bites me? I don't like biting. What if I am lost? Or a storm comes. I don't like storms. I like sweets. Have you got sweets?'

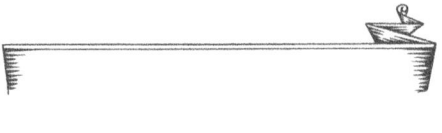

Chapter 41

'I've got sweets,' Toady-loo says, ignoring all her instincts and stepping out from behind the tree.

The ogre's eyes widen, and he opens his mouth to cry or scream or shout. She's not sure.

She quickly conjures up a sweet – a rhubarb and custard, her mum's favourite – and holds it out for the boy.

His mouth snaps shut, and he scratches his belly, frowning.

She walks slowly toward him, more of a creep than a walk, a sort of creep, shuffle, mooch; she doesn't want to scare him.

She holds out her hand, as she lowers herself to the floor.

He looks at her, eyes wide, and a single, fat tear snakes down his chubby little face.

'Oh, darling boy,' Toady-loo says, shuffling forward on her bum, and scooping him into a hug. He's bigger than her and heavier than her, but his little face, all green and blotchy, his wide eyes, so friendly and innocent have hooked her.

He takes the sweet and she rocks him until he's calm and happy.

She points at him. 'Sticks?'

He nods, grinning.

She points at herself. 'Toady-loo.'

'Toady-loo?'

She nods, and stands up, brushing the dirt from her coat. She offers him her hand.

He struggles to his feet and looks at her, taking her hand and grinning.

She feeds him sweets all the way home, and then grins as her tiny cabin comes into view.

A cabin big enough for a witch and a human. Not an ogre.

She takes a deep breath; there's not much her and Dave argue about. This might be one of them, but when she looks at this giant baby, who wouldn't eat a frog, her heart melts.

She closes her eyes and uses her incredible magic to make their little cabin bigger.

The trees surrounding the cabin, bend, shrink, and move back. Everything moves to accommodate her magic and make the cabin bigger.

Dave comes round the side, wiping his glasses with his shirt.

'What's this, Toady? Feel like rattling around in the house? Fed up of being snug and cosy with me?'

He laughs as he pops his glasses back on and then he screams, staggering backwards and holding out his hand to his wife.

'Come here,' he says, his voice low and tremulous. 'There's an ogre.'

Toady-loo laughs and rolls her eyes. 'I know Dave. I'm holding his hand.'

Dave opens his mouth to speak, and faints.

Toady-loo laughs and magics him inside the newly sized cabin. Sticks fits easily through the front door, and she pops Dave on the couch, placing his glasses on the table beside him. She kisses his head and tucks a blanket over him.

'Nasty shock,' she says, turning to Sticks. 'Hungry?' she asks him, rubbing her own tummy.

He nods and follows her through to the kitchen.

'Ooh, I like this,' she says. Not only are the ceilings higher and the rooms bigger, but her kitchen has had a makeover. The cabinets are freshly painted and there's a stash of fruit and sweets on the counter.

Sticks grins and grabs a banana, before placing himself on the floor.

She magics up some toys for him, not sure what ogres like to play with.

He grabs a ball and bounces it.

'Did you run away?' she asks him.

He nods, wiping the food from his mouth and then grabbing another banana.

'Why?'

He shrugs, then bites his lip.

'Mum and dad wanted to eat me,' he says, his voice low and sad.

Toady tries to cover her shock, but she's not sure if she's managed. They wanted to eat their own baby. That's why nobody likes ogres.

'Do you want to go home?' she asks him, and he shakes his head, his expression panicked.

'No. Please, no.'

Those words are enough to make her mind up. Dave might take a while to come around, but this baby needs a home, and she's got one. This baby needs a mum and dad, and her and Dave would be perfect.

Unconventional. But perfect.

Chapter 42

Dave comes around, a look of fear still on his face.

'Tell me that was a dream, Toady,' he says, sitting up and putting his glasses back on.

He spots Sticks on the floor surrounded by balls, bricks and sweets.

Toady-loo holds her hand up, and then slides over to sit beside Dave. She takes his hand.

'We always wanted a baby,' she says.

His eyes are so wide, his eyebrows disappear in his hair and his mouth is agape.

She closes his mouth gently with her hand. She already knows he'll give in; he always does. And so does she. She gave in when he wanted to move to the cabin in the middle of the woods so he could fish every day. She doesn't moan even once when he cleans his golf clubs daily despite never playing a game, and she indulges his every whim with regard to anything he wants. He took a risk and married a witch, when there were lots of normal human women who'd have been glad to marry such a gentleman. And she took a risk when she turned down one of the greatest wizards who ever lived, for the quiet, bookish, handsome fellow who smiled shyly at her every day.

He closes his eyes and then opens them again.

'He's still here.'

'He's just a baby,' she says, stroking Dave's arm.

Dave raises his eyebrows at her, clearly unimpressed.

'Will he eat me?' he asks, eyeing up the giant toddler who's now laughing with Dumpling the frog.

'He wouldn't hurt a fly,' she says, and Dave laughs. 'I mean it. He was going to eat Dumpling, but he didn't.'

'And where did he come from? Are we going to have angry ogre parents hunting him down and finding us instead?'

Toady-loo shakes her head. 'They wanted to eat him.'

He shakes his head.

'I suppose the cabin being a bit bigger is nice. Maybe I can have a hobby room?'

She grins and kisses his cheek. 'You can have anything you want.'

'Really?' He waggles his eyebrows and slides an arm around her.

She pokes him with her elbow.

'Not in front of the baby,' she says, and he groans.

He stands up with a sigh, and then goes to sit on the floor with Sticks. He sits cross legged and watches him.

Sticks grins and points at himself. 'Sticks,' he says.

Dave sighs and points at himself. 'Dave,' he says.

'Dave,' Sticks says.

'Dave,' Dave agrees and builds a tower out of bricks. Sticks knocks it down laughing.

Dave smiles at Toady-loo.

'The things I do for you.'

'The things we do for each other,' she says, and joins them on the floor.

Sticks smiles at them.

'Sticks stay here?' he asks them, and Toady-loo nods. Dave nods too, wondering how marrying the woman he loved ended up with him sitting on the floor playing games with an ogre.

An ogre who is nearly as tall as him, and is definitely twice as wide as him, if not more. An ogre who could crush him with one meaty fist despite being only a few years old.

'Promise he won't kill me,' Dave whispers, and Sticks' eyes fill with tears. They plop down his cheeks, fat and sad.

'Sticks won't kill you. You're Dave.'

Dave shakes his head, ashamed of himself.

'Sorry, Sticks. I know you won't eat me, and I won't eat you.'

Sticks laughs, a deep belly laugh, and ruffles Dave's hair, almost giving him whiplash.

'You can't eat me. I'm too big. I promise I won't eat you. I'm a good ogre.'

A good ogre. Dave willingly builds the bricks into towers for Sticks to knock down, over and over again, wondering again what his wife's got them into now.

What do you do with a naughty toddler ogre who won't eat his vegetables or go to bed on time, when he could knock you flying with the flick of his wrist? How do you get him to toe the line when he's going to end up so much bigger than he is, so much stronger than he already is?

'We can do anything,' Toady-loo says, kissing Dave's cheek and then leaning over to kiss Sticks' cheek too.

'Family?' Sticks asks, pointing at himself, then Toady-loo and then Dave.

'Family,' Toady-loo says, completely sure of the fact.

'Family,' Dave parrots, not sure at all, but also knowing that when he looks into the ogre's eyes, he sees nothing but kindness there, nothing but friendliness, nothing but love.

Chapter 43

And as Sticks grows up, there is still nothing but kindness, friendliness and love not just in his eyes, but in his demeanour, his whole personality.

He cannot see an injured animal without having to fix it; he cannot see a friendless child without wanting to play with them.

The only thing that worries his mum and dad, Toady-loo and Dave, is that other people don't know him like they do. They don't see the gentle manners and sweet nature.

All they see is an ogre.

'Damn kids,' Dave says, slamming his drink on the table, causing it to spill.

'Shush, he'll hear you.'

'Sorry,' Dave whispers. 'They just annoy me. He's a sweet kid, always trying to fit in, willing to do anything they tell him to, just to stay in their good books.'

Toady-loo sighs, massaging the bridge of her nose with one finger.

'I know, I know. It doesn't help that most of them are witches or wizards and he's not.'

'Exactly. They trick him, or bamboozle him, or bewitch him.'

'No, Dave, they don't. They just string him along until he does something stupid they've told him to do and then they run off and let him take the fall.'

'No magic involved?'

'None. Hmm.'

'What's hmm. Is that a hmm I'll like or a hmm I won't?'

Toady-loo slaps her forehead with her palm. 'Damn it, Dave, I'm a flipping witch.'

'I know. And a very good one,' he says, kissing her cheek.

'So I'll just put magical protections on him, magical spells that stop the other kids from harassing him.'

Dave sighs. 'But they're not harassing him, not in his eyes. He thinks they're his friends.'

'But they're not. They only play with him to make him the butt of their jokes. They only like him because they want to take the mick out of him. They only keep him around because he's an ogre, an oddity, a freak-'

The squeak of the stairs makes them both whip their heads around, to catch Sticks on the bottom step, lower lip sticking out, fat tears plopping down his bright green cheeks.

'Crap!' Toady-loo says, as he bolts through the front door.

They both rush outside, but despite the sheer size of him and the bright colour of his skin, there's no sign of him.

'Damn it,' Toady-loo says, tears filling her eyes. 'It hurts when your kid hurts, doesn't it?'

'Doesn't it?' Dave says, taking off his glasses and rubbing at his eyes. 'He's an absolute darling boy, why can't anybody see it?'

Toady shrugs. 'Because he's an ogre and we're surrounded by humans, witches, elves, pixies... all the good guys.'

'So he's the bad guy?'

'Ogres are, and a lot of people can't see past that. Remember your reaction when you met him?'

Dave nods, shame colouring his cheeks.

'You shouldn't feel bad. Ogres are bad news. But Sticks isn't.'

'He's the best news we ever got,' he says, and takes his wife in his arms. 'We'll go and look for him. He might be in the swamp.'

'He might be,' Toady-loo agrees, and they head out in different directions to look for their son.

Chapter 44

Sticks lumbers through the woods, tears blinding him, but his size meaning he can barrel through the bushes and trees and make a path of his own.

Are his mum and dad right? Are his friends only friends with him because they want to make fun of him?

He plonks onto the wet floor, and cries.

He feels like stuff like this shouldn't bother him anymore. He's been with his mum and dad, a witch and a human, for seven years, and he's ten now, which sounds quite big, unless you are ten and then it feels very small, and far too small to deal with such big feelings.

Is there a little bit of him that knows what his mum and dad just said is true? Does he see the looks his friends give each other sometimes, the subtle digs they make at him, which they brush off as banter, the way he'll hear them talk about doing something he wasn't invited to and feel so left out he wants to cry, but have to brush it off, and smile like he didn't hear them talking about it, even though he thinks maybe they want him to hear them, and it really doesn't bother them if he did hear it.

Is it silly to still want to be friends with people who only give him crumbs? Who don't see the real Sticks?

He draws in the dirt with his finger, turning his bright green skin muddy.

His mum and dad are wonderful. People use the word adopted but it doesn't feel right. He thinks of them as his real mum and dad, because they say and do everything a real mum and dad do. They certainly wouldn't sell him or eat him, and he's pretty sure his dad knows he won't eat him now that so much time has passed.

But he knows that some people think his mum and dad are stupid for taking him in and calling him their own. He even heard Dave's mum say that once they had children of their own, they could send Sticks back to whatever swamp he came from. He never saw her again.

His dad had hugged him extra tight and for extra long that night, and whispered, you're not going anywhere, which had made Sticks cry happy tears.

It's not easy being an ogre. It's even harder being an ogre when nobody wants to be your friend, and not because they don't like you, but just because you're an ogre. Are they scared of him? Probably. Do they take the time to get to know him? Not really. They let him in to the periphery of the group. They let him join in when they need him. When they need a goalie to help their team win, because he's so big he fills the net. Or when they need someone tall to help get the best berries from the high up branches. Or when they throw stones and break a window and need someone to blame.

And Sticks always took the blame, because that's what friends do – right?

Except nobody ever took the blame for him. Nobody ever called to his house to ask him if he wanted to come out to play. Nobody ever wanted to sit by him.

He knows he's a good ogre, a kind ogre, a friendly boy. His mum and dad tell him all the time, so why doesn't anyone else see it?

Or are his mum and dad lying?

Chapter 45

An elephant eared slug slithers along in the dirt beside him and Sticks gently scoops him up.

'Hey buddy,' he says. 'Oh, you've got a splinter.'

He can see the thick sliver of wood sticking out of his tail end.

'Shall I help you?' he asks, his voice soft, his giant fingers close to the splinter.

The slug gives a wriggle, which Sticks takes as a yes.

Tongue sticking out as he concentrates, he grabs the end of the splinter in a pincer grip, and gently, ever so gently, pulls the splinter free.

A tiny drop of bright green blood oozes out, and Sticks holds his finger against it.

'Nearly done,' he says to the slug, who wriggles again, this time making his ears shudder. Sticks tickles him behind the ears with his free hand, and the slug smiles.

When the bleeding stops, he sets him gently on a leaf.

'Off you go, bud,' he says, and the slug gives one more wriggle before squelching away.

Sticks watches him go, tears in his eyes. At least animals like him.

'That was kind,' a voice says, and Sticks turns his head, this way and that trying to figure out who's talking to him.

'Over here,' the voice says, and Sticks peers through the branches of the tree.

'Down here,' the same voice says, and Sticks lowers his gaze.

Perched on a pebble is the smallest, cutest little fairy he's ever seen. Her hair looks like candy floss and her eyes are fiery. She flutters her wings and flies up to him, hovering just in front of his face.

'You're kind,' she says.

'I am,' he says. It's not bragging if it's true.

'In that case, I need your help,' she says.

Sticks nods and smooths down his tunic. 'What do you need?' he asks.

She beckons to him to follow her, and she flies slowly through the woods, away from where he lives and plays, and from where his friends tease and make fun of him, and down past the river.

'Where are we going?' he asks. 'I don't usually go this far from home.'

She stops, wings fluttering, keeping her in one place.

'Do you want to go back?'

He hesitates. 'Someone needs help?'

'My mum,' she says, her voice trembling. 'She got hurt by a fox, and her wing is ripped. I don't know if it can be saved.'

'If it can be saved, then I can do it,' he says, proud of his healing abilities.

He follows along behind her, and she flies nice and slowly so he can keep up. He's big and often clumsy. When his friends make fun of him for having two left feet, he ends up falling more often, which makes them laugh more.

If he ever looks upset, one of them will ruffle his hair, and tell him not to be sad.

And he usually listens to them, because you should listen to your friends.

'Here,' she says, and then pauses. 'It's not going to work. You're too big. You can't come in.'

'Can she come out?' Sticks asks.

The fairy shakes her head. 'No. Her wing is torn, but I think her leg is broken too.'

Sticks bites his lip. He knows who can help.

'Go inside, tell your mum I won't be long. I'm going to get my mum.'

The fairy visibly pales. 'Your mum?'

Sticks grins. 'My mum is a witch, not an ogre, and my dad's a normal bloke called Dave.'

'I'll come with you,' the fairy says. 'My name is Pip. Let me just tell my mum.'

Sticks waits for Pip and then they head back to Sticks' house, as fast as they can. Sticks is gasping for air as they go, but calling for his mum and dad too. He knows they're out looking for him; he knows they'll be worried about him running off, and worried about what he heard. Which really seems so silly now.

'Mum!' he sees her in the distance, her purple hair flying as she rushes around calling his name.

'Sticks!' The relief in her voice is evident and she grabs hold of him and hugs him fiercely, despite his size.

'Mum, this is Pip.'

Toady-loo notices the tiny fairy, and smiles.

'Hello, Pip. Sticks, come home, me and dad are sorry we upset you.'

'It's fine mum,' Sticks says, shaking his head. 'We need your help.'

Toady-loo doesn't ask questions, just follows them through the trees until they get to the fairy's house.

'My mum is hurt, but Sticks,' she says, smiling at him, 'can't get in the tree house, and my mum can't come out.'

Chapter 46

'We need your magic mum,' Sticks says, and Toady-loo nods. The fact that her son is okay, and talking to her, means she'll do anything to help him. She would anyway, but she's flooded with relief.

Toady-loo holds her hands up in front of her. She's a born witch not a taught witch, so she doesn't need a magic wand, just her hands.

As they watch, the tree trunk slowly and seamlessly starts to split in half.

Toady-loo pauses.

'Go inside,' she tells Pip, with a big smile. 'Reassure her that it's okay.'

Pip nods and flutters inside the split trunk.

Toady-loo uses her magic to completely split the trunk into two, so they can all see inside the tree house.

The tree trunk isn't completely hollowed out; floors and rooms have been fashioned.

Pip grins at the look of astonishment on Sticks and his mum's faces.

'We were really lucky to find this place,' she says. 'Usually fairies and pixies live in tree houses, that are carved into the outside of the trunk, or built into the leaves and branches. This place belonged to three miniature woodchucks, who made this lovely home inside the tree instead of out.'

'It's lovely,' Sticks says, peering in at the tiny furniture fashioned from leaves and twigs and wood.

'I can fix it,' Toady-loo says.

Pip's mum looks alarmed, but she must trust her daughter, because she has a smile pasted onto her face, and Toady-loo can tell she's trying not to panic.

To have your home ripped open and find a witch and an ogre on the other side must be disconcerting.

'You're in safe hands,' Toady-loo says, sending some calming magic toward Pip's mum. She could mend the fairy's wing and leg in seconds with her own magic, but she knows that Sticks needs this.

Sticks tells his mum in a low voice what he needs – water to clean the wounds with, spider's web to sew the wing together, honey paste to help heal the leg.

He sets about his work, and for such a massive ogre, he could not have been more gentle, more delicate. His tongue pokes out from his mouth as he cleans, mends and tends to Pip's mum.

'Your leg isn't broken,' he says, and Pip's mum smiles.

'My name's Judy,' she says. 'Thank you for helping me.'

Sticks beams and applies a little more honey paste with a flourish.

Toady-loo grins. Her son, and he is her son, is transformed when he's helping people and it breaks her heart that his friends are unkind to him, that they don't see the beauty inside him, the sweet, kind, selfless nature of an ogre, that's so at odds with what he was born to be, that it's even more special.

He doesn't need her help to heal; it's inside him, something he instinctively knows how to do, but while she knows it's a bad idea to magically protect him from life – from mean friends, or bad situations, she sends a little magic his way, a small ball of magical light that will live inside him and help him with his healing, just by making it a little bit better than it is now. And it's already amazing.

'How do I thank you?' Judy asks, fluttering her newly mended wing and wiping a tear from her eye.

'No need,' Sticks says. 'I love mending and healing.'

'You have a knack for it,' Toady-loo says, reaching over to gently ruffle his hair. Sticks snuggles into her. 'Thanks mum.'

'Why don't you two see if you can pick some berries, while I mend the house,' Toady-loo suggests.

The two youngsters head off, and toady-loo smiles at Judy.

'Your daughter is sweet.'

'Your son is too.'

'Thank you. Not many people can see it.'

Judy waves a hand. 'It's written all over him.' She pauses. 'You could have healed me just as easily with magic, couldn't you?'

Toady nods. 'But Pip didn't know that, and Sticks needed to do it – and I have a feeling they were meant to find each other.'

'Me too,' Judy says. 'She's got a lovely group of friends – orcs, goblins, ghosts. I think Sticks would fit right in.'

Tears spring to Toady-loo's eyes. 'Really?'

'Really.'

Judy holds out a hand, and Toady-loo gently touches it. 'Thank you. He needs real friends.'

'Don't we all,' Judy says, and as they listen to their children laugh and joke as they bring back a hoard of berries, Toady-loo and Judy realise that they might end up just as good friends as their children.

Chapter 47

Dayne wipes a tear away.

'Oh, Sticks, Pip sounds like so much fun. Where is she now?'

Sticks lowers his gaze. 'She moved across the seas, when we were both eighteen.'

'Did you love her?' Dayne asks, a cheeky little grin on her face.

'I did. But not like that,' Sticks says, a blush colouring his green skin. 'Never like that. Just like friends. Best friends.'

'I never had a best friend,' Dayne says. 'So you should both count yourselves lucky.'

'Wasn't your mum your best friend?' Ettie asks, and Dayne nods sadly.

'Yeah, she was, actually.'

'Tell us about her,' Ettie says, sending some healing her way. Grief is such a cruel emotion. Loving someone means grieving more when you lose them, but what a price to pay.

Dayne shrugs. 'I'm enjoying sharing our stories, but I'm not sure I'm ready to talk about her,' she says, with a shake of her head.

'Whenever you are,' Sticks says.

'I'll let you know,' Dayne says. 'So, you were always a healer, but when did you open your shop?'

Sticks sits up, a proud expression on his face.

'My twenty first birthday. My mum found the place, and I fixed it, painted it, got it ready. My dad helped.'

'Is that why you don't want me to use my magic this time round?' Ettie asks.

Sticks nods. 'Me and dad did it all. Mum tried to help, and I'm sure she eased things along in her own unique way.' He grins. 'I miss them.'

'I don't miss my parents anymore,' Ettie says.

'I think I'll always miss my mum,' Dayne says, and then stands up, shaking out her wings.

'Right. We're getting melancholy now. I'll tell you about my mum one day, but for today – shall we go and see how Posey's getting on?'

'Great idea.'

The three of them stand outside her door.

'Do you think she'll ever forgive me for what I said,' Sticks asks, his voice quiet.

Ettie touches his arm. 'I'm sure she will. We all say things sometimes.'

'I just meant trolls in general, not her.'

'I know,' Dayne says, shrugging. 'It's easier for me, because all pixies are a delight.' She looks at Ettie. 'Witches can be evil.' Then she nods at Sticks. 'And everyone knows ogres are bad news. But pixies. I dare you to say one bad thing about pixies.'

She folds her arms, a cheeky grin on her pretty little face.

Ettie and Sticks look at each other and at the same time say, 'Bugsy!'

They fall about laughing and Dayne sighs, hands up in the air. 'Okay, you got me. But my dad's a one off.'

'Frank!' Sticks says.

Dayne sighs. 'Okay, so he's pretty rubbish, but generally, you don't hear anything bad about pixies. Admit it.'

Ettie giggles and nods. 'You know we're teasing you. Pixies are a delight, and you are the most delightful.'

Dayne preens and Sticks knocks the door.

Posey opens it, a grin on her face.

'Ready?'

Sticks can't stand still; he's desperate to see what she's done.

'Shall we go through to the kitchen?' Ettie asks. 'We can take a look at Posey's drawings, and maybe I can rustle us up some tea? You must be starving after how hard you've worked today.'

Posey nods. 'I am, but I don't want to intrude.'

'You wouldn't be,' Sticks says. 'We'd love you to join us.'

Posey looks at him, assessing him, and then nods. 'Okay. That would be lovely.'

'Shall we eat first?' Dayne says, a cheeky smile on her face, and Sticks looks fit to explode.

'Joking!' she says, before he blows a gasket.

Sticks looks at her darkly. 'Not funny.'

Dayne flutters close to him, fluttering her eyelashes and her wings. She knows he won't stay mad at her for long.

Chapter 48

Posey spreads out her drawings, and Ettie uses magic to hold them flat on the table.

'These look great,' Sticks says, turning his head this way and that.

'This is the front door,' Posey says, and points out the front door, the back door, the hatch the animals can use to go in and out, the different areas of the shop, and the different rooms in his healing space.

'It's so big,' she says. 'I've made space for storage, medicines, extra rooms for ill creatures.'

Sticks beams. 'It's magnificent,' he says, and holds up a hand to high five Posey.

Posey hesitates, but then high fives him back.

'I've made a list of all the equipment we need,' she says, looking at Ettie. 'And in normal time, I estimate it'll take ten days. If you can work your magic, then, who knows.'

Ettie nods. 'I need to check my spell books, but I think I've got an idea.'

'And you've got a crew?'

Dayne nods. 'My dad and my five brothers. Ettie's going to make them all big – and me too. We can all help.'

'I can help,' Ettie says. 'But my skills are less than zero. I've always used magic, so I can't even use a paintbrush.'

'We'll teach you,' Sticks says. 'If you want to learn.'

Ettie shrugs. 'We'll see. I'll be busy conjuring up hammers and nails, I reckon.'

'I'm so excited,' Sticks says. 'Look at the alehouse bringing you here, Posey. It knows exactly what we need, sometimes before we do.'

'It is strange,' Posey says. 'I was having a pretty bad day until I found the job advert.'

'We were all having pretty bad days until the alehouse brought us here,' Dayne says. 'There was a goblin here too, called Graily, but she's gone to Paris to learn to cook.'

'Though she could already cook,' Sticks says, remembering her delicious pastries.

'Though Ettie does a wonderful job too,' Dayne says.

Ettie grins. 'On that note, what do we all want to eat?'

Posey shakes her head. 'I can't get used to this. Getting fed at home was a battle. There was never enough, and I'd often end up with the leftovers from the tavern. You can just magic up anything you want?'

Ettie nods. It's so normal to her, she forgets how novel it is for non magical folk.

'Not just food, either' Dayne says. 'She made me tools, she can do anything.'

Ettie laughs. 'Enough. I'm just a witch. And I failed more times than I succeeded,' she adds, looking at Posey. She feels like there's more to the troll's story than she's letting on.

But she also knows that they also say what they need to say when they need to say it. If they need to say it at all. Do they all have secrets? Probably – she does. Are there secrets that should stay secrets? Probably.

'So, Posey, what do you want to eat?'

Posey blows out her cheeks.

'Everything?'

They all laugh.

'Has your first day worn you out?' Dayne asks.

Posey shrugs. 'I'm used to hard work. My mum does a little bit in our house, but not the tavern, and my stepdad and my brother are worse than useless. And I always did far more than my mum, so I actually did less today because I had help from you guys.'

Sticks grins. He hopes she's forgiven him.

'And it was blinding not to have to do the dishes,' Posey says, giving Ettie a salute.

Ettie smiles. 'Magic is useful.'

'Useful?' Posey shakes her head. 'If I had magic…' She trails off, and Ettie gets that same feeling; that there's more to her story.

'So, food?' Ettie reminds everyone.

'I'd love pie and mash,' Posey says.

Ettie nods. 'Any particular kind of pie?'

'Roasted goat,' Posey says, and then cracks into a grin. 'Not because of the goats that go over the bridge, mind you, it's just goat's my favourite.'

They all laugh. Sticks clears his throat. 'Can you forgive me, Posey? For what I said about trolls?'

Ettie conjures up goat pie and mash, and cutlery for Posey.

'If I was angry I wouldn't have done the drawings,' Posey says, and then sighs. 'I know what people think about us. Heck, half the time I think the same thing. But I know that being a troll doesn't define me, even if it sometimes limits me.'

'Hopefully it won't limit you anymore,' Dayne says. She points at the drawings for Hooves and Horns. 'You are welcome here as long as you want – same as the rest of us, but if you ever want to find work as an architect, then Hooves and Horns can be part of your body of work. People will love to see what you're capable of.'

'Great idea. Thanks guys. I do feel really welcome, and happy here.'

'The alehouse is a safe place,' Sticks says. 'And it's looking after all of us.'

Once they've all eaten, and the huge array of bowls, plates and cups is cleared magically away, Ettie snuggles up by the fire under her blanket.

'I'm going to read for a bit,' she says.

'I'm going to bed,' Dayne says, with a huge stretch. 'I need to rest if we're building a shop tomorrow.'

Sticks gives a squeal of excitement.

'Thank you, Posey, I'm so grateful to you.'

Posey shakes her head. 'It's nothing.'

They all smile at each other, because they know that's not true.

Chapter 49

When Ettie wakes in the morning, Posey is already sitting in the den, knees tucked up to her chin, a pensive look on her face.

Ettie sends magical healing her way, and then sits in her usual seat.

'Good morning,' she says, smiling warmly at Posey and using her magic to make the fire a little warmer.

'Morning,' Posey says. 'I slept like a log. I wasn't sure that I would.'

'Do you want to talk about it?'

Posey shrugs. 'Not really.'

Ettie shrugs too. 'You know we all came here after bad days. But none of us is obliged to talk about it.'

'It's not that I don't want to,' Posey says, 'just that I don't want to. Does that make sense?'

Ettie laughs. 'I know exactly what you mean. Talking about it might make you feel better in the long run but talking about it will make you feel bad initially. None of us will put pressure on you. The alehouse brought you here, so for however long you stay, we all know you're supposed to be here.'

'You believe that?'

Ettie nods, tucking her feet underneath her. 'I was in the magical academy,' she says, feeling like sharing her story will help Posey, even if she doesn't open up, she'll know that they've all been through it. 'I kept failing my end of year exam, but I kept repeating the year. For seven years.'

'That's a long time. You're tenacious.'

Ettie laughs. She'd never framed her failure in that way. She'd never thought that sticking around year after year showed resilience and tenacity; she always just felt like it reinforced her failure.

'I didn't feel tenacious,' Ettie admits. 'I felt like I kept getting it wrong and would never get it right. After I failed my last exam, the new head teacher threw me out.'

'He threw you out?'

'Long story short,' Ettie says. 'But my parents aren't in my life. I didn't know anyone outside of the academy and I had no friends. Only one, and she's a professor at the academy. The new head threw me out the same night – he didn't even let me stay until the morning.'

'No way.'

'Yup. I was alone, scared and hopeless. I had nowhere to go, no money, and just a few boxes of my stuff.'

'What happened? How did you get here?'

Ettie closes her eyes for a second. The sick, panicked feeling she felt that night has come rushing back, twisting her stomach and making her feel ill.

'They sent me away in a carriage, but I didn't know where I was going; I had nowhere to go. Then a feather – and a ladybug came into the carriage, and that's definitely a story for another day – but the feather led the way here.'

'Like my job advert.'

'Exactly the same,' Ettie says. 'It's why we know you're supposed to be here. Whether you're running from something, or to something, it's none of our business, but the alehouse knows what we need, and we're just going along with it.'

'That actually sounds really nice. Just giving into a higher power.'

Ettie grins. 'That's exactly what it is. Give in, and settle in. I don't know how long you'll stay but you're welcome to stay forever. It's what I plan to do.'

'Really?'

Ettie nods and tucks her feet the other way. 'I'm a homebird. I don't like new places or people. I like what I know.'

'And you don't mind living a small life?'

'There's nothing wrong with small,' Ettie says, knowing it's true. 'We all want different things. Some of us have big dreams – and I love that. Heck, I'll even cheer you on. From the comfort of my home. My safe space.'

Posey smiles. 'I like it here. And I like all of you.'

'Even Sticks?'

'Especially Sticks – there's something so endearing about him.'

'You're right. It's because he's so different to how we imagine an ogre will be. And you're the same – I've never met a nice troll. Until now. That's another thing this place does – it turns your world upside down, and your ideas on their head. Everything might change, but it's okay. The alehouse knows what we need. Even if we don't.'

Posey stands up and stretches. 'I guess I should open the bar.'

Ettie nods. 'I'll make you some breakfast.'

She magics Posey up a bowl of honey and cinnamon porridge.

'Once we get back from the palace, I'll come and help you again.'

Posey nods her thanks, and tucks into her porridge.

Chapter 50

Sticks comes in, nose first, sniffing, like a puppy.

'Smells good,' he says. 'Morning Posey. How did you sleep?'

'Really well, thanks,' she says, licking her spoon. 'Before I head to the bar, I just want you to know there's no bad blood between us.'

Sticks beams and opens his arms for a hug. Posey steps into his embrace, and he's careful not to squash her. His hugs are always sincere but gentle; he can be gentle and careful when he heals, but he's caused pain with an over enthusiastic hug more than once. He broke his dad's ribs once. Luckily his mum magically fixed them, and his dad didn't mind.

It was the day they finished the shop and put the sign up outside.

'I'm so happy you've forgiven me,' he says. 'And I'm so happy you're helping us with the shop.'

'That's the first call of business,' Ettie says, magicking up an array of food items for Sticks.

He grins and pounces on the jammy, pastry things that Graily used to make.

'We're going to the palace?'

Ettie nods. 'Then we'll come back and help Posey in the bar. Then I need to work on a time spell. I don't know if I should try to stop it or slow it.'

'Whichever's easier,' Sticks says with a shrug, and Ettie grins. She loves the faith they all seem to have in her and her magic. Truth is, she's never played with time before.

And she's not sure that she should.

'Morning,' Dayne says, flying into the room, and taking a nose dive into one of Sticks' croissants and stealing a bit for herself.

Ettie magics up more food and a cup of tea for all of them.

'I cannot wait to be big!' Dayne says. 'I'm so excited.'

Ettie laughs. 'Wait and see if your dad and brothers want to help first.'

Dayne shakes her head. 'Nuh-uh. You promised me big, regardless of whether or not they help.'

'Don't panic me,' Sticks says. 'We need their help.'

'Hey, if I'm big,' Dayne says. 'I'm worth ten of them. Maybe more.'

Ettie laughs. 'I don't doubt that. But I can't see them turning this down. It's not every day pixies get to be big, and it's not every day they get to work on something so exciting.'

Sticks smiles. 'It is exciting, isn't it?'

'I think so,' Ettie says.

'Me too,' Posey says. 'I can't wait to see my plans come to life.'

'Let's go then,' Dayne says. 'I can't wait.'

They say goodbye to Posey, and Ettie magics them up to the palace.

Briella is there outside, walking with Nathaniel.

'Morning,' she says, clearly pleased to see them.

'Morning. We need a favour,' Ettie says, and Briella laughs.

'You guys are always up here, asking for something.' She's smiling, and they all know she's teasing. 'What is it this time?'

'We need to know if Bugsy and his sons could help us with something.'

'Take them away from their royal duties?' Briella asks, a cheeky smile on her face.

'Yes please,' Sticks says. 'We're refurbishing the shop in the building next to the alehouse.'

'And we need a crew,' Dayne says.

Briella smiles. 'I think they might be too tiny to help,' she says. Then she looks at Ettie and points. 'Unless you're planning a little bit of magic?'

Ettie nods. 'I am. I want to slow or stop time and make them all human sized. We have an architect, and she's drawn up plans. I'm going to magic up the supplies.'

'That sounds great. You know the King is away, but I know my father. He'd be happy to give them some time off. Since we locked the foxes up, things are running pretty smoothly.'

Ettie nods. That's good news. The foxes were wreaking havoc before Bugsy and the orcs helped take them down.

'Go and ask your father,' Briella says. 'As long as he's happy to help, we're happy to let him.'

She takes hold of Nathaniel's hand, and with a wave, they continue their stroll around the grounds.

Dayne smiles. 'You guys stay here. I'll talk to my dad.'

'Do you think he's going to say no? That you'll need to persuade him?' Sticks asks, the worried expression back on his face.

'No. But I want to ask him about Frank too. Find out if he's spoken to him, and figured out what he's up to.'

Ettie nods. 'We can wait for you. It's a beautiful day.'

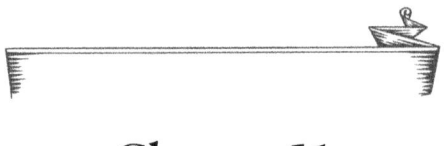

Chapter 51

Dayne comes back to join them, but she's not smiling. She looks worried.

'He said no?' Sticks says, stomach filling up with dread.

Dayne shakes her head, and smiles. 'Sorry, no. He said yes. He's really excited. They've got some things to take care of today, and so they'll be with us first thing in the morning.'

Sticks grins. 'Phew. You had me worried then. So why don't you look happy?'

'Frank is missing. He didn't come back to the palace last night. Dad hasn't seen him since the day before yesterday.'

'Does he have any theories?'

Dayne shakes her head. 'No. He reckons he'll turn up.'

'But you don't?'

'I think he'll turn up,' Dayne says. 'But I'm worried what he's doing in the meantime.'

Ettie tuts. 'You can't worry about him.'

'Oh, I know. He's old enough and ugly enough to worry about himself. But Mrs Dinklepants was scared. And what if he's doing that to other people?'

'Why don't we go to see the other people you used to help?' Sticks suggests. 'We've got some time today to try and figure out what he's up to.'

'We've got time,' Ettie agrees with a shrug. 'Posey won't need our help until the lunch time rush.'

'You really don't mind helping me?' Dayne asks, and then she waves her arms around, with a laugh. 'That was stupid. Of course you don't mind helping me. Let's go.'

'Where to?' Ettie asks, as Dayne tucks herself into Sticks' pocket with a grimace.

'Dumpling's been in here hasn't he?'

Sticks looks sheepish, but then he shrugs. 'Yes, but you don't need my pocket anymore. Now you fly, you never want to tuck in with me.'

Dayne rests her head on his chest. 'Do you miss me?'

Sticks shrugs, bashful. 'Of course I do – you and me had much better conversations than I do with Dumpling.'

Ettie grins. 'Come on, where to?'

'The Dewberries,' Dayne says. 'Derek didn't mention Frank to me when I went to see him, but I know he's scared of him, and embarrassed to be a giant who's scared of pixies.'

'He might have kept quiet then. Let's go.'

Ettie magics them there, and they land with a woosh.

Dayne flies up to the door and knocks.

'How does he hear that?' Ettie asks.

'Giants have superior hearing,' Sticks says.

'They do?'

Sticks and Dayne nod.

'Like bats. Only giants.'

Ettie shrugs. 'You learn something new every day.'

'I'm not sure Frank does,' Dayne says, darkly. 'What the heck do you think he's up to?'

'I don't know,' Sticks says. 'If I was him, with a cushty job at the palace, and digs too, I wouldn't be putting a foot out of line.'

'Or a wing,' Ettie adds. 'But you know him best. What do you think?'

Dayne frowns. 'I've been racking my brain trying to think. I don't understand why he'd threaten Mrs Dinklepants. He doesn't need money; he's got a job. He doesn't need to be menacing people anymore – the King has allowed them all to be legitimate.'

Ettie sighs. 'So there's only two reasons why he'd be doing it.'

'Go on,' Dayne says, flying out of Sticks' pocket.

'He either likes it – enjoys messing with people, and roughing them up, and his legitimate work for the King doesn't allow him to get too mean.'

'Or?'

'Or someone's forcing him to do it.'

Dayne shakes her head. 'No, no way. I can't see him being forced to do anything against his will.'

'Then he's just nasty.'

Dayne is about to knock the door again, when it swings open, just a fraction.

'Who's there?' Derek's voice is gruff, and Dayne immediately knows something is wrong. She knows this gentle old giant too well.

'Let us in,' Dayne says, her voice soft, flying up to the small gap where Derek has opened the door, so she can see his face.

She cries out when he does; his eye is black and there's a cut on his cheek which is bleeding.

'Derek, let us in. You need help.'

He opens the door fully, and they all traipse inside. Ettie can't help but smile softly when she looks up at him, despite the pain he's clearly in, because craning her neck to look up at a giant reminds her of being with Liss.

Sticks doesn't have to look as far.

'Ettie, you need to heal him.'

'You could do it too, Sticks.'

He shakes his head. 'My healing takes time.'

Ettie nods. She knows Sticks is missing tending to ill animals, but he's right. Her magic is immediate.

'Did Frank do this?' Dayne asks, as they all take seats.

Sticks smiles despite himself; giant furniture makes him feel rather small and dainty.

Derek nods, and tears fill his eyes and plop onto the floor.

'I'm so ashamed.'

'Don't you dare!' Dayne shouts at him, harsher than she intended to be. Derek lets out a wail. Dayne flies closer to him and leans against his face.

'I'm so sorry. But I'm the one who's ashamed. My brother works for the King now; there's no reason for him to go around doing what he's doing.'

Dayne is crying too, and Ettie tries to fill the room with some healing magic, and calm.

She clears her throat, her heart breaking when Derek rests his doleful gaze on her.

'Did he say anything? Frank?'

Derek winces at his name.

The giant nods.

'He said, Philomena sends her love.'

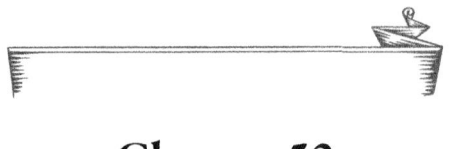

Chapter 52

'What! Philomena, as in Philomena the fox? That doesn't even make sense. She owed money to my dad too. Why would Frank be beating people up for her?' Dayne looks furious and confused all at once.

Ettie shakes her head.

'That's definitely what he said?'

Derek nods, gently touching one of his ears. 'Like a bat,' he says, and Ettie smiles.

'Like a bat. Okay, so he came here, hurt you, and said it was for Philomena. Did he ask you for money?'

Derek shakes his head. 'No. But I'd have paid him, if it would have stopped him hurting me.'

'There's no way Frank has anything to do with Philomena,' Dayne says, her expression dark. 'She burned our house down. His house.'

Derek shrugs, and Ettie pats his arm. She can tell it took a lot for him to tell them what happened. It must be so humiliating for a giant to admit that a pixie got the better of him.

'Is there anything I can help you with?' Dayne asks.

Derek shakes his head. 'I'm okay,' he says, though his tone says otherwise.

The three of them leave, sadness settling over them like a heavy blanket.

'Poor Derek,' Sticks says.

'Poor Derek, poor Mrs. Dinklepants...' Dayne says. 'I hate my brother.'

Ettie sighs. 'If he's still hurting people now, then I hate him too, but there's no way he'd be working for Philomena, surely?'

Dayne shrugs. 'I hate to say it, because he's my brother, and I defended him to Derek, but he's horrible. Out of all my brothers, he's the worst one. Always the worst.'

'Bad enough to team up with the foxes? Work for the foxes?' Sticks asks, his expression forlorn.

Ettie shakes her head. 'The foxes are all locked up. There's no way Philomena could be working with Frank.'

'The prison is at the palace,' Dayne says. 'It's not like Frank couldn't go there to see her, if he really wanted to.'

Sticks bites his lip. 'Dayne, he's your brother. Do you really think he'd stoop that low?'

'We could go to see Philomena ourselves,' Ettie suggests. 'See what she has to say.'

'You think she'd admit it?'

'I think we might be able to tell if she's lying. Why would Frank do her bidding?'

Dayne shrugs again. 'I don't know. I hate thinking so badly of him, but he used to beat people up for my dad, why not for someone else?'

'Because of what Philomena did to your house.'

'But then why would he say he was doing it for her, if he wasn't?'

'It doesn't make sense.'

'It doesn't. Let's go back to the alehouse; I always think more clearly when I'm there.'

'Me too. And we can see if Posey needs our help.'

'And we can figure out what the heck Frank is up to.'

'Maybe he's blaming Philomena to put your dad, and the King, off the scent. So nobody will know it's him.'

'But everyone knows Frank,' Dayne says. 'Even if he says he's doing someone else's bidding it's still him. We're pretty notorious.'

Sticks nods. 'That's true, Ettie. You don't know much about the area, what with being stuck up at the school for so long, but everyone here knows them. Not just in Daisy Creek. I'd heard of them and I lived in the Honey Lands.'

Ettie sighs. 'When something doesn't make sense like this, it's usually not true. So we need to figure it out.'

Dayne tucks herself into Sticks' pocket, and Ettie transports them all back to the alehouse.

Instead of going through the front door, they go around the side, and into the bar as though they were patrons.

Posey has it all under control; they can tell immediately.

'Hey!' She calls out the greeting when she sees them. 'Hungry customers,' she adds, and Ettie grins, magicking up plenty of food for everyone.

Sticks sneaks over to his custard tap, and takes a quick drink.

Dayne flies out of his pocket. 'Hey, don't splash me with custard.'

'I don't waste a drop,' he says, grinning and wiping his mouth on his sleeve. 'You know that.'

Dayne nods. 'Except what's on your sleeve.'

Sticks looks worried, and tries to twist his arm around so he can lick off any stray drops. Dayne laughs.

Posey joins them at the table, and Ettie conjures her up some food.

'All good?'

Posey nods. 'Yeah. Everyone's relaxed. They come in, I give them drinks, they pay, they sit, they chat, they go.'

'Sounds better than our morning,' Dayne says. She's never felt such hatred for her stupid brother.

'What happened?' Posey asks, taking a sip of ale.

Chapter 53

'My brother,' Dayne says, as though that's explanation enough. 'Frank doesn't need to hurt anyone anymore,' Dayne says, fluttering her wings in frustration. 'But is that stopping him? No, because he's a thug. So even though he works for the King, he's still going around beating people up.'

'That's awful.' Posey says, sipping more ale, and then eating more chicken.

Ettie conjures up more, and Sticks helps himself.

'It is awful,' Dayne says, sadly sipping some tea.

'I don't understand it,' Ettie says. 'Why would he do it?'

Dayne shrugs. 'I don't know. But when I get hold of him, I'm going to knock him out. Twice.'

'You can't really knock-' Ettie bites her lip to stop herself because Dayne gives her a fierce look.

'Good enough for him,' Sticks says. 'Imagine being so horrible that a giant is scared of you. Derek could squash your brother like a bug.'

Dayne tears of a piece of chicken skin, watching the grease dribble over her fingers. She eats the chicken and licks her fingers. 'That is delightful,' she says. 'Derek would never hurt Frank. He's so scared that he can't even see how tiny and annoying Frank is. I have to fix this. It doesn't look like my dad's been able to stop him.'

'How are you going to fix it?' Sticks asks, licking his chickeny fingers.

'I'm going to visit all the other people I used to help until I find him, until I track him down, until I get my hands on him and his stupid, nasty, useless-'

'Hey sis, who are you so peeved off at?'

Dayne turns at Frank's voice, fury mingled with aggravation and annoyance at his cheek for just waltzing into the alehouse like he hasn't been terrorising tiny hedgehogs and giant giants.

She turns to face him, pulls back her arm and punches him right in the face with all her strength.

He falls to the floor.

Dayne rubs her hand, and Ettie and Sticks lean over his tiny, unconscious body.

Posey pours Dayne some ale, which she drinks down in one mouthful.

'Damn, that was some punch,' Ettie says.

'You've knocked him clean out,' Sticks says, grinning at her.

Dayne shrugs. 'He deserved it. Who does he think he is? Did he think I wouldn't know?'

Ettie lifts him onto the table and they all stare at him. Dayne hovers above him, waiting for him to come around.

'What will you do when he wakes up?' Sticks asks.

'I'll knock him out again,' she says, glaring at them all, just daring them to disagree.

None of them say a word.

Posey serves a few customers, and Ettie uses her magic to clean the bar room, and magics up some more food for the few remaining patrons.

None of them seem to have noticed the kerfuffle with Frank.

Dayne sits beside him, quivering with rage.

'I hate him,' she says. 'I actually hate him.'

'I hate my brother too,' Posey says. 'I know the feeling.'

'Is he as bad as this one?' Dayne asks, nudging Frank's still body with her foot.

Posey shakes her head. 'He doesn't terrorise anyone, except me. But he's lazy and annoying. I'd knock him out if he tried to hurt me.'

Dayne nods. 'Good for you, brothers are the worst.'

'Was he always this bad?' Ettie asks, softly. She can completely understand why Dayne is so furious with Frank. He's not just beating people up for no good reason, he's also jeopardising what they have with the King. Not everyone who did what they had all done would be given a second chance. They've been given a chance to work for the King and a place to live. By pulling the same old nonsense he used to do, with his father and his brothers, he's putting everything at risk.

He's also annoying Dayne. She vouched for him with the King, and Ettie knows she'll be mortified if the King finds out what he's been up to.

Dayne shrugs. 'He wasn't always so bad. When my mum was around...'

'Tell us about her,' Sticks says. 'We'd love to hear all about her. We don't even know her name.'

'Mabel,' Dayne says, wiping at the tears that fill her eyes whenever she talks about her mum or even just thinks about her.

'Tell us about Mabel,' Posey says, pouring more ale for Dayne, in her tiny little pixie sized mug.

Chapter 54

Dayne runs after her brothers, her tiny legs pumping as fast as she can possibly make them go. And she knows it'll never be fast enough; she knows she'll never keep up. How can tiny pixie legs ever keep up with beautiful pixie wings?

She throws herself down onto the floor and rolls around in the grass instead.

'Loser!' Frank shouts before pelting her with acorns.

'Ow!' Dayne shouts out, wanting to cry but refusing to. She won't let her brothers see her cry; she won't let anyone see her cry.

She jumps up, shaking the grass out of her wings; her wings that don't work and never have, and starts running again.

Her brothers laugh and fly closer to her this time, and she watches them soar and swoop, and race the butterflies with envy on her face. She can't help it. She knows it's not her fault her wings don't work, and she knows her mum and dad love her anyway; they always tell her so.

The imperfections make you perfect.

Is that true? She doesn't know and she doesn't care. She just wants to be happy, and chasing after her brothers, no matter how many times they fly away from her, makes her happy.

'Ready?' Micah asks, and she nods.

They don't do this very often, because they complain that she's too heavy – which is just a lie because she's tiny – but when they do, it makes her feel like the luckiest, happiest pixie in the world. Adam takes her other hand, and then they fly, with her between them, and she laughs as the wind takes her words, tears streaming down her cheeks because the breeze stings her eyes, and her cheeks bright red from the cold.

They fly with her until they reach home, and then they set her down at the bottom of the tree house.

'Take me up!' she begs, but they laugh and fly away from her.

Grumbling but secretly happy, she makes her way up the roughly hewn steps to find her mum and dad.

She's the youngest in the family, and although the boys tease her, she's the apple of everyone's eye.

The boys love to bring her gifts, and she calls them, my boys, whenever they aren't there.

'Mum!' she calls as she climbs.

'In here,' her mum calls out, her voice weak.

She hasn't been well for ages, and Dayne is fed up. She misses their days out at the river, or at the market. She wishes her mum had energy.

'Hey mum,' Dayne says, joining her in bed and snuggling up beside her.

'I'm feeling better,' her mum says, and Dayne hugs her.

'Does that mean we can go to the river soon?'

Mabel nods. 'We'll make a day of it,' she says. 'All of us.'

'Definitely,' Dayne says, cuddling up and instantly falling asleep.

Bugsy comes into the room with a drink for Mabel.

'Look at her,' he says, gently ruffling Dayne's bright turquoise hair, and then kissing her cheek.

'Don't wake her,' Mabel says. 'She's been out with the boys; she's exhausted.'

'She's a sweet pea,' he says, settling beside her and taking his wife's hand.

'Don't let her fool you,' Mabel says, staring down at her daughter fondly. 'She can be feisty.'

'Good,' Bugsy says with a grin. 'I don't want five daft sons and a whiny daughter. I want five daft sons and the bravest, strongest, kindest, most beautiful daughter.'

'I think you've got all of that and more,' Mabel says. 'She never complains.'

'Tell me about it,' Bugsy says. 'If it was one of the boys who had wings that didn't work, we wouldn't hear the end of it, but she's always positive, always happy.'

'She's our sunshine,' Mabel says, smoothing Dayne's hair.

'I'm going to work hard,' Bugsy says. 'Make more money, see if I can save up, and get her wings fixed.'

Mabel smiles. 'Really? You work all the hours already.'

'I know. But I'll work all the more if it means I can look after my family. Once the boys are a bit older, they can help me out. Frank's already started.'

Mabel smiles and lies her head against the pillow. 'I'm definitely feeling better, but not best.'

'Go to sleep,' Bugsy says, leaning over to kiss her forehead. 'I'll let my two angels sleep. I'll bring you some food in a while.'

Mabel closes her eyes, snuggles under the blanket, and Dayne cuddles closer to her.

Chapter 55

'Mum, they've gone without me again,' Dayne says, joining her mother in the garden, at the base of their tree house.

'Don't worry,' Mabel says, pulling her in for a cuddle, and kissing the top of her head. 'Us girls don't need them. Let me show you this.'

They spend the next three hours gardening, planting seeds, and fixing the tiny fence that goes around their lot.

Mud smudging both her cheeks, but her eyes sparkling, Dayne takes her mum's hand.

'I love learning all this stuff,' she says.

'You pick it up so easily,' Mabel says. 'I love my boys, but they follow their dad. You and me, we're the same.'

They rub noses, their version of a kiss, and then they pick some berries to eat.

They only need one each, and that's too much really.

Dayne rubs her stomach. 'That was delicious. But I ate too much.'

'Same,' Mabel says. 'But I might take one more and make a pie for your dad and the boys.'

'I can help,' Dayne offers, and Mabel nods.

'Good idea. You make it, and I'll supervise.'

Dayne giggles. 'That makes it sound like school.'

'Life is like school sometimes,' Mabel says. 'Even at my age I learn something new every day.'

'Really? Even at your age?'

Mabel ruffles her hair. 'Cheeky. Even at my wrinkly, old, decrepit age.'

Dayne laughs. 'Sorry, old lady. Let's make some food.'

'Does it bother you?' Mabel asks, as she walks up the stairs with Dayne instead of flying, 'That the boys are working with dad now?'

Dayne shrugs. 'No. I reckon I'll help him once I'm done with school.'

Mabel frowns. 'I'm not sure about that. Dad's...'

'Dad's what?' Dayne asks.

'Nothing,' Mabel says. 'Nothing for you to worry your sweet head about.'

Dayne hugs her mum, and they spend the next few hours in the kitchen, chatting, laughing and cooking.

Mabel tastes a mini pie fresh from the fire.

'Dayne, that is delicious, you're really coming along.'

Dayne beams. 'I can help dad, mum. You mustn't worry that just because I'm a girl or younger or my wings don't work.'

Mabel takes her hand. 'Darling, I don't think you can't help your dad. You being a girl, or younger, or not able to fly has nothing to do with anything. But your dad isn't cutting hair anymore.'

'He's not? What's he doing then?'

'Something I don't want you involved with,' Mabel says, and she refuses to say anything more.

Dayne hides behind a leaf later that day watching her mum and dad argue, and her stomach churns. They never argue; they're always impossibly happy.

'Hey.' Her mum finds her in her room, watching the moon through a gap in the trees.

'You're quiet tonight,' Mabel says, hugging her, and tucking her blanket tightly around her.

Dayne shrugs. 'I'm okay.'

'Grown ups fight sometimes,' Mabel says, brushing her fingers through Dayne's hair. 'It doesn't mean anything.'

'It means you're fighting,' Dayne says.

'True. But it doesn't mean we don't like each other, or love each other, or love you and the boys.'

'I don't like it.'

'I'm sorry you saw it. But we're good. Hey, while the boys are busy tomorrow, shall we take a picnic to the top of the old black mountain?'

Dayne nods. 'That sounds fun. I love you mum. And I love dad. And I love my boys. Even Frank.'

'Even Frank?'

'He's meaner than the others.'

'Is he now? I'll have a word with him.'

'You don't need to,' Dayne answers, cuddling closer to her mum. 'One day I'll be a little bit bigger and stronger than I am now, and when he teases me, I'll punch him in the nose.'

Mabel hides her smile, kissing Dayne's hair again.

'Love you, feisty girl.'

'Love you too, mum.'

Chapter 56

Dayne wipes tears from her eyes, and kicks at Frank again. 'I can't talk about her. It's too sad.'

'She sounds wonderful,' Ettie says, holding out her finger to gently touch Dayne's hand.

'She was. But I miss her too much. And if I think about her too much it gets too sad.'

'I'm sure,' Sticks says. 'I feel sad when I think about my mum and dad because I miss them so much, and I know I'll see them again.'

Dayne smiles. 'I'll be glad to meet them. Whenever it is.'

'What are we going to do about your brother?' Posey asks, as Dayne lifts his hand and watches it flop back down beside him.

'Punch him again,' Dayne says, sitting next to him, hand balled into a fist.

Ettie shakes her head. 'Don't. He's here now, which means he can't hurt anyone else, and he'll have to explain himself to you.'

'I don't think there's anything he can say which would stop me hating him,' Dayne says.

'You don't have to like him,' Sticks says. 'We just have to stop him.'

'Mission accomplished,' Dayne says, poking him in the side.

Frank winces and slowly opens his eyes.

Dayne lifts her fist to punch him again, but he rolls out of her reach, and flies away.

Sticks grabs hold of his wings, ever so carefully, making sure he doesn't rip them, but preventing Frank from flying any higher.

'Hey!' Frank glares at Sticks but Sticks just shrugs. He's not letting him go.

'Dayne, I love you and your freaky bunch of friends, but if this fat git doesn't put me down, I'm going to slice his neck open.'

Sticks pales but doesn't let his grip falter.

Frank shoots him another evil glance.

'I mean it. I'm very quiet. You won't hear me sneak up on you when you're sleeping in your swamp.' He makes a hand across his throat gesture and Sticks' hand starts to shake.

'Dayne,' Sticks says, a pleading in his voice.

'Cut it out Frank. You don't get to threaten my friends. And you've got a damn cheek calling them freaks, when you're the one going around threatening giants and tiny hedgehogs.'

Frank glares at Dayne now. 'Sis, I'm losing my patience fast, you know we don't do that anymore, and I don't like this lump holding onto me, and you knocking me out. I'm not going to apologise forever.'

'This isn't about apologising forever, Frank, this is about you still pulling the same crap you were then.'

'I'm not pulling any crap. And can you put me down.' He spits the words at Sticks, and Sticks looks at Dayne. She nods, and he sets Frank down on the table, before taking a step back. He's embarrassed to admit that the tiny pixie scares the living daylights out of him.

'I'm the same,' Ettie whispers, giving his arm a little rub.

Sticks smiles, though he looks like he might throw up.

Dayne points at Frank. 'You're still terrorising people. Tell me it's not true.'

Frank looks pretty aggravated, but he holds his hands up. 'Sis, I'm with dad now, up at the palace, working my backside off for the King. I don't have time for any crap now.'

'Mrs. Dinklepants and Derek the giant both told me you'd been at their places harassing them for money, since you started working for the King.'

'That is a load of crap,' Franks says, his eyes narrowing. 'There's no way I'd do it. Dad'd have my hide if I even thought about it. Beside we've got a good thing going on up at the palace.'

Dayne shakes her head, and then turns to Ettie and Sticks, an 'I don't know what to think' look on her face.

Ettie clears her throat. 'Frank. Do you promise it wasn't you?'

'Hey. I don't owe you a promise, or nothing else,' he says, frowning at her. Ettie refuses to shrink away from him, even though she really wants to.

He steps toward Dayne and takes her hands. 'Sis, you damn near broke my nose, and I should be furious, and I only came here to ask if you wanted me to bring anything when we come for Sunday lunch, but I'm telling you, this is nothing to do with me.'

Ettie sighs. 'It must be some sort of magic.'

They all turn to her. 'If Mrs. Dinklepants and Derek said it was Frank, it must have looked like Frank. They're hardly going to want to blame him for something someone else did; they'd be too scared.'

Frank puffs up a bit, and Dayne slaps at him. 'Don't be so impressed with yourself for being a dinkus,' she says. 'Everything you and dad and the others did to these people is sickening. You should be embarrassed that they're scared of you, not proud.'

Frank has the grace to look a tiny bit ashamed.

'Sorry, sis,' he says. 'I am. I haven't done anything.'

Dayne turns to Ettie. 'What sort of magic makes someone else look like Frank?'

'And more importantly,' Sticks says, feeling very brave for speaking up. 'Why?'

'Yeah,' Frank says. 'Who's trying to get me in trouble? When I find out, I'll knock them out. And maybe I'll get you to help me,' he says, grinning at Dayne, and gingerly touching his bloody nose.

Chapter 57

Dayne stares at Frank until he squirms, but she believes him. And really, it didn't make sense that he was still harassing old customers, not when he'd been given a clean slate, a job with the King, and somewhere to live.

'Can I go?' he asks, not as cheekily as he normally would.

Dayne looks at Ettie and Sticks who nod.

'You can, but if I find out you had anything to do with this...'

Hands up again, Franks flies close and kisses her cheek. 'Look, kid, I know I was a pain to you, always making fun of you, and stuff, but I've changed.'

Dayne makes a face.

'What? You believe dad can change, but not me? I'm even looking forward to coming up and helping this idiot with his shop.' He gestures at Sticks who reddens and takes a step back.

'Dad hadn't seen you,' Dayne says, suspicious again, 'so how do you know about the shop?'

Frank blushes. 'Look, it's nothing to do with putting the willies up ridiculous hedgehogs... I'm seeing someone at the palace, and I don't want dad to know.'

'Seeing someone?' Dayne asks. 'Like seeing them?'

'Yes. Seeing them, courting them, falling in love a little bit.'

'Who?'

'I'm not telling,' Frank says. He kicks at the floor, unable to look at his sister. 'I don't want to jinx it.'

Dayne grins. 'Okay. I believe you. But if it gets more serious, I want to meet her.'

'Of course. One day. So, what's the plan for getting this shop up and running,' he says, glaring at Sticks, but with a tiny glimmer of excitement in his eyes. 'I hear this one,' he gestures at Ettie, 'is going to make us a little bit bigger.'

'I am,' Ettie says, feeling weirdly proud to be acknowledged by Frank for something good, unlike Sticks.

'Bigger's not necessarily better,' he reminds them with a scowl.

Dayne clips him round the ear. 'It is for building a shop. Doofus.'

Frank rubs his ear but takes the slap. 'Tomorrow?'

'Tomorrow.'

Dayne is grinning as he flies out of the bar.

'I believe him,' she says.

'Me too,' Posey says. 'I've seen my brother lie a million times, usually to get me in trouble, he's definitely telling the truth.'

'Which begs the question,' Ettie says, 'who is pretending to be Frank, and why?'

'I can't make it make sense,' Sticks says. 'I'm too hungry and too scared. Dayne, your brother scares the life out of me, and I've looked after spit firing dooshlebugs. I know how Derek feels.'

'He is scary, though he's mellower than he was. And he's in love,' Dayne adds, beaming. 'Love might make him all warm and fuzzy.'

Sticks snorts, and Dayne laughs.

'Okay, maybe not.'

'So, is it a worry for another day?'

'Who's pretending to be Frank?' Ettie asks, shaking her head. 'No, I think it's a worry for today. We've got a shop to build tomorrow, and I want to go through my spell books, just to make sure I know what I'm doing making you all bigger.'

Dayne looks a tiny bit alarmed and Ettie laughs.

'I'm good. I'm not nervous anymore.' She turns to Posey. 'When I met these guys I had puppy dog ears, because I magicked them up during my exam – that I failed, by the way – and then I couldn't get rid of them.'

'But she's passed her exams now,' Sticks says, 'and if she can make a custard tap, she can make tiny pixies bigger.'

'I have faith in you,' Dayne says. 'I was only teasing when I looked scared. We have more faith in you than you have in yourself.'

'Thanks,' Ettie says. 'I would like to check, though.'

'So why don't we have some more food, and then head out, we could visit some of the other people my family terrorised,' Dayne says, looking sad.

'You're not responsible for what they did,' Ettie says. 'You never were. But good idea. We can see if anyone has anything to say that might help us figure out who's pretending to be Frank. And why.'

Ettie conjures up some more food and drink, and then some for the bar's customers, who come sniffing around, and the four of them eat and chat and laugh.

Chapter 58

They make sure Posey is happy, and then head outside.

'Where are we going?' Ettie asks, turning to Dayne.

'Closest one from here, would be Gilpin. He's a dwarf. Pretty frosty. But always grateful when I went to help him. He lives just outside of Daisy Creek.'

Ettie nods, Dayne flies into Sticks' pocket and Ettie and Sticks hold hands.

They land with a whoosh, and Dayne points at a row of crooked little cottages.

'He lives in the third one. Remember, he can be frosty.'

Ettie hangs back, as does Sticks, and they let Dayne fly up to the front door.

Ettie steps forward and knocks for Dayne.

'Sorry,' she says, wondering if it was patronising.

'It's fine. I'd usually throw stones at his window until he came to the door to yell at me,' Dayne says, and Ettie smiles. There are so many small inconveniences she's never considered because she's not a tiny pixie.

The door swings inwards, and a pointy nosed, narrow eyed, green haired dwarf glares at Ettie and Sticks, and then notices Dayne hovering in front of him.

'Look at you!' he says, a grin completely changing the way he looks.

Ettie smiles; he might be frosty, but she can tell from his reaction what he thinks about Dayne and how much kindness she clearly showed him.

'I know!' Dayne says, flying around in a circle, fluttering her wings extra fast.

Gilpin steps into his house and gestures for them to follow.

Ettie steps inside, but Sticks can't quite make it through the door.

Ettie raises a hand to magic him inside, but he shakes his head. 'I don't want to break anything. I'll wait out here.'

Ettie nods and touches his arm.

The cottage is as tiny and crooked inside as out. Ettie's hair is touching the ceiling, and if she still had her puppy ears, they'd be completely squashed.

Gilpin sits, and nods for Ettie to take a seat.

She perches on the edge of a chair. This must be how Sticks feels. Just a bit too big. Of course, the alehouse accommodates him, but this place can't.

'I suppose you're here about Frank?' Gilpin asks. 'I heard from one of the goblins in the market that your father has a new job, so I knew he wouldn't be bothering me. I was surprised when Frank turned up.'

'I'm so sorry,' Dayne says. 'I wanted to come and see you, to explain that my dad had stopped doing what he used to do, before anyone else told you.'

He waves a fat hand. 'It's fine. Word gets round. But Frank – he annoyed me.'

'That's the thing,' Dayne says. 'I know it looked like Frank, but we think it was someone pretending to be him.'

'Hmm.' Gilpin strokes his purple beard, staring at her, head cocked to one side. 'You wouldn't cover for him. You spent too long trying to make up for what he and the others did.'

'Exactly. But we can't figure out who it was or why,' Dayne says. 'Any ideas.'

Ettie leans forward. 'Now you know it might not have been Frank, is there anything that struck you as odd, anything that stood out?'

Still stroking his beard, Gilpin closes his eyes briefly. 'I tell you one thing that struck me as odd.'

'Go on,' Dayne says.

'Your brother was always clean shaven, but when he came to see me, he had a fuzzy little beard, and really hairy knuckles.'

Dayne grins at Ettie.

'Sounds like a fox to me.'

'A fox?' Gilpin asks. 'I heard about that business with Philomena and her ilk. You think she's behind this?'

'She's locked up,' Dayne says. 'But it's definitely not Frank. I saw him today, and I believe him.'

'And this impersonator mentioned Philomena when he was at Derek's house.' Ettie adds.

'Ah, how is Derek?' Gilpin asks, and Ettie smiles. She hasn't seen the frosty side of the dwarf, that Dayne mentioned. Maybe now he's not beholden to her family, he's more relaxed.

'He's good.'

'I haven't seen him for a long time.'

'He's okay – though he's fed up with my family aggravating him.'

'But of course, if it's something to do with Philomena, then it's nothing to do with you.'

'True – but I still have to fix it. If the King hears about it, it could cause all kinds of problems.'

'Which is why whoever's doing it, is doing it,' Ettie says, smacking her palm to her forehead. 'We couldn't figure out why someone would mention Philomena.'

'It's probably nothing to do with her, but everything to do with someone who's annoyed at Frank,' Dayne says, and then her face falls. 'Which could be any number of people.'

'Yeah,' Ettie says, nodding her head. If this is someone's idea of revenge against Frank and his family, just to get him in trouble with the King, and maybe lose them their job with the King, then it could be anyone Frank has ever roughed up.

'It's a long list,' Gilpin says. 'Though I'm glad you got some clarity on it.'

'Yeah, and I'm sorry I didn't get round to visiting before now,' Dayne says.

Gilpin holds his hands up. 'I'm just glad I don't have to see them anymore. And I don't spend money I haven't got anymore.'

'That's good!' Dayne says, beaming at the dwarf. 'You seem happier for it too.'

'I am. Happy and free.'

Dayne smiles and flies up off the chair she was perched on. Ettie stands too, hair brushing the ceiling again.

'We'll be off, but come and visit me,' Dayne says.

'Where are you?' Gilpin asks, a sad look on his face. 'I heard about the treehouse. Those damn foxes.'

'I'm in Puddle Town,' Dayne says. 'In the alehouse.'

'I know it,' Gilpin says, stroking his beard. 'I thought it shut down – used to be a busy old place. On the crossroads?'

Dayne nods. 'Well it's getting busy again, and you're always welcome there.'

Gilpin grins and holds up a meaty fist. Dayne holds up her tiny fist and flies at him, fist bumping him so lightly she can tell from his expression that he's not sure she's even touched him.

'Thanks Dayne. I'll pop and see you next time I'm in that neck of the woods.'

Dayne grins, and Gilpin lets them out of the front door.

Chapter 59

Sticks is leaning awkwardly against a tree. He lifts a hand in greeting, and Gilpin waves at him.

'We think we've solved one thing,' Ettie says, as Dayne flies into his pocket and they join hands.

'Go on,' he says.

'We couldn't figure out how Philomena would be involved when she's in prison or why anyone would want to pretend to be Frank,' Dayne says. 'It's just too stupid.'

'But we think it might be someone who wants revenge on Frank, or Bugsy, or all of them as a family. Which includes the foxes – Gilpin did say that the fake frank had hairy knuckles.'

Sticks nods. 'So they go round causing trouble, muddying the water by mentioning Philomena, and hope the King gets wind of it...'

'Exactly!' Ettie and Dayne shout at the same time.

'Then my dad and my brothers lose their jobs, and where they live.'

'Sounds feasible,' Sticks says, scratching his belly.

'I think so. But there are so many people who hate my family, it might be impossible to figure it out.'

'But we need to figure it out,' Ettie says. 'Not just for Franks' sake – but for the people who are still being harassed.'

'So we make a list of everyone you ever visited to offer them help,' Ettie says. 'And we visit them, and we...' she trails off.

Dayne shakes her head. 'We need to catch them in the act, and stop them,' she says.

'But how?' Sticks says. 'They've visited the hedgehog, the giant and dwarf, and we don't know who else. By the time we figure that out...'

'Mrs Dinklepants, Derek and Gilpin,' Dayne says, pointedly.

'Ooh, I know!' Ettie says, her eyes shining. 'Magic!'

'Magic what?' Dayne asks.

'Magic tracking,' Ettie says. 'Whoever is doing this – for whatever reason, though we think we've cracked it – they have to be using magic, to make them look like Frank. Gilpin said they were hairy, but that could be a fox or a bearded man, it's not really helpful.'

'Okay,' Dayne says, flying in a circle, stretching her wings.

'Magic tracking?' Sticks says, nudging Ettie because she seems to have lost her train of thought.

'Yes. Whoever went to their houses was under some sort of spell or enchantment to make them look like Frank.'

'Right?'

'So it'll have left a mark.'

'Really?'

'Yes, magic always does. But you can't see it. And it doesn't last forever.'

'That doesn't help,' Dayne says, feeling a little bit exasperated.

'But you can see it if you're looking for it,' Ettie says. 'Imagine a cake. Once it's eaten there might still be signs that it was there.'

'Not if I've got anything to do with it,' Sticks says.

Ettie laughs. 'Maybe not. But there'd be crumbs, or an empty plate.'

'Okay so we're looking for magic crumbs?' Dayne asks.

'Kind of.'

Ettie turns back to Gilpin's house and holds her hands up in front of her.

'If I get a magic… crumb then we can follow it.'

Dayne squeals. 'Really?'

Ettie nods. 'I'd forgotten all about it. We did a module on it at the academy. I wasn't very good at it.'

Sticks rubs her arm. 'You weren't good at anything at the academy,' he says, gently. Then he shakes his head. 'Sorry, that sounded better in my head. I meant that you were all nervous when you were at the academy. Now you're not. You know how good you are, we know how good you are, you've passed your exam, even got a certificate….'

Ettie smiles at him. 'I knew what you meant. I wasn't great at the academy, but I remember this, because it was so intriguing. To think that every spell I ever did, left a trail that was invisible to anyone who wasn't looking for it.'

'It's pretty cool,' Dayne says.

Ettie grins and holds up her hands again. 'I can see a trail of grey, it's almost like smoke. But that's me,' she says.

'Anything else?' Dayne asks, so excited now that they might figure this out and fix it before it causes any real harm.

'Yes,' Ettie says, slowly moving her fingers around and walking closer to the front door. 'There's a purple whisp. It's not very strong – maybe because the person who visited didn't do the magic, but had the magic done to them.'

She turns right abruptly. 'It's going this way. It's faint but I can see it.'

She walks slowly, bent at the waist, her eyes tracking what Sticks and Dayne cannot see.

'This is odd,' Sticks whispers and Dayne giggles, flying ahead and then doubling back so she doesn't distract Ettie.

They cross the dusty road, and wind through the trees. Ettie is ahead of them, still bent over and muttering, her hands moving slightly as she walks.

She stops.

Chapter 60

'It ends here,' she says, in a whisper.

'Here?' Sticks whispers too.

'Right here?' Dayne asks, flying over to hover next to Ettie.

Ettie nods, frowning. 'But there's nothing-'

Her words are lost, because she's fallen through a hole in the ground.

'Ettie!' Dayne shouts out, and flies into the hole after her.

'Girls!' Sticks shouts and jumps in after them. He doesn't get far because he's too big. He's stuck with his legs in the hole and his belly and everything else on the outside.

'Damn me being a bloody great ogre,' he mutters, as he pulls himself out. He sticks his head down the hole. 'Girls! Girls, are you okay? Got to be a damned fox,' he mumbles, sitting down in the dirt, right next to the hole.

ETTIE LANDS WITH A bump and is faced with three fairly large tunnels.

'I'm here,' Dayne says, flying close. 'Foxes?'

'Got to be. But which way?'

Dayne shrugs. 'I can fly ahead and check?'

'It could be dangerous. Where's Sticks?'

'Too big,' Dayne says, and Ettie nods.

'Poor Sticks.'

'Lucky foxes though. I reckon he'd kill them if he got hold of them after what they did to his shop. So do we reckon it's someone who knows Philomena?'

'Bound to be. I figured it could be anyone, but I suppose they've got more reason than most to hate your dad and your brothers.'

'True. But we can't let them go round harassing people, even if it is to get revenge.'

'No, we can't. Okay. Go really slowly and quietly. Fly down and listen out for any noise. If you hear anything come back to me, and we'll confront them together.'

Dayne nods. She's as brave as a tiny pixie could be, but she also knows how easy it was for the foxes to kidnap her last time. She's too small to put up a fight.

DAYNE FLIES THROUGH the cold, dank tunnel, wishing she was bigger than she was. It's one thing to feel brave and know you could kick someone's butt – didn't she have the best teachers – but she's so tiny, there's no way she could stand up to a fox and do anything other than fail.

There's a light burning ahead and she drops to the floor. She tucks against the side of the tunnel, breathing in the earthy smell, and walking slowly forward. She can't afford to be seen. She peeks around the corner. The good thing about being so small, is that it's easy for her to hide, easy for her to sneak about, easy for her to see Mrs Dinklepants sitting on a stool, eating a cake.

She shakes her head. This must be a fox enchanted to look like Mrs Dinklepants – there's no way she would be here, in the fox's lair, unless...

Dayne flies forward.

'Mrs Dinklepants!' Her voice is low but panicked. 'Quick – I can help you – I can get you out of here.'

Mrs Dinklepants drops her cake, and her eyes dart side to side.

Dayne holds out her hand. Mrs Dinklepants is small enough that she can take hold of her and try to pull her to her feet.

'I wish I could see the look on their faces,' Frank says, coming through from the shadows and holding out another cake to Mrs. Dinklepants.

Dayne jumps away from Mrs Dinklepants, dropping her hand. She's shaking her head, but she can see with her own eyes what's going on, even though she doesn't want to believe it.

Frank laughs – and now she knows it's not him, she turns to snap at him.

'You think you're so clever, but we figured it out.' She turns to look at the hedgehog, who doesn't even look ashamed. 'But you? I don't understand why you're here, with him...'

Mrs Dinklepants smooths down her dress. 'My brother married Philomena's sister. They're family. You're not.'

'So everything I did to help you meant nothing?' Dayne can't help but feel put out.

'It helped,' Mrs Dinklepants says with a shrug, 'but it doesn't change the facts.'

'And the facts are?'

'Your family is bad news. Your family got Philomena and her boys locked up. I blame you.'

Dayne shakes her head. 'You know what? Your sad little game of revenge won't work, because I know the King and when I tell him what you've done, Frank himself could go and rob the crown jewels and the King would believe me.'

Dayne flutters her wings; she has one advantage now that she can fly that she didn't have when she was kidnapped. She can escape.

She flies back the way she came and then turns to Mrs Dinklepants.

'All you've done with this pathetic play is prove that you're as bad as my dad and my brothers.'

Mrs Dinklepants bristles and Dayne laughs.

'I mean it. You hate my brothers and my dad because they intimidated and hurt you – and yet they only did that because you owed them something. You've let your puppet-' Dayne gestures at the fox disguised with magic as Frank, 'hurt people, people who haven't done anything wrong, and you can try to justify it as revenge or family loyalty, but we all know that's just crap. You're a low life, and if I ever see you again, it's not Frank you'll need to worry about. It's me.'

She turns and flies quickly back through the muddy tunnel.

'Ettie, let's go now.'

For all her harsh words, Dayne is absolutely devastated. She sat with Mrs Dinklepants, ate her cakes, shared laughs with her. Dayne always knew she helped all of the people her family harassed out of guilt, but she always felt lucky that she made some real friends – like Gilpin, like Derek, like Mrs Dinklepants.

Ettie scrambles out, Sticks helping to pull her up, and the three of them stand in the woods.

'Well?' Sticks asks.

Chapter 61

Dayne wipes angry tears.
'Well, I know who it is.' She turns to Ettie. 'Can we get away from here? Far away?'

Ettie nods and joins hands with Sticks. Dayne flies into his pocket.

They land beside the river behind the alehouse.

Dayne flies over to the water's edge.

The others join her.

'Go on,' Ettie says softly.

Dayne turns to them, still barely able to make sense of what she just saw.

She sighs. 'It was a fox – though they were disguised as my brother.'

Ettie tuts. 'Do you want me to go back in there, magic him back to what he should look like?'

Dayne shakes her head. 'Nah, I don't really care – it was clearly a fox, and it was Mrs. Dinklepants.'

'Mrs Dinklepants?' Ettie shakes her head. 'No way!'

'It was. She said that her brother married Philomena's sister, or her sister married Philomena's brother. Someone married someone, which made them family, and so they were just trying to get revenge.'

'I thought she seemed a bit spiky,' Sticks says, wrinkling his nose. 'What a witch.'

'Hey!' Ettie says, giving him a nudge with her elbow. 'That gives witches a bad name. Although...' She cocks her head, thinking. 'A witch must have helped them – where else would they have got the magic from to change the fox into frank?'

Dayne wipes her eyes. 'Right now, I don't even care.'

'We'll tell the King. He needs to have them arrested. They can't go around beating people up...'

Dayne sighs. 'It's what my dad used to do. And nobody arrested him, or my brothers.'

They are quite for a moment. It irks all of them to think that Mrs. Dinklepants and the fox might get away with what they've been doing, all in a bid to get Frank in trouble.

Sticks holds out his huge hand, and Dayne flies onto his palm. He brings her up to his face, and she leans on his cheek.

'I thought me and Mrs; Dinklepants were friends.'

'It's a running theme around here,' Sticks says. 'Lox betrayed me, Liss betrayed Ettie, and now the hedgehog has betrayed you.'

Dayne doesn't even correct him this time by saying the hedgehog's name.

'I feel sad,' Dayne says, wiping away another fat tear.

'Of course you do. Betrayal stings.'

'What did you say to me, Sticks? When I was upset about Liss? You told me that you can't take it personally when someone hurts you; they're just doing what they do.'

'It feels personal,' Dayne says. 'It was an attack against my family.'

'A stupid attack, designed to make you look bad.'

'But we'll talk to the King,' Sticks says, scratching his belly and then rolling up his trousers and dangling his feet in the water. 'Ooh that's nice. The King will believe us over some spiky dirt bag.'

'I hope so.'

'You know so,' Ettie says, smiling softly. 'And if he doesn't – we can show him the magic tracking and he can see for himself.'

'He'll believe us,' Dayne says. 'I know he will, I just can't believe she did that to Frank and to me.'

They are quiet for a moment, three friends, listening to the river babbling, the birds singing, and the gentle rustle of the leaves in the trees.

'This place always makes me feel better,' Dayne says.

'Me too,' Ettie says.

'Me three,' Sticks says, lying on the grass, letting his feet dry.

'Well, at least we figured it out,' Ettie says. 'And I really can't see them carrying on with their silly charade. Now we know, and now they know that we'll tell the King. Their plan to get your family in trouble won't work. They'll probably stop their nonsense.'

'I hope so. I know my family hurt a lot of people, and maybe it's not enough to just stop.'

'You're not saying you agree with what they did?' Sticks asks, sitting up.

'No. But I know a lot of people got hurt. And just because my family stopped what they were doing, doesn't mean that real harm wasn't done, that real damage wasn't inflicted. People might still feel angry about it…'

'What are you thinking?' Ettie asks, and Dayne smiles.

'I think I have an idea.'

'Go on,' Sticks says.

'But I think we'll need some help.'

'From?' Ettie asks, wondering where Dayne is going with this.

Dayne grins.

'A certain red-crested, bobble headed pigeon.'

Ettie shakes her head, still not sure where Dayne is going with this.

'I'll explain,' she says.

'And if the bobble head is coming here, they can take our letter for Graily.'

'Let's go in and help Posey and then I'll tell you what I'm thinking.'

Chapter 62

Posey is sitting with her feet up on a bench. The bar room is empty of customers and absolutely pristine. All the dishes are done, all the tables are wiped, and the floor is shiny and clean.

'What would we have done if you hadn't shown up?' Ettie asks, slipping onto the bench beside her.

Sticks sits opposite. 'Or if you'd run away because of what I said about trolls?'

Posey laughs, and touches his arm, waiting for him to raise his eyes and meet her gaze. 'Sticks – I'm fine and we're fine. There might have been some offence at first but now, we're fine. Trolls are horrible. I'm just the exception.'

'Like me!' Sticks says. 'Nobody likes ogres.'

'We do!' the three girls say in chorus.

They all laugh.

'How was your afternoon?' Ettie asks Posey.

'Absolutely no trouble. People come in and they drink and then they leave. I really like it here.'

'We really like having you,' Dayne says. 'And I don't know how you keep such a cool head with so much to do.'

Posey shrugs. 'I'm used to it. That's not to say I wouldn't rather be a full-time architect, but...'

'But for now,' Ettie says.

'Exactly.'

Sticks yawns. 'I'm suddenly so tired – I think I need a little sugar rush.'

'You don't need an excuse to use your custard tap,' Dayne says, with a laugh.

'It's yours,' Ettie says.

'I haven't let a customer near it,' Posey adds.

Sticks grins and blushes. 'I feel a bit greedy.'

'Not at all. What's a custard tap for if not to drink from?'

He grins and leaps off the bench.

While he's guzzling away and burping, the girls sit in silence trying not to giggle.

'I need to check my magic for tomorrow,' Ettie says after one particularly huge burp from Sticks. 'I think I'm going to try to stop time.'

'That would be cool,' Posey says.

'I cannot wait to be big!' Dayne says, an excited grin on her face. 'With all this other nonsense I'd almost forgotten about the shop.'

'Did you get it sorted?' Posey asks, raising her voice to drown out the large custard-induced burps coming from behind the counter.

'We did. It was Mrs Dinklepants.'

'The sweet, old hedgehog?' Posey asks, eyes wide.

'Yup. Who'd have thought it.'

'You never can tell,' Ettie says. 'Some people are very good at hiding their true colours.'

'And some of us are open books,' Dayne says, grinning at Sticks, who's lumbering towards them, looking custard drunk and oh so happy.

'That was–' He pauses to let out another huge burp. 'Sorry – delicious.' He grins, his ears turning pink.

'Now I'm hungry,' Dayne says. 'Not for custard, or for anything that makes me burp like that. No offence,' she says, patting Sticks on his arm.

He grins. 'I'm not offended. In some cultures, burping after food is a sign of respect.'

'Really?'

He nods. 'But custard is only a starter, really, I'm still hungry.'

'For?'

'Anything,' he says with a shrug.

'Let's have some food, and then we've got some letters to write,' Dayne says, with a smile.

'Letters?' Ettie asks. 'This is getting more and more mysterious.'

Dayne grins.

'I need some sleep,' Posey says, stifling a yawn.

'Is it too much on your own?' Ettie asks, and Posey shrugs.

'Nah – I'm not saying help isn't appreciated – especially your magic help – but to be honest I like being busy and there's a mindlessness to some of it, like washing and drying all the mugs, that I kind of enjoy. Stops me thinking too much, you know.'

They all nod. They all know there's more to her story, and they all know that when she's ready, she'll share with them.

'I'll start,' Dayne says, fluttering her wings. 'Chicken pie.'

'Egg and cress tart,' Sticks says, licking his lips.

'Cheese and ham toastie,' Posey says, her voice still lilting at the end of her sentence.

Ettie easily conjures up all they've asked for and more. She magics up a pot of tea and several mugs, including a tiny cup and saucer for Dayne.

Chapter 63

Ettie stretches and yawns.

'It's been a long day, but I'm going to go up to my room and make sure I'm on the right track with my magic for tomorrow.' She wrings her hands. 'I know you all trust me, but I don't want to get this wrong. But first, tell us what you're up to.'

Dayne grins. 'Okay so there's a bunch of people my family have hurt. And there's a bunch of people we'd like to come to the opening of the shop when it's done. So I was thinking of inviting everyone to the shop opening. People my family need to apologise to, and all of your old customers,' she says, looking at Sticks. 'That way there'll be loads of people for the shop, but also my dad and my brothers can see everyone they ever hurt and apologise to them all. Sort of all in one fell swoop. What do you think?'

Ettie beams. 'I think it's a marvellous idea. I hadn't thought about a grand opening for the shop.'

Sticks puffs out his chest and blushes. 'I'd love that,' he says. 'A real celebration to make up for what happened before.'

'Exactly. Do you think I should run it by my dad and my brothers first?'

'They're not going to like it,' Sticks says, opening his mouth wide and cramming in the last of his tart.

'I know. Nobody likes being called out on the stuff they've done wrong,' Dayne says. 'But I feel like we all need it.'

'It might do them good,' Ettie says. 'You're not asking for atonement necessarily, just acknowledgment and an apology.'

'I reckon it'll go a long way,' Sticks says, crumbs falling from his mouth. 'You're lucky you've got your dad and your brothers close. If you can clear the air and get all the bad blood out of the way, you'll all be happier for it.'

'I am lucky. You miss your parents, don't you Sticks?'

He nods, looking a little forlorn. 'It's just with the shop and everything. I'd like them to be here. But they're busy. They'll come back when they're ready.'

'They will. And they'll be so proud of you,' Dayne says.

'I reckon I'll go and have a little swing in the hammock,' Sticks says. 'Let my food go down. See you for supper?'

Ettie laughs. 'You're so full, you look green.'

Dayne giggles, because Sticks is green.

'Ah, that'll pass,' Sticks says, poking out his tongue. 'Always does.'

ALONE IN HER ROOM, Ettie pulls out a spell book, and sits on her bed, flicking through the pages.

She still gets a thrill whenever she holds a spell book – and it reminds her of first going to the academy. She misses it. She misses Liss.

She can admit to herself, though, that she's infinitely happier here than she ever was at the academy, and while she doesn't have as close of a bond with Sticks and Dayne quite yet, she knows she will. She's only been at the alehouse a matter of weeks, and already they feel like family.

Liss is family too, and although she's itching to see her, and help her with whatever she needs, she also knows that if she goes nosing around the academy and Milton really is bad news, she could end up putting her friend in danger. However helpless she feels right now, she'd never do that.

The academy was home for a long time, but it was also a place she felt lost in, a place she didn't feel like she belonged in, a place that reminded her daily of her failures.

Here she's reminded daily that she's a great witch, with real magical ability. Which is why she needs to get this spell right for tomorrow.

She has to make all the pixies bigger and she has to stop time.

Easy!

She's humming as she flicks through the pages, excitement building.

DAYNE IS HOLDING A tiny quill and a tiny piece of parchment. She loves how easy it is for Ettie to conjure up anything she might need in tiny pixie-sized versions, but she's also so excited to be bigger tomorrow.

She spent years pretending she didn't want to fix her wings, as though using magic to help her fly was cheating in some way, and flying was something she should just get used to not being able to do. It was a limit she placed on herself, and she's so glad Ettie helped her to fly.

Being bigger – if only for a day – feels similar. Before she'd have acted all tough and insisted there was nothing wrong with being a pixie; she didn't need fixing to be any bigger, and yet of course they'll all be able to help Sticks better if they're bigger.

They're building a shop big enough to fit an ogre and who knows how many magical creatures. It needs to be super sized, and pixie just won't cut it.

She starts writing her list, and once she has all the names down, she places it on the table near the ever-roaring fire, and the list of names Sticks gave her of customers. Then she heads out to speak to her father and her brothers.

They'll do the right thing – or at least she hopes they will.

STICKS IS SNORING GENTLY, one arm and one leg dragging on the floor as he snoozes in the hammock.

Amma smiles at him, watching the way his chest rises and falls as he sleeps.

She's fed and watered all the animals and she can't wait for tomorrow to help him, and who knows who else, refurbish the building into a shop.

'Hey lazy bones,' she says, giving his arm a little shake.

Sticks wakes with a start, wiping the drool from his chin. He scrambles to sit up and grins at Amma.

'How are all our babies?'

Amma blushes slightly, and grins. 'They're good. Dad.'

He laughs. 'They're going to love the shop when it's done – they'll have so much space.'

'You're going to love it too. I know you love a snooze, but you seem a little lost with nothing much to do.'

He scratches his chin and finds a bit of egg from his tart. He licks his fingers. 'You know what, you're right. I haven't given it much thought, but I am lost. And a little bit moochy. I want to get back to work, back to healing.'

'It'll do you good. I can't wait either.' She pauses and tucks her hair behind her ear. 'I've missed you.'

'I bet you've missed the stink of the place too,' he says with a grin. 'I went in to see them all earlier, and the beggars were pretty smelly.'

Amma laughs. 'They smell. But I'm used to that – I've got brothers.'

'Are you still going to be able to help tomorrow?' Sticks asks.

'Try stopping me,' Amma says. She touches his arm, and then hugs him. 'It'll be wonderful to have Hooves and Horns up and running again, Sticks.'

'It will. I reckon we could promote you too, now Lox has gone,' he says, his expression darkening when he remembers his duplicitous best friend and the trouble he almost got into because of him.

Amma squeals and stretches up to kiss his cheek.

'Really?'

'Yeah,' Sticks says, grinning, and rubbing the spot where she kissed him. 'I need a deputy manager.'

Amma grins. 'I have to go and tell my mum! Thanks Sticks.'

Sticks grins, watching her go, and then climbs back into the hammock. He can hardly believe he'll have a shop again.

When he first saw the flames engulfing Hooves and Horns, he never thought he'd be happy again. Then Amma and Blast came around the corner with all the animals and magical creatures, all safe, and he was elated.

This new shop is going to be even better.

He cannot wait.

Chapter 64

Ettie reads through the directions for the spell one more time. She's sure she knows what she's doing – but then she did give herself puppy dog ears that she couldn't get rid of for the longest time. Her stomach twists: she hates it when she doubts herself. She hates how she can remember every stupid thing she's ever done, every awkward encounter she's ever had, every single time when she can tell she said the wrong thing at the wrong time to the wrong person, but she cannot think of a single instance where she got it right.

She taps her forehead. 'Be nice,' she whispers to herself about herself. It's so hard when you're your own worst enemy. How do you win against yourself, when you seem to revel in pointing out your own flaws?

She shakes her head. She's got this.

Witches are funny old things – there are some who seem to be born with every single bit of magic they might ever need or want. They don't need a spell book; they are walking, talking, doing spell books. Then there are others who know a lot, but need to double check their methods. She falls into this camp. She knows, but she wants to check that she knows.

She has to make pixies big and time stand still.

No biggie.

She laughs to herself, then laughs even more because if anyone could see her muttering and laughing to herself about herself, they'd surely think she'd gone mad.

She's not mad; she's just under a lot of pressure.

But she's got this.

She takes the spell book downstairs with her. She'll keep it with her tomorrow – like a good luck charm. And she'll be fine.

She hopes.

Dayne is in the den, cuddled up on her miniature chair, twirling a strand of her bright turquoise hair around her finger.

'Your hair's growing,' Ettie says, taking a seat in her favourite spot right by the fire.

'Yours is changing colour,' Dayne says, still fascinated by the way Ettie's hair was different streaks of grey when she met her, and now has all different coloured strands running through it. 'I think it changes with your mood,' Dayne says, sitting up a little straighter.

'Could be,' Ettie says with a shrug. 'I don't pay attention to it.'

'You should,' Dayne says. 'It's beautiful.'

Ettie laughs. 'Okay. Did you get your list done?'

'I did. I think it's complete.'

'And your dad…?'

Dayne sighs. 'It took a bit of work, but my dad ended up with an even better idea than mine.'

'Really?'

'Yes – I was with you, just thinking they need to apologise, to set things right, but…'

She fills Ettie in on the conversation she had with her dad, his idea, and the way he eventually talked her brothers into going along with it. By giving them all a clip around the ear.

Ettie laughs.

Dayne grins. 'So, we just need some magically prepared invites, and we can address them and get them sent.'

Sticks lumbers into the room, a grin on his face.

'Evening. I just saw Amma. She's going to be my deputy manager.'

'Oh, Sticks, that's great news.'

He nods and jumps onto his sofa, swings his legs around and tucks his hands under his head.

'It means if I'm busy healing or hammocking or chilling in my swamp, Amma will be there to help.'

'Hammocking. Is that even a thing?'

'It is now,' he says with a laugh. Then he sits up. 'How did you get on with the spells?' he asks Ettie.

She nods and holds up the book, proof that she has it all under control.

Dayne squeals. 'I cannot wait to be big. Look out!'

Ettie laughs. 'Why? What are you planning to do to us?'

Dayne grins. 'Just, you know, be big. Elbow you out of the way, steal your custard,' she says winking at Sticks, who panics before seeing – hoping – that she's joking. 'You guys are safe, it's my brothers who need to look out. Make me bigger first so I can frighten them.'

Ettie grins. 'Will do. I'm excited too. You're going to have your shop by the end of the day tomorrow, Sticks.'

He shakes his head, pink spots on his cheeks. 'I can't say thank you enough, to either of you, any of you, everyone. Your magic Ettie, you and your family, Dayne, Posey. Imagine her just coming along exactly when we need her.'

'She's amazing. I love her hair,' Dayne says.

'Shall we see if she wants to join us. We could have a nice cup of tea, some snacks...' Sticks trails off hopefully.

Ettie nods.

'I'll go and knock for her.'

Ettie comes back with Posey in tow and Dayne claps.

'Yay! Supper and chill out time is just what we all need – and definitely what you need after a long day working.'

Chapter 65

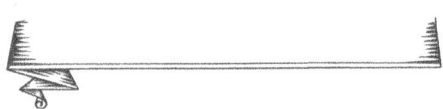

The den expands without any of them noticing, making room for another sofa, so that Sticks has his giant one, Dayne has her tiny one, as well as her pixie sized chair and table, Ettie still has her chair, and there's another sofa for Posey. It's squashy and green and covered in flowers.

Ettie laughs, pointing at it.

'That wasn't there just now, was it?'

Sticks and Dayne laugh. 'We did not notice that show up.'

'This place,' Sticks says, shaking his head.

'This place is weird,' Posey says, but she throws herself down on the sofa, letting out a sigh. 'Damn this is the most comfortable thing I've ever sat on. I just need a blanket.'

Ettie waggles her fingers, before the alehouse can oblige, and a fluffy, flowered blanket lands on Posey's lap.

She sighs again.

'I might never leave.'

'You're welcome to stay,' Ettie says, beaming.

'Snacks!' Dayne calls out.

'Snackage!' Sticks says grinning from ear to ear.

Ettie laughs. 'Order up,' she says, and they all call out their preferences.

'Hot, buttery toast.'

'Treacle tart and custard.'

'Cheese and pickle.'

'Hot chocolate.'

Ettie loves how quickly she's able to magic up each item and she knows in her heart that her magic is getting better, quicker and stronger since she left the academy.

Didn't she hear that once? That the real learning starts once you leave school.

Sticks lies down, and throws chunks of cheese in the air, catching each one neatly in his mouth.

'You're good,' Dayne says with a whistle.

'I don't waste food,' Sticks says. 'It's too good.'

'It is good,' Posey says, staring wide eyed at Ettie. 'You're amazing.'

Ettie shrugs.

Dayne giggles. 'She won't let you compliment her,' she says. 'She gets too embarrassed.'

'Not embarrassed,' Ettie says. 'Just awkward. I'm a witch, it's what we do.'

'But you do it so well,' Posey says. 'If I was a witch, I'd magic my family far, far away, somewhere they could never find me.'

Ettie smiles sadly. 'You don't get on?'

Posey sighs. 'Sorry, guys this is lovely. I don't want to spoil it with my pity party.'

'It's not a pity party.'

'The best thing about having people to share things with, is sharing things with them,' Sticks says. 'That's what we're here for.'

Posey sighs.

Dayne sits up straight and looks at her intensely.

'Posey. You're here for a reason. We need you. And you need us. You turned up right when we needed someone to run the bar – which you can do with your eyes closed. And right when we needed an architect. And you're just magically one of those too. You didn't come here by accident.'

Posey nods, sombre. 'No, I know. I'm meant to be here. And yeah, maybe I'm meant to tell you all about my horrible mum, and my terrible stepdad and my flipping awful brother, but maybe not tonight. This is too nice to spoil. I want more food, I want more drinks, I want another fluffy blanket. Ooh, and some fluffy slippers. I want to be safe and comfy and have nothing on my mind other than a full belly and the promise of a good night's sleep.'

She takes a big breath, and they all smile at her.

'If that's what you want,' Dayne says with a happy sigh. 'That's what you get. Ettie!' Dayne points at Ettie, who promptly conjures up fluffy blankets for all of them, and fluffy slippers for Posey.

Posey tucks them onto her feet.

'Yes! That's what I'm talking about.'

They all laugh and Ettie conjures up even more food and even more drink, until none of them can move and they are all happy but moaning from being over full, and too tired and exhausted to get themselves to bed.

Chapter 66

Ettie wakes earlier than usual and pads down in her comfy slippers to the den. She smiles at the fire, still burning low, always burning, and sits in her seat.

She picks up the list of names and addresses that Dayne wrote out and peers at her tiny handwriting. Using magic, she makes the parchment and the words bigger.

There are thirty-seven names on the list; thirty-seven names that belong to the people Dayne's family harassed.

It's strange that Bugsy probably started out by helping people – lending a little money here and there because he had it but ended up breaking bones – and possibly worse – because he had to keep them in line and get his money back.

Ettie shakes her head. She's glad sometimes that she had a fairly uneventful childhood, followed by so many years at the academy – her life is pretty boring. She misses her parents, but she never yearns to see them, the way she knows Sticks wishes he could see his parents again.

They're on a monster hunt, apparently, which sounds so much up Sticks' street, she's sure the only reason he didn't join them was the shop.

All being well his shop will be finished today – as long as her magic does what it's supposed to do, and then they'll have the grand opening party on Saturday.

She conjures up a pile of invites – thirty-seven of them for Dayne's guests, fifty five for customers who used to shop at Hooves and Horns, and one that's a little bit different, which she rolls into a scroll and slips into her pocket. She also grabs Graily's letter – it's time that was sent out too.

'Morning,' Posey says, walking into the room, stifling a yawn with one hand, her fluffy blanket draped over her shoulders like a cape.

'I slept like a baby but I'm still tired. What's that about?'

Ettie laughs. 'I was the same when I got here. I don't think I've felt as peaceful in my life as I do in this place. I think you're probably just catching up on sleep, rest, peace of mind.'

Posey scoffs. 'Yeah – there wasn't a lot of that at home.'

Ettie conjures up a cup of tea for her.

'Here,' she says, and Posey smiles her thanks.

'I like it a lot here,' she says.

'We do too – and we like having you.'

They sit in an easy silence, and then Posey clears her throat.

'I don't have a terrible story to tell. My life was okay – just not perfect.'

Ettie shrugs. 'Is life ever perfect?'

'It feels close to it here,' Posey says, tucking her feet underneath her. 'I feel safe.' She lifts her cup to Ettie. 'I'm well fed and well watered.'

Ettie grins. 'Me too! I've never eaten as much in my life.'

'You're a brilliant witch.'

'And you're a lovely troll.'

They both laugh.

'Morning,' Dayne says, flying into the room, and squealing at the pile of invitations in front of Ettie.

'Are those what I think they are?'

Ettie nods. 'They are!'

'What are they?' Posey asks. 'May I?' She gestures at the pile and Ettie nods.

'Of course.'

Posey picks one up, reading it quickly, a smile covering her face.

'That's nice. Do you think it'll work?'

Dayne shrugs.

'I think so.'

'Time will tell,' Ettie says, and using her magic once again, all the invites are rolled into scrolls, address labels attached.

'We just need Sticks now to get that pigeon thing.'

'Did I hear my name taken in vain?' Sticks asks, huffing into the room.

'Why are you out of breath?' Ettie asks, conjuring mugs of tea for him and Dayne.

'Just doing a little bit of stretching,' he says, ignoring the mug of hot tea, and reaching down to touch his toes. He gets as far as his knees, and that's a strain.

'Stretching?' Dayne asks, her little nose wrinkled. 'Why are you stretching?'

'Limbering up,' he says, a huge grin on his face. 'Today's the day.'

Dayne squeals and turns to Ettie. 'I completely forgot. Make me big, witch!'

Chapter 67

Ettie bursts out laughing, and then pats the spell book on the table, hoping and wishing and praying that she gets this right, and that she doesn't mess up her friend in a way that can't be undone.

Dayne flies up and hovers directly in her eyeline.

'Ettie, I trust you.'

Ettie nods and lets out a big, deep breath, centring herself and drawing on the knowledge and the power she knows she has, even if she doesn't seem to always remember that she knows she has it.

She holds her hands up, and smiles. They're not shaking.

'You've got this,' Dayne whispers.

Sticks and Posey are on the edge of their seats, watching.

Ettie locks eyes with Dayne and whispers some words that none of them can hear.

Then with a loud whoosh and a pop and a weird dull fog that fills the air, the magic is done.

'It worked!' Dayne screams out, her voice even higher in pitch than usual from the excitement.

Ettie opens her eyes and comes face to face with Dayne.

She's not pixie sized anymore.

Dayne flings her arms around Ettie and they hug and laugh and cry a little bit.

'I've wanted to hug you since we met,' Ettie says, tears streaming down her face.

'Me too!' Dayne says. And they hug again.

'Come on now. My turn,' Sticks says, standing up and opening his arms wide. Dayne still barely meets his chest, but she jumps up into his arms and they hug and laugh and cry a little bit too.

'I'm not hurting you, am I?' Sticks asks, wanting to hug his new friend tighter, but desperate not to hurt her.

'No. It's like having a bear hug from a bear,' Dayne says, wiping tears away.

'Imagine how quickly I could fly anywhere at this size,' she says, laughing and flapping her wings.

She knocks the invites all over the floor; her wings are so big now.

'Sorry!' she says, turning quickly, and batting Ettie with her wings.

'Watch out!' Ettie says, laughing, and magicking the invites into a neat pile again.

'Sticks, we need the pigeon thing to send all these.'

'Right-o,' he says, and then gathers Dayne into another hug.

Dayne laughs and then hugs Posey before she sits on his sofa.

'Ooh this is comfy,' she says with a sigh.

She can't stop grinning. None of them can.

'I can't stop looking at you,' Sticks says. 'I love you pixie sized, but it's really funny seeing you so big. Good thing you don't want to knock Frank out anymore,' he says, chuckling.

Dayne giggles. 'I love it. I feel so huge though, and a bit cumbersome,' she says, flapping her wings softly.

'You'll get used to that,' Ettie says.

Sticks opens the window and without warning lets out the most ear splitting, high pitched weird sounding shriek.

Ettie laughs, hand on her heart. 'What was that?'

Sticks looks bashful. 'Sorry – I should have given you a warning. That's' the call – you know for the red-crested, bobble headed pigeon.'

'Right. And that... noise will work, will it?'

A fluttering of wings gives them the answer to Ettie's question.

The pigeon flies in, and Sticks greets it warmly.

'Morning, son. That pile of scrolls is for you.'

The pigeon, as efficient as before, ducks his head in a nod, and then some way, somehow manages to gather all the scrolls into a bag that appears out of nowhere. He then loops the bag around his ankle, and despite the weight of it being heavier than he is, he flies towards the window.

'Wait!' Ettie says, and rushes to him.

'I forgot this one.'

She takes the scroll from her pocket, and hands it to the pigeon, whispering quiet instructions to him.

He blinks slowly at her, then ducks his head in a nod, before flying out of the window.

Sticks claps her back. 'Nearly forgot someone, did you, silly!'

Ettie coughs. 'Yes. Nearly.'

Chapter 68

'Breakfast anyone?' Ettie asks.

They all nod and she conjures up toast and jam and croissants and ham, some scrambled eggs and bagels.

Dayne picks up a croissant that fits easily in her hand.

'Now this is disappointing. I can usually sit on one of these like I'm riding a horse.'

They laugh as she easily bites off a third and chews on it, a smile of happiness on her face.

Posey clears her throat.

'I'd love to help you guys with the shop,' she says. 'And I had an idea.'

'Go on,' Ettie says.

Posey takes out a piece of parchment from her pocket.

ARE YOU HANDY?

LEND A HAND NEXT DOOR FOR FREE ALE AND SNACKS

Dayne squeals and claps her hands.

'That's such a good idea.'

'You don't mind?'

'Mind what?' Sticks asks.

'Mind the bar not being open? Mind me sticking my nose in?'

'You're not sticking your nose in,' Ettie says. 'You're helping – and it's a genius idea. The more help we get the better.'

'And we need you there,' Sticks says. 'It's your design. You need to work with Bugsy, make sure it's all done right.'

She beams.

'Morning,' Amma says, sticking her head in the room.

'Come in,' Sticks says, getting up to make room for her on the sofa.

Amma smiles, and shuffles past Dayne to sit down and then squeals.

'Dayne! Look at you!'

Dayne squeals too and they hug.

'It's because Sticks can't get this shop sorted without my muscle,' Dayne says, flexing her arm.

Sticks grins. 'I'll take all the help I can get.'

With that, Bugsy, and Dayne's five brothers fly through the window, and let out whoops when they see the size of Dayne.

'Look at you, sis,' Micah calls out. 'I better not mess with you – you'll squash me.'

'I could anyway,' Dayne says, standing up. 'Big, small, I was always tougher than you.'

Micah laughs and flies over to sit on the table in front of his sister.

George, Adam, Frank, and Josh follow suit, each of them waving or saluting or smiling at their sister.

'Do you feel okay?' Bugsy asks flying over and landing in the palm of her hand.

Dayne nods. 'I feel exactly the same, just big.'

Bugsy grins, then looks over at Ettie. 'And you can make us small again? You know, once we've done all the free labour on the shop?'

Dayne closes her hand around him, and he yells out indignantly.

'Dad – it's not free labour – it's help. Helpful help, freely given with good grace. You'll be fed and watered like you'd never believe, and Ettie's going to stop time, so you're not even wasting a day.'

'Stopping time?'

Ettie nods. 'I'm going to set up a time bubble around the shop, so whenever anyone enters the bubble, time stops, but once they leave the bubble, it's the exact same time as they went in.'

'Ooh that's clever,' Sticks says, beaming. He clears his throat. 'Um, Mr Bugsy and um, Dayne's brothers, thank you. I really appreciate the help. And, um, Frank, I hope there's no hard feelings, you know, from the other day...'

Sticks blushes. He won't admit it to anyone, and he can hardly admit it to himself, but he's scared that Frank will want revenge and once he's bigger, he'll be able to get it.

Frank grins. 'Don't you worry. I'm here, and I'm happy to be here.' He glowers at his sister.

Dayne grins and claps her hands together.

'Who's first?'

Ettie clears her throat. 'I think we should go outside. The alehouse is very accommodating, but we don't have room for the four of us and all of you once you're not pixie sized.'

They troop outside, and Bugsy whistles when he sees the river. 'This is nice – be good to have a dip in here, boys.'

The boys all nod and murmur their agreement, and Ettie grins.

'Great idea – I'll do a picnic by the river for lunch.'

Dayne grins. 'We don't spend a lot of time in the water – we're so small that it's easy to be swept away. Of course, the boys could fly out of the water if that happened to them, but I never could. And sometimes, if wings are soaked through, it takes them a minute to dry.'

Bugsy nods. 'My great aunt Sarah drowned. Terrible business.'

Ettie clears her throat again. 'Ready?'

Bugsy nods. 'Ready as I'll ever be.'

Closing her eyes to centre herself and forget that so many people are watching her, and counting on her, Ettie does the required magic and when the fog clears, Bugsy is standing there, slightly taller than she is.

She steps back. Ooh, he's far more menacing when he's not pixie sized, and he was bad enough when he was tiny. She would not want to cross him.

He grins, and does a little jig. 'Look at this!' He grabs Dayne in a bear hug and she laughs.

The others queue up in front of Ettie and she makes light work of changing each of them from pixie sized, to big.

'To Hooves and Horns,' Sticks says, fist in the air.

Chapter 69

The gang of pixies, a witch, and ogre and a troll can barely contain their excitement as they troop round to the front of the derelict building.

Posey pulls out the blueprint she drew up of the building and the list of materials they'll need.

Bugsy gives a loud whistle, and the boys immediately fall in line.

Dayne giggles and Sticks takes a step backwards.

'Right. We won't get anywhere if we don't have some shape about us.'

He points at Ettie. 'You, what are you going to do?'

Weirdly having an overwhelming need to giggle, Ettie bites her lip.

'I'm going to magic up the supplies as and when we need them per Posey or anyone else's instructions. I'm going to keep the ale flowing and the snacks coming. I'm also going to bring other people into the time bubble, if anyone turns up.'

Bugsy nods, and then points at Posey.

'Liaising with Ettie for materials, and I'm handy as hell. I can build, paint, plaster...' she trails off, and Bugsy nods.

'Excellent.' He nods at Sticks.

Sticks clears his throat and salutes.

Dayne and Ettie stifle their giggles.

'Sir, I'm going to do as I'm told. Sir!' he salutes again, flustered, and then grins.

Amma steps forward. 'I'm not strong or very capable, but I'm a willing pair of hands. I can fetch and carry as long as it's not too heavy and I can bring people cups of tea.'

She steps back beside Sticks, shaking a bit.

Bugsy nods, and whistles again. His boys all stand to attention.

'Boys, you know how I like to work. Quick and clean, no messing about. We'll have plenty of breaks – if you earn them – no dillydallying. Let me see,' he says, taking hold of the blueprint.

They watch him, eyes raking over the whole thing, and then the list of materials.

'Got it,' he says, and then grins. 'This is going to be fun.'

If anyone disagrees with his assessment, they're definitely not going to speak up, and so with a nod from Posey and direction from Bugsy as where to have the stuff magicked to, Ettie conjures up the first load of materials.

WHILE BUGSY BARKS ORDERS, and everyone immediately obeys, Ettie takes a step back and works her magic.

She needs to build a time bubble, that includes the alehouse. It's a big job, but she's sure she can do it.

Tuning out the noise of the crew, she stands on the road, so she can see the alehouse and the shop next door.

She holds out her hands, muttering the spell, and willing it to work.

The look of joy and hope on Sticks' face as they all stood outside the wreck of a building, and she just knew he was imagining what it will look like when it's done, made her ache for it to all work out perfectly for him.

He deserves it.

She grins. She thinks it's done, but she needs to test it.

She gestures for Dayne, and Dayne flies over and hugs her.

'How good is this?'

'So good – we never would have got this done without your dad and your brothers.'

'They love it,' Dayne says, waving her hand. 'My dad loves bossing people around, and he's good at it. He loves a project, and this is the biggest thing any of them have ever worked on. They're having a ball.'

'It looks like,' Ettie says, and it does – Bugsy and Dayne's brothers all have big grins on their faces. Posey looks happy, cross referencing her blueprint and her list of supplies conferring with Bugsy and then adding notes to her drawings, her tongue poking out as she works. Amma is shadowing Sticks, who looks excited by what they're doing and scared of the pixies in equal measure.

'I need to check my magic,' Ettie says.

Dayne nods. 'What do I need to do?'

'Stand on the pavement over there. When I go in the bubble start counting. I'll go in the bubble, into the shop, out into the garden, into the alehouse through the backdoor, and then out of the front door.'

'Just count?'

'Out loud.'

Dayne nods, and Ettie hugs her before heading across the road.

There's a slight shimmer in the air, nobody would notice it unless they were looking for it. She nods at Dayne.

'Now!'

She takes a step to the side, and walks through the shop, stopping to magic up some more wood for Posey. She slips outside, and walks along the river, thinking how nice their picnic will be there, especially if the lovely weather holds up. Then she goes into the alehouse, through the kitchen, and out of the front door. She can see Dayne looking at the spot she last saw her at.

She shouts out. 'Here!'

Dayne whips around a massive smile on her face.

'One,' she says, with a laugh.

'That was you just starting to count?'

Dayne nods. 'Amazing. You went all the way around?'

Ettie grins. 'And I magicked some wood for Posey on the way.'

'I think it worked!'

They high five each other.

Chapter 70

Content that the time bubble spell is working, Ettie rallies round the crew, bringing tea, ale and snacks, conjuring up more and more supplies as she's asked to by either Posey or Bugsy, and by magically keeping things a little tidier than they might otherwise be.

Bugsy, Dayne and her brothers are pristine – they've clearly worked together before, and they're a military operation, but Sticks is clumsy and cumbersome, and at one point has more paint on his feet than the wall.

Ettie smiles, as she sends each of the workers a magical dose of energy and rest combined, so they don't feel too tired. It's one thing to make time stop still, but they are still working in that paused time – they are putting up walls, sawing wood, painting, sweating and swearing.

'Here,' she passes a mug of ale to Posey, whose cheeks are pink with excitement and exertion.

'Thanks,' Posey says, drinking it down in one go. Ettie refills it. 'I love this,' Posey says, looking around the now less derelict building.

It's incredible how quickly it's taking shape. The walls are up, dividing the space just as Sticks envisaged it. The pixies can still fly, so they're flitting high and low, almost blurring with the speed they're working at.

'I'll speak to the King,' Ettie says, 'next time we see him, and tell him what you've done here. Then if he ever needs an architect, he'll know where to find you.'

'Really?' Posey grins, and downs her ale. 'Thanks Ettie. I best get back. I do not want to cross Bugsy.'

Ettie laughs. None of them do.

Dayne flies over. 'How good is this?' she asks, gesturing at the space.

'I can hardly believe how quickly it's all coming together,' Ettie says. 'I couldn't really see the vision before, but now. It's going to be great.'

'So much space, and yeah, it's easy when you know what you're doing and you have people to help. Your magic is great too – we'd have probably had to wait weeks for all these supplies.'

Ettie smiles. 'Thanks Dayne. I actually feel pretty useless. I can barely wield a paintbrush.'

'And you don't need to.' Her tummy gives out a forceful grumble.

Ettie grins. 'That might be a sign for me to get the picnic ready. Give everyone a five minute warning.'

Ettie heads out the back and conjures up picnic blankets, some tables and benches and another hammock. She magics up a load of sandwiches, pork pies and sausage rolls. She fills tankards with ale, and cups with tea, and makes a whole load of tiny cakes with different flavoured icing.

She grins as she hears the workers heading outside.

They devour the first lot of food in minutes, and she quietly and quickly replenishes the platters and adds extras as she thinks about them. She looks at each crew member, when they're not looking at her, and sends a magical tonic their way. She loosens their muscles and eases their aches. She gives them extra energy and takes away the knots in their shoulders. She quietly magics away the scuffs on their shoes and the dirt from their skin.

Bugsy taps his stomach. 'Beautiful,' he says, and then peels his top and trousers off. Standing there in his pants, stretching this way and that, Dayne tells him off, but Bugsy lets out a huge belch and then runs into the water.

Floating on his back he calls out. 'This is bliss.'

Dayne's brothers join him, stripping off to their pants, and revelling in the cool joy of the river. They splash and duck each other and don't stop laughing

Dayne is gazing at them all, head cocked to the side, tears in her eyes.

'I hated them for so long,' she says. 'I never thought I'd get a day like this with them. Look at them.'

'Oh I am,' Posey says, and Dayne looks alarmed. She's definitely ogling them, and Dayne isn't sure she likes it.

'I've never really noticed how good looking some pixies are,' Posey says, her eyes roaming over the lads as they splash in the water. 'They've always been too small for me.'

'Not today they're not,' Ettie says with a wink.

Dayne makes a face. 'Gross. Those are my brothers,' she says, wrinkling her nose.

Ettie laughs and Posey cackles.

'You okay, Sticks?' Ettie asks. He's sitting cross legged on the picnic blanket, Amma sitting close beside him.

'Good,' he says and can't stop smiling. 'The place is going to be smashing.'

Amma stands up. 'I'll go and check on the animals,' she says. 'Do you want to give me a hand?'

Sticks rubs his belly. 'Nope. I haven't eaten enough,' he says, reaching for a cake, and cramming it in his mouth.

'Amma's been great,' Ettie says.

Sticks nods. 'Yeah, she's good. A bit of a weakling, but she's trying.'

Ettie smiles. 'She is trying. Very hard.'

Chapter 71

The time goes on, and Ettie lies down, shielding her eyes from the sun with her hand. There's no need to rush this break; no time has passed since she made her bubble, and they're all having so much fun, she doesn't want to be the one to call a stop to it.

Sticks is snoozing in the old hammock, and Bugsy's in the new one. Dayne is playing in the river with her brothers, and Posey is sitting cross legged beside her, head tipped back, basking in the sun.

'This is so good,' Posey says. 'When I lived at home, there wasn't much down time. I'd stay in bed as long as I could, every single day, and I'd always get woken up, dragged downstairs to help out.'

'Doesn't sound fun,' Ettie says, carefully. She won't pry into whatever the circumstances were that brought Posey here.

'It wasn't,' she says with a sigh. 'But this is. This is pixies and ogres and me and you, and Amma, all mixed together for one sole purpose – a purpose that doesn't even benefit most of us.'

Ettie smiles and sits up, conjuring up a cup of tea.

'You're right. That's what's so magical about the alehouse – I think it brings out the best in all of us, I think there's a special kind of magic here, in the bones of the place.'

'I think so too.'

They are quiet again, each lost in their own thoughts, until a loud whistle startles them.

Bugsy is pulling on his clothes. 'Let's go.'

Dayne and her brothers immediately troop out of the river and pull on their clothes, despite the fact that they're soaking wet.

Ettie sends a little drying spell their way.

Sticks wakes with a snort when Bugsy pokes him in the side.

'Come on lazy bones. This is your shop, not mine.'

Sticks falls on the floor scrambling to get out of the hammock, pink spots on his cheeks.

Ettie helps him up.

'He scares me,' Sticks mumbles.

'Me too. And you know he's just being...' she trails off because Bugsy is helping them so much, it doesn't feel right to criticise him. His manner could do with a bit of a tweak, but really, considering how quickly the shop is coming together, they shouldn't complain.

Amma is already inside the shop when they get back.

'Ready to go again?' Sticks asks her.

'Of course,' she says, touching his arm. 'Anything for you and the animals.'

Sticks lets out a huge burp and turns to Bugsy.

'What's next, boss?'

Bugsy and Posey conflab over the blueprints, and then give everyone their orders. Ettie sends them all energy and enthusiasm via her magic. She feels stupid though. Helpless.

Posey passes her the list.

'If you can magic this lot up, we'll be good for the next couple of hours. This is like magic, the way it's coming together.'

Ettie laughs. 'The whole thing could have been done in two minutes if Sticks would have let me use magic.'

'And where would the fun have been in that?' Posey asks with a grin.

Ettie shrugs to herself, because Posey has gone to help Dayne with something or other, and so she busies herself with what she's best at.

She might not be able to build a wall, or paint one, but she can feed everyone, and water everyone. She can clean up, and she can keep everyone smiling.

She bustles around doing her best, but her favourite thing is watching everyone work.

Bugsy is militant. He's organised and precise, and as well as dishing out orders to everyone, he's busy getting things done himself. He flies back and fore between the work he's doing, the work he's asked everyone else to do, and Posey.

They often have their heads together, conferring over the drawings she made of the shop, and the list she made of what was needed to get it all done.

Dayne is one of the boys today, getting stuck in exactly the way her brothers are – no job is too big for her, and she's barely looks up from her work.

Sticks is trying his best, but Ettie can see that he's struggling so she sends some confidence his way. Amma is still glued to his side, and Ettie wonders if the gangly, orange elf, hasn't got a crush on him.

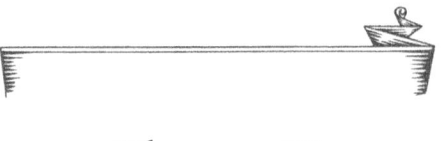

Chapter 72

Dayne flies over to her, sweaty but unable to stop smiling. 'I can't believe how much we've got done.'

'Me neither. It looks great.'

'Sticks looks happy,' Dayne says, nodding at him.

'He's going to be so happy when it's done. I think he misses it,' Ettie says, wondering what their days will look like once Sticks has his shop back. 'Do you ever think about what you want to do with your life?' Ettie asks Dayne.

'Deep question,' Dayne says, shaking out her wings. 'I know I could get used to being big.'

'Really?'

'Yeah – I really like it. This world isn't built for pixies.'

'The alehouse makes things your size though, and I can, if you need me too.'

'I know,' Dayne says, and hugs Ettie. 'But I don't feel vulnerable like this.'

'I never thought about that,' Ettie says.

'Yeah, being small is perilous,' Dayne says with a shrug. 'Especially being small when my wings didn't work. That's why the foxes managed to kidnap me; I couldn't get away.'

'You poor thing. If you ever want to be big, just ask.'

Dayne laughs. 'I love being a pixie, and now I can fly it's so much easier. I don't walk along worrying that something might eat me anymore.'

'No wonder you haven't given thought to what you want to do with your life – you've just been trying to stay alive.'

Dayne laughs and sits on a pile of bricks. Ettie magics her up a drink.

'You're thinking about Sticks working in his shop?' Dayne asks, and Ettie nods.

'I know we're all at the alehouse, but we don't do much – especially with Posey, and even without her, I don't think I want to spend all my days serving drinks...'

'What would you like to do?' Dayne asks her. 'If Sticks is working and the bar is taken care of?'

Ettie shrugs. 'When I was at the academy, I never wanted to leave, so I assumed I'd be like Liss, and teach.'

'And now?'

'I don't know. What about you?'

Dayne shrugs. 'I don't know. I spent so long running round putting out the fires my dad and brothers had started, I never thought about what I wanted to do. I like fixing things and helping people.'

Ettie smiles. 'You're good at both of those.'

'A worry for another day?' Dayne says, catching her dad looking at her, a frown on his face. 'Uh oh – dad's spotted me slacking.'

Ettie laughs. 'I'll bring everyone drinks and snacks – that should distract him.'

'Thanks,' Dayne says. 'Wanna help in a bit?'

Ettie shakes her head. 'No – I'll only do it wrong.'

'Help me paint,' Dayne says. 'You can't get that wrong.'

'I could,' Ettie says with a sigh, and hugs Dayne again before going round the whole crew, conjuring up food and drinks. She sends a little magic to each of them. More energy, more patience, more of anything they might need to get them through this long day.

'Hello!' she hears the call from outside of the shop and heads out to see who it is. Maybe someone who was after a cold drink of ale but wants to help instead.

There are several customers that she recognises from the bar room, all craning their necks to get a look inside the shop.

'We saw the sign,' a tall, green haired goblin says, seemingly jittery with excitement.

'We want to help,' an elf says. 'I know Sticks from the old shop. Terrible business. What can we do?'

Ettie laughs. There are seven customers, all smiling and eager and ready to help.

She feels a little bit tearful as she calls Posey, Sticks and Bugsy over.

The whole crew ambles over, and she takes the opportunity to give everyone more drinks.

'What's this?' Sticks asks.

'Help!' Posey says, also recognising several of the customers from the bar room.

An ogre, almost as tall as Sticks grins. 'I'm visiting my nephew today, and he's dragged me here. And I find you, a fellow ogre.'

Sticks grins and the two of them embrace.

'There's not many of us that are a good fit for polite society,' the ogre says with a laugh.

Sticks claps him on the back. 'You've never been here before – in the alehouse and the shop, everyone is welcome. Even ogres.'

Chapter 73

Bugsy gives a loud whistle.

'We need the help.' He starts doling out orders, and Ettie doles out her thanks. Dayne is squealing with happiness at the way people are happy to help and the progress they're making.

Sticks sits for a moment, mopping his brow with a hankie.

Ettie puts a hand on his shoulder. Dayne stands the other side of him and does the same.

'Look at this,' he says, eyes full of tears.

Ettie wipes a tear of her own.

'People are good,' Dayne says. 'We've had some bad luck thanks to some particularly nasty people, but really, this is people.'

They look around the shop – the limited parts they can see now that so many walls have gone up. Bugsy and his boys are machines. They haven't slowed down for a minute; it was the best idea to get them here helping.

Amma gives a little wave as they watch her carrying a small pile of stones to one of the new volunteers.

Posey comes over to join them.

'What's this? An unofficial break? Don't let Bugsy catch you.'

They all laugh.

'We were just saying that people are good and kind and helpful.'

'They are,' Posey says, leaning against the wall. 'Not always, but often.'

'Often enough,' Ettie says. 'Often enough.'

They are silent for a moment, watching the bustle of the shop, the easy going and willing manner of the new helpers, the way Bugsy and his sons are so exacting.

'It's incredible to watch,' Sticks says. 'I don't know how to thank anyone.'

'You don't need to do anything,' Dayne says. 'We're all happy to be here and happy to help.'

'Speak for yourself,' Micah says, giving her a cheeky poke in the side as he passes. 'Slacker!'

Dayne laughs but flies after him. Ettie squeezes Sticks on the shoulder. Posey grins at her.

'Ready to magic more supplies?'

Ettie groans. 'I don't know. It's just such hard work.'

They're laughing as they head outside, and Posey tells her what she needs and Ettie magics everything into neat piles.

'I'm just going to head next door for a minute,' Ettie says, but Posey has already moved onto the next thing.

Ettie sends everyone in the shop another blast of magical assistance and then heads to the den.

She sits on her favourite seat; feet tucked under her and conjures up a cup of tea for herself.

She closes her eyes and takes a deep breath, quietening her mind, and listening to the dull roar of the fire.

It's been incredible to see the shop taking place so quickly, and she's so glad she's been able to help with materials and food and drink, but she's seen an awful lot of people and between the bustle and noise and palaver, she just needs a quiet minute or two.

Then maybe she'll surprise Dayne and grab a paintbrush.

She grins.

Eyes opened, she looks around the den, still amazed that she feels so at home, so at peace, at somewhere that is still so new to her.

She loves the alehouse, she loves the accommodations it makes – like the space it makes for Sticks, the individual bedrooms it made for all of them, the downstairs room it made for Posey.

'How do you do it?' she whispers, feeling silly for talking to a house.

The fire roars louder and she chuckles. She's never alone here, and that's a really comforting thought.

'Hello?'

She jumps up, another customer willing and able to help, she recons, but when she heads through to the bar room, and sees a woman and a man, she somehow knows who they are, and she knows she needs to hide them.

'Ettie?' the woman asks, and Ettie nods.

The man shuffles awkwardly beside her.

'I know we're early,' the woman says, 'but we were just too excited to wait. Is he okay?'

Ettie nods. 'He is now. Losing the shop broke him.'

The woman puts a hand to her heart and the man takes her other hand.

'But he's good now. The new shop will be finished today, and he's surrounded by good people.'

The woman nods.

'We can't wait to see him.'

'Do you mind waiting a bit?' Ettie asks. 'They are so busy next door and I want him to really enjoy seeing you.'

The woman nods. 'Of course. Tell us where to go.'

Ettie grins.

'By the way, I'm not sure if she was on her way to help here,' the woman adds, 'but we just saw a rather sad looking giant on the side of the road, about five minutes away.'

Ettie's stomach clenches. Liss.

'I need somewhere to hide you,' she says out loud, knowing the alehouse will come to her aid. 'Let's see.'

She takes them through to the house, and next to the room the animals are staying in, and Posey's room, there's a new bend in the hallway and around the corner, is another door.

Ettie opens it up, and it's a lovely sitting room, with sofas, and armchairs, books on shelves and drinks and snacks laid out.

She pats the wall.

'I've stopped time in here, and the shop next door,' Ettie says. 'And I'll bring him here once we're done.'

The woman nods and hugs her, and the man shakes her hand.

Ettie rushes out.

She has to see if the giant outside is Liss, even though she knows it is.

Chapter 74

Ettie rushes along the road. She can see Liss; she'd be able to see her from a mile away.

She's sitting on the side of the road, taking up so much space, and Ettie's heart quickens when she gets closer.

This is her best friend. However strange she's been acting, whatever mess she's caught up in at the academy, it was Liss who always looked out for her, and Liss who kept her at the academy for all those years.

Ettie runs onto her open palm, and Liss lifts her up. Ettie leans on her cheek, knowing how Dayne must feel when she's with her.

'You've been crying,' Ettie says, touching the tears on her cheek.

Liss nods. 'I don't have long. Professor Milton doesn't know where I am, and if he knows I'm missing, he'll look for me.'

'Can you tell me what's going on?' Ettie asks her. 'I got your letter.'

Liss shakes her head. 'Not yet, though I will. I just needed to get away for a moment. I'm so sick of pretending. I'm not a good liar.'

Ettie sighs. This is her best friend of seven years. She knows her so well; she's family. But the way she treated her after she left the academy and went back to help Graily, broke her. She knows why, or at least she knows what Liss told her, but there's a small part of her that knows she won't ever trust her the same way again. Never fully.

It's sad.

'You look sad,' Liss says.

'I am,' Ettie says. 'I know you said in your letter that you were undercover, but the way you spoke to me broke my heart.'

'I know, and I will never forgive myself, but I had to make him trust me.'

Ettie nods. 'On the day I left the academy, I used my magic to call your bracelet. You ignored me.'

Liss hangs her head. 'Ettie. I'm sorry. It had already started. Milton was watching me – very closely. He knew you were leaving, and I had to make it look like I didn't care.' She lifts her empty wrist. 'I broke it, by accident,' she adds.

Ettie sighs but doesn't even offer to make her another one. What would be the point? 'Do you want to come and see where I'm living?'

Liss hesitates. 'I need to get back, if he-'

Ettie grins. 'I've stopped time. In the alehouse and the building next door.'

'I won't fit in the alehouse,' Liss says, sadly.

Ettie smiles. 'You probably would, it's enchanted, but we can sit outside, by the river. It's all in a time bubble.'

'Clever witch,' Liss says, with a soft smile.

Ettie grins. 'I passed my exam. Professor Parfait watched me do magic while he was here watching our friend to see if she could go to France with him. I didn't even know he was assessing me.'

'You passed?'

Ettie nods, and Liss lets out a whoop that almost makes her eardrum bleed.

'Sorry,' she says, her voice a whisper. 'I knew you could do it.'

'I did it,' Ettie says, surprised that she's still so proud of herself.

'And Professor Parfait helped your friend?'

'He did. She's gone now – they went to France. He was unhappy at the academy.'

Liss sighs. 'Everyone's unhappy at the academy. And I want to talk to you about it, but I'd really love to not talk about it for a while.'

Liss follows Ettie along the road, and into the garden. She steps over the house with a single step and sits on the floor by the river, taking up almost all of the space.

'Sorry,' Liss says, trying to shift so she's not squashing the flowers, and then breaking one of the picnic tables instead.

'It's fine,' Ettie says. 'I'm used to you.'

'I'm used to me too,' Liss says. 'But I forget how well the academy caters for giants. It's not so easy anywhere else.'

'Though you made it over the house easily,' Ettie says with a grin.

'I can go quite far, quite fast,' Liss says, laughing.

They both laugh.

'Make me smaller?' Liss asks, her head to the side.

Ettie shakes her head. 'You've never asked me to do that before.'

'I didn't trust that you could,' Liss says, with a cheeky smile on her face. Ettie punches her arm, even though she knows Liss won't feel a thing.

'I just want to be somewhere else and be someone else for a little bit of time. I'm sick of being me.'

Ettie tuts.

'Please. I want an afternoon off. If I'm in a time bubble it means Milton won't miss me. That means I can talk to you, catch up with everything that's happened. See where you live. Bathe in the river.'

Ettie nods. 'I can do it if you want me to. I made a bunch of pixies bigger this morning, I can easily make a giant smaller.'

Chapter 75

Ettie uses her magic, muttering the words and moving her hands around and then Liss is no longer a giant. She's the same size as Ettie and the two women hug and laugh.

'Why didn't I ask you to do this before?' Liss asks.

'Because the academy caters so well for you,' Ettie says. 'And there were other giants there. And because I'm small and you're big and that's the way it was.'

'I like this,' Liss says. 'Maybe I'll just stay small and run away. Milton won't know where to find me.'

'You never would. If you're meant to be helping at the academy, you'd never walk away,' Ettie says and Liss shrugs.

'True. But I don't want to go into it. Show me round?'

'I will,' Ettie says, 'but I need to go and see if the others need any help first.'

'I can help,' Liss says, rubbing her hands together. 'What are we doing?'

'We're refurbishing the old, derelict building into a shop – Hooves and Horns.'

'Cute name,' Liss says. 'I'm handy. Let's go.'

Ettie grins, and they head into the shop. There's so much going on. Bugsy is still doling out orders, flying around but still calm and in control. Dayne is working away with Posey. Amma and Sticks are together. The volunteers from the alehouse are busy too.

Posey notices her and raises a hand in greeting.

'Perfect timing. We need you.'

Ettie grins.

'What do you need?'

Posey reads out the list, and with each item, Ettie magics it up.

Liss grins and takes her arm, giving it a squeeze.

'You are so much better now – quick and effortless.'

Ettie smiles. It's true; her magic is part of her now, not something extra that she worries and frets about, but something she does without thinking about, like walking or breathing.

'Another helper?' Posey cocks her head at Liss who nods.

'Absolutely. Just tell me what to do.'

Posey grins, and Liss follows her with a wave at Ettie.

Dayne flies over.

'That looked weirdly like your not-very-friendly friend, Liss.' She frowns. 'But smaller.'

Ettie nods and places a hand on Dayne's arm. 'Look, I know you don't like her, and I know you think she's a terrible person, but I know a bit more now.'

'Go on,' Dayne says, shooting furious looks in the direction Liss went with Posey.

'This is what she told me.' Ettie cocks her head. 'It feels like the truth,' she says with a sigh, 'or maybe I just want it to be the truth.'

Dayne raises an eyebrow, as if to say, well, yeah.

Ettie grins and hugs her. 'I love that I can hug you, and I love that you care so much. I don't know all the details, but according to Liss, there's something going on at the academy, with the new head.'

'You think?' Dayne says, with a short laugh. 'He threw you out. That professor that went to France with Graily left because he hated it there.'

'Parfait,' Ettie says, reminding her of the professor's name. Not that it matters. 'Yes, but she said she's helping the magical council investigate him.'

'Hmm,' Dayne says, clearly unconvinced.

Ettie holds her hands up. 'Okay, I know, it could be a convenient excuse for treating me like crap, or it could be true.'

'And right now, you want to believe it's true because she's your oldest friend?'

Ettie nods. 'Is that sad?'

Dayne hugs her. 'No, it's actually beautiful. Trust is hard to earn and hard to keep, and I'm only jealous because I've never had a best friend.'

Ettie bumps her with her hip. 'I can have more than one best friend…. If you like?'

Dayne grins. 'That sounds good.'

'And you can make a million friends now you're out from under your dad's shadow,' Ettie reminds her.

Dayne nods. 'I know. But the same goes for you. You've told us that Liss was your only friend…'

Ettie shakes her head. 'But nobody ever told me how hard it is to make friends when you're a grown up. You put a bunch of kids in a room, and they just become friends. Put me in a room with anyone and I feel like a loser.'

'Well, you shouldn't,' Dayne says. 'You're the kindest witch I've ever met.'

Ettie smiles, and they hug again.

'It's going to be so weird when I'm tiny again,' Dayne says.

'I know, but now we know how easy it is to make you big, if you ever need a proper hug, then I can make you big in an instant.'

Sticks ambles over. 'What are you two gassing about?' He rubs his belly. 'People are getting hungry around here.'

Ettie grins. 'People? Or you?'

Sticks shrugs. 'I'm people.'

Ettie doesn't need telling twice.

Chapter 76

She heads back out to the river. The sun is still high in the sky because no time has passed since they started working, but she doesn't want to conjure up another picnic; it seems a bit boring.

What would she want to eat after a long day of hard work?

She smiles, and magics away the picnic blankets, conjuring up, instead, two long wooden tables with plenty of chairs around them. Crockery and cutlery magically appear with a swish of her fingers, and she adds pitchers of ale and mugs.

Poking her head inside the door, she calls out.

'Food's ready.'

It takes almost five minutes for all the workers to trudge out of the dust and the sweat of the shop and head her way. As each one passes her, she flourishes a finger and cleans the dust from their clothes, the dirt from their skin, and tidies their clothes and hair.

They take their seats.

'I thought you said dinner was served?' Bugsy says, with a wink, gesturing at the empty plates and cups.

Ettie holds up her hands and within a second there are platters and platters of steaming hot roast beef, buttery mashed potatoes and crisp vegetables. She conjures up a mushroom pie for Sticks, popping it straight onto his plate, and she adds jugs of gravy and stacks of roast potatoes to the table too.

There are groans of joy and sighs of happiness as everyone – including the volunteers – fill their plates and tuck in.

Ettie fills her plate, and Liss touches her arm.

'Amazing. I wish everyone at the academy could see you now.'

'She's got her certificate,' Dayne says, pointing at Liss with her fork. 'She's certified.'

'I know,' Liss says, biting her lip.

'I know what you mean,' Ettie says to Liss. 'But I don't feel that panicky need to prove myself anymore.'

'Look at what she can do,' Dayne says, pointing her fork again. 'She can stop time. Make small people big. And big people small.'

Liss nods and lowers her voice. 'Dayne, I know you saw me at the academy be really horrible to Ettie, and I can tell you're angry with me, but I promise I had good reason. Reasons Ettie knows about.'

Liss puts her hand over Ettie's and Dayne glares at her.

'I saw exactly what you said and did at the academy,' she says. 'And I know what Ettie thinks of you. I don't like it, but if she trusts you, I can put up with you.'

Liss looks like she wants to argue, but Dayne jabs her fork at her, and then turns to her brother Josh, and they start chatting about the progress they are making.

Ettie bites her lip to hide a smile.

There were many times at the academy when Liss stepped in to stick up for her, but there were many times when she didn't. Times when she wasn't there, or times when Ettie could tell, she was just weary of always having to stick up for Ettie.

It feels nice to have Dayne on her side. She's like her father in that way; formidable.

Liss eats her food, quietly, and Ettie digs in. Although she hasn't done any physical work, the magic makes her tired.

Bugsy gives a whistle, and everyone turns to him. He's holding up his mug of ale.

'The shop is looking incredible. We're not far off finishing – which makes us all absolute legends.'

Everyone laughs.

'This toast is for all of us. My boys, my girl, her friends, and all of you who came for a cheeky pint and ended up getting roped into this.'

More laughter.

'To the legends!'

They all lift their mugs and then take big drinks from them.

Sticks stands up. 'I can't thank you, any of you, enough. I'm just an ogre, and I don't have the words to let you all know how much this means to me. But for me, the animals, Amma.' He gestures at her, and she blushes, prettily. 'It means everything.'

They all lift their mugs again.

Ettie clears the platters and then magically fills the table with cakes and puddings.

And custard.

She grins at Dayne and then at Sticks, whose eyes have spilled over with tears.

'It's too much,' he says. 'All the help, the shop, the custard...'

Ettie and Dayne giggle, and then go over to give him big hugs.

Chapter 77

'I think I should go,' Liss says, while everyone else is finishing off more cake and puddings than they can realistically eat – especially if they want to get any more work done.

'You don't have to,' Ettie says, patting her friend on the arm. 'Dayne is just sticking up for me.'

'I'm glad you've got someone to stick up for you,' Liss says. 'I didn't realise how lonely I'd be once you left the academy. You've got all these new friends...' She trails off, feeling sorry for herself.

'You'll always be my friend,' Ettie says, conscious that she's left off the word 'best'. Even if she had the greatest reason in the world to treat Ettie the way she did in front of Professor Milton, it still stings. Couldn't her best and only friend have trusted her with the truth?

Liss smiles sadly. 'I know where to find you now,' she says.

'Please don't be a stranger,' Ettie says.

'I won't,' Liss says, but Ettie isn't sure she's telling the truth.

'I'll follow you out to the road,' Ettie says. 'And make you giant again.'

Liss nods. 'Honestly, Ettie, I didn't mean to hurt you, I just had this mission, and I didn't know what to say to you, and now I wish I'd just told you...'

'I wish you had too,' Ettie says, and then hugs Liss awkwardly, before walking her out to the main road.

With a flourish she turns her back into a giant, and whatever else they might have said, whatever else Liss might have wanted to say, the moment is gone.

Liss lifts a hand, and Ettie cranes her neck to look up at her face. She looks sad. But then Ettie is sad, too.

She watches her go, trying not to cry. It feels like a very final goodbye.

'Hey,' Dayne says, nudging her with her foot. 'You okay?'

Ettie shakes her head. 'Liss was my best friend for so long, my only friend, really. I just wish she'd told me the truth. If she's on some secret mission at the academy, she could have told me. I would have still had to leave, but I wouldn't have felt so broken hearted. And even though I know the truth, I still feel betrayed.'

'And she just told you all about it?'

'No, Professor Parfait brought me a letter from her. The day he took Graily. I didn't like to say.'

'You didn't think I'd believe her?' Dayne asks.

Ettie shrugs. 'Maybe. I suppose I thought you'd judge me, think I was stupid for believing her, think I was a pushover.'

Dayne shakes her head. 'I don't think any of those things. I think you're lovely and Liss was your best friend. Of course you want to believe her. But I think you're right. She should have told you what was going on.'

'I think so.'

'I think so too. And I think she might regret that she didn't."

'I don't want to be mean to her, or punish her,' Ettie says, walking back to the river side with Dayne. 'But I feel differently about her now. I'm on edge. Wary.'

'Because she lied once. It's understandable. Ettie, I was there. She was spiteful to you when we went to the academy, and I know you say that she says it was to cover up what she's doing there, but I don't think she had to be quite so mean.'

Ettie nods. That's the trouble. Liss would say that she was mean so Professor Milton wouldn't suspect anything, but did she have to say such nasty things? Such personal things? Or did she secretly enjoy getting some digs in? That's what it felt like.

Tears fill her eyes, and Dayne pulls her into a hug. 'Hey, don't cry. Don't let her spoil our day. You might feel different next time you see her.'

'True,' Ettie says, though she's not sure.

'And if you don't, then it doesn't matter. You don't have to stay friends with someone who makes you sad.'

Ettie nods, but the thought of losing Liss, despite it all feels sad. 'I'm confused,' Ettie says.

Dayne kisses her cheek. 'Stop thinking about it. Give yourself some of that lovely magic you always give me when I need to feel better.' She laughs. 'Yes, I know you do it, so does Sticks.'

Ettie laughs. 'Okay. I'll magic myself to feel better.'

'Now let's rally this lazy bunch and get the shop finished.'

Chapter 78

The river is packed with people laughing and splashing, Sticks is in his hammock. And Amma is sitting on the grass, paddling her feet in the water.

Posey and Bugsy are head to head, going over the blueprints.

'How's it looking?' Dayne asks, hugging her dad, and then resting her head on his shoulder.

'Good.' He grins. 'I thought you were barking mad when you said we could do this whole thing in a day. This should have taken me weeks, even with a full crew.'

Ettie grins, and Bugsy winks at her. 'Did you do more than just freeze time?'

Ettie shakes her head and holds her hands up. 'No. Sticks wanted to build this place without my magic, and I've kept out of it. I've sent a little bit of energy your way – to all of you, as the build has gone on. But the hard work, the sweat and dirt. It's all you.'

'It's looking incredible,' Posey says with a huge grin. 'This is the first time I've seen something I've designed come to life. It's so exciting.'

'I bet,' Ettie says. 'I hope you get to do it more often.'

'Me too. It's so much fun. And the help we've had is amazing. We're nearly done.'

'We've left a wall for you to help us with,' Dayne says, looking at Ettie.

'There's one plain wall left,' Posey says, 'so we think everyone should sign their name on it before we paint over it.'

Sticks comes over. 'Ready to go?'

They all nod, and slowly the others come out of the river, and dry off. Ettie sends them all some energy, some enthusiasm, some good vibes.

'Final push,' Bugsy says, pointing at each person and giving them their job.

'Don't forget to sign the wall,' Posey calls to them as they each head off to their task.

'Look at it,' Ettie says, squeezing Sticks on the arm.

'I can't,' he says. 'I get tearful just looking around.'

'It's amazing.'

And it is.

The once empty building isn't an empty shell anymore, it's a shop. The front is huge, with shelves and shelves ready to fill with pet supplies for people to buy for their own magical creatures. It's bright and airy and they've fashioned plenty of windows so the whole place is light.

Through a door to the back of the shop, there's separate rooms for the animals who need treatment, a proper table for Sticks to put animals on while he examines them, and rows and rows of shelving ready for medicine.

He has his own office, with a bookshelf ready to be filled with books, and then some store rooms for equipment and supplies.

'What's this room?' Ettie asks, pushing open the door to a bright yellow room, with a heavy duty lock on the outside.

Sticks shrugs. 'Just in case we get troublesome creatures,' he says, just a bit too nonchalantly. Ettie knows he's planning something shifty, but she's not sure what it is.

He pushes open the door to the garden, and they all troop outside.

The garden has been transformed with ropes for animals to swing from, tree houses for them to climb up to and shelter in, various steps and rocks for them to jump around on, and of course the river running through.

'This area is netted,' he says, taking them through a large wooden gate, to an area that's outside but with a netted roof, and sides. 'For the birds, and flying dragons,' he says. 'And flying anything, really.'

'Sticks, this is wonderful,' Dayne says, giving him a massive hug.

'I couldn't be more chuffed,' he says, beaming from ear to ear. 'I just need books, equipment, stuff to sell, and then I'm away.'

Ettie grins and opens her hands. 'I can help with all of that.'

'I know,' he says, ears pink from happiness.

'Last wall,' Bugsy says, flying over and handing Ettie a paintbrush. 'Apparently we're all going to put our names on this last wall, and then paint over them.' He makes a face and rolls his eyes. 'Seems a bit pointless.'

Dayne pokes him. 'It's not pointless dad, it's special. Everyone who helped gets to know they've left their mark here, even if nobody can see it.'

Bugsy laughs and ruffles her hair. Dayne shrugs him off.

'It's a lovely idea.'

Ettie and Sticks and Dayne group together for a cuddle, and then one at a time they write their names on the wall.

Ettie
Sticks
Dayne

Then watching everyone else write their names, the three of them tear up.

'I can't believe this,' Sticks says, gesturing at everyone.

'I can,' Dayne says. 'Who wouldn't want to help you? After what happened at the shop?'

'But people are so kind. There's nothing in it for them,' he says. 'Ooh, I could give them a discount on their first pet.'

'You could, but people like to be kind, even if there's nothing in it for them,' Ettie says.

A peaceful feeling settles over the three of them, as they watch Bugsy, Posey, Dayne's brothers and all the helpers from the bar sign their names with paint.

'We'll wait for it to dry, and then we'll paint over it,' Dayne says.

'I like it,' Ettie says, and she does. It seems special to have all their names written there, and then covered over, a little secret.

Amma touches Sticks on the arm.

'I need to get going, but I'll be back in the morning to help deck it all out.'

Sticks nods and lifts his fist for her to bump it.

Ettie grins, and Amma smiles, and Dayne is watching them closely.

She looks at Ettie, who grins and nods.

'Thanks, Amma. You're a star,' he says, and Amma heads off, a blush covering her orange skin.

Chapter 79

There's a loud herald from outside that several of them recognise.

'The King?' Sticks says and Ettie and Dayne nod.

'Or Briella,' Dayne says.

They head outside to take a look, and it's Briella.

'Hello,' she calls out, climbing out of the carriage. 'We thought we'd come and say hello. I hope you don't mind?'

'Of course not,' Sticks says, with a big grin. 'Do you want to help?'

Briella giggles and smooths down her exquisite powder blue gown. She's wearing white satin gloves.

'Maybe not,' she says. 'Is that okay?' She spots Dayne and gasps. 'Look at you, so big!' She gives Dayne a massive hug. 'You look wonderful.'

Dayne grins.

'Can I take a peek inside? Alaysia, come on out.'

Briella's sister, the other Princess, pokes her head out of the carriage, her face all pale and her eyes sad. They've never met her before and the girls both curtsey and Sticks bows.

She looks a little alarmed to see him, so he shuffles backwards a bit. He hates it when he scares people.

Briella tuts. 'Come on, Alaysia. You've met ogres before.' She rolls her eyes. 'She's a little better, but still milking it.'

Alaysia steps out of the carriage. She is much shorter than her sister, short and delicate looking, and very pretty.

Alaysia smiles. 'My sister said some fresh air would do me good.'

'She's right,' Sticks says with a grin, desperate to make a good impression. 'Whenever my fat bottomed, toxic farting pigs get grumpy I know they need fresh air.'

Alaysia gasps and fans at her face as though she might faint any moment at the mention of such creatures, and both Ettie and Dayne have to look away so they don't burst out laughing.

Briella lets out a snort of a laugh. 'Oh, Sticks!'

'What?' he looks confused and Briella just pats his arm. 'Show us your lovely shop,' she says, smoothing over his comment.

Alaysia gives him a stinking look and then follows her sister, stepping daintily, and lifting her skirts so she doesn't get her beautiful pink dress dusty.

Briella takes no such care; she bounds into the shop, and whistles.

'This is wonderful! And Bugsy and the boys did all this?'

Alaysia stands beside her. 'Bugsy is here, and his sons?'

Briella nods. 'I gave them time off. I knew daddy wouldn't mind.'

'But they're so small,' Alaysia says.

'Not today they're not,' Briella says, and points across the way. Bugsy and Frank come around the corner.

'I see,' Alaysia says, fanning her face again.

'Will they finish today?' Briella asks.

'They will,' Dayne says. 'Hey, do you want to paint your names on the wall? It's for everyone who helped.'

'We haven't helped,' Briella says, with a smile.

'Of course you did,' Sticks says. 'You gave us our work force.'

Briella smiles. 'Lead the way.'

They watch with smiles as Briella and Alaysia add their names to the wall.

Frank comes over, and nods at them both.

'All right, sis?' he says, leaning against the wall, and flinging his arm around Dayne.

'Fine,' she says. 'Happy. You?'

'I'm glad I'm here,' he says, watching the princesses paint.

'Me too. I'm sorry I knocked you out.'

He shrugs. 'Bygones.'

She laughs. 'That's not like you – maybe this new woman has changed you.'

Frank glares at her and heads back to work.

Dayne shakes her head. What did she say?

'I think it's wonderful,' Briella says. Father will be back for the open day; I'll be sure to bring him over.'

Alaysia clears her throat. 'Will Bugsy be here for that? And the boys?'

Dayne nods. 'Everyone will be here. It'll be a great day.'

'I might come,' Alaysia says. 'Fresh air will do me good, don't you think?'

They all nod, and Briella makes a surprised face.

'Are you ready to go?'

'I don't mind watching everyone work,' Alaysia says, her eyes scanning the parts of the shop she can see.

'We'll go,' Briella says, making the decision for them. Alaysia pouts but doesn't argue. That wouldn't be very princessy.

Dayne steps closer to Briella before they leave and fills her in on what happened with Mrs. Dinklepants and the fox pretending to be her brother. It's not up to her to decide what happens next – Briella can tell the King and the King can figure it out.

They all wave goodbye, back out on the road, and the three of them smile.

'I like Briella. I'm so glad we're friends.'

'Friends with royalty,' Sticks says. 'If my mum and dad could see me now!'

Ettie grins. 'If only!'

Chapter 80

'That's us done,' Bugsy says coming over to join them as they come back inside. He puffs out his chest, with a grin. 'Reckon we did you proud?'

Sticks nods. 'More than proud, Sir, I couldn't have asked for more.'

Bugsy grins and playfully punches Sticks in the arm. Sticks tries to hide his wince, and Bugsy chuckles.

'We'll be back for the grand opening,' he says. 'Reckon there might be more good food on offer?'

Ettie nods. 'Absolutely. Thank you. Thanks all of you.'

They are all happy and there's lots of hugs and back pats and joy as they all troop out of the shop, and Sticks locks the front door with the shiny new key.

The other helpers head off with promises to come back for the open day, and Ettie smiles at the pixies. 'Ready to be pixies again?' she asks.

'I reckon I might stay big for a little bit longer,' Dayne says, when Ettie looks at her, hands up ready to magic her back to being pixie sized.

'Not me,' Bugsy says. 'I don't need to be big.'

He stands beside Ettie and gives her a kiss on the cheek. Ettie blushes. He's a scary man, but he's also very charming when he wants to be.

She flourishes her hands and makes him pixie sized again. Then she does the same for the rest of Dayne's brothers, and then there are more thank you's and more goodbyes, and suddenly it's just the four of them, and time is going by again.

Posey lets out a sigh. 'I know you stopped time, and gave us all some weird magical energy, but I am tired. I want nothing more than a sleep. Preferably until tomorrow morning.'

'I'll come with you to your room,' Ettie says. 'I can magic you up some snacks and drinks in case you're hungry through the night.'

Dayne smothers a yawn. 'I won't be long either,' she says. 'What a day.'

'A magical day,' Sticks says, eyes filling with tears again. 'I know I said I didn't want this done with magic, Ettie, but it was magic that made it possible. The time thing, the materials, the energy...'

Ettie grins. 'I thought I was subtle.'

'Nothing subtle about it,' Posey says. 'It's like being hit by a brick. A lovely brick of peace and energy and happiness all at once. But you can feel it. It's a physical thing.'

Ettie shakes her head. 'I never knew that.'

'Yeah – the same as when you do the one to cheer us up. We can feel it.'

'You never said,' Ettie says, folding her arms over her chest.

'Why would we? We didn't want you to stop. It's lovely.'

'Really? Even though it's obvious.'

'It's good – it's like a warm hug without having the hug. When you send us anything, we know you're thinking of us.'

'It makes me warm and fuzzy,' Sticks says, 'like I've got a belly full of custard.'

They all laugh.

'Speaking of custard,' he says, and lumbers inside the alehouse to have a top up.

Ettie goes with Posey to set her up for the night, and then finds Dayne in the lounge, lying back on Sticks' squashy sofa.

'This is so comfy,' she says. 'I can't get over it.'

'It looks comfy,' Ettie says. 'I've never sat in it. Sticks is always in it.'

She sits beside Dayne. 'I've got a surprise for Sticks.'

'Ooh,' Dayne grins, clapping her hands. 'You know I love a surprise.'

'I know, so do I. When we sent out the invites for the open day, I sent a letter to Sticks' parents too.'

Dayne's eyes are wide. 'I thought they were on a monster hunt. How would it get to them?'

Ettie grins. 'The magic of a witch writing to a witch.'

'That's a thing?' Dayne asks and Ettie nods.

'Yes. They're here.'

Dayne looks around the empty room. 'Here? Where?'

'Not in here. In the alehouse. I'm going to get them now. The alehouse found a room for them, and I'm going to bring them in here before Sticks comes in.'

'He's going to cry.'

Ettie nods. 'Which is why I wanted to hide them until we were finished with the shop.'

'Good call,' Dayne says. 'Oh, I love this. Go and fetch them.'

Ettie does, and the four of them have a delightedly joyful introduction, and then sit by the fire waiting for Sticks.

The room seems to get a bit bigger, another sofa appears for his parents, and a big, squashy armchair for Dayne.

She tucks her knees under her, eyes wide.

'He's going to be so happy,' she says.

Toady-loo grins. 'We've missed him so much. I can't believe we didn't know about the shop. Poor Sticks – that was his pride and joy.'

'Wait until you see the new one,' Dayne says. 'Everybody wanted to help him.'

'They did?' Toady-loo asks, her hands clasped on her lap, biting her lip.

Ettie and Dayne nod at the same time.

'He's got a lot of friends,' Dayne says. 'All different types of people.'

Dave grins, and pats his wife's knee. 'We knew he'd be okay.'

'He's more than okay,' Dayne says, giggling. 'He's got a custard tap.'

Chapter 81

'Are you two talking about me again?' Sticks asks, lumbering into the room, licking custard off his chin.

Ettie and Dayne are grinning, and just watching him, waiting for him to see his parents.

He looks up, wondering why they aren't answering, and it's then that he sees his mum and dad.

His eyes widen, as his mouth drops open, and tears pour down his cheeks, arms hanging at his side, like he's not sure what to do and isn't even sure that what he's seeing is real.

Toady-loo grabs him into a hug, though she barely comes up to his elbows, and Dave joins them in a huddle.

Ettie and Dayne look at each other, both wiping a tear away.

Sticks is shaking his head, stuttering and mumbling and crying.

'Where did you, how did you, what's going on?'

Ettie laughs. 'I sent for them, Sticks. We knew you needed them.'

'Why didn't you send for us?' Toady-loo asks, batting him on the arm, and then hugging him again.

'I didn't want to disturb you,' Sticks says, his bottom lip quivering.

'You sausage,' Dave says, craning his neck to look up at his son.

'We would have come in a heartbeat.' Toady-loo says, resting her head on his tummy.

'We did come in a heartbeat,' Dave says. 'As soon as we got the letter.'

Sticks turns to Ettie and Dayne. 'You did this?'

Ettie nods, and Dayne points at her. 'She did. But I wish I'd thought of it – it's such a good idea.'

Sticks sits heavily on the sofa; he just can't stand any longer.

He wipes his eyes. 'Thank you. I can't believe you're here.'

'We are – for as long as you need us,' Toady-loo says, able to wipe at his tears and kiss his cheeks now that he's sitting and she's standing. Dave does the same, kissing Sticks on the forehead.

Sticks sniffs. 'I don't know what to say.'

Ettie and Dayne grin.

'We knew you missed them. And we knew that you didn't know where they were...'

'He could have summoned us if he needed to,' Toady says, as though she's keen to make sure Ettie and Dayne know that Sticks could have got hold of them if he needed to.

'I'm sure,' Ettie says, thinking of the magic she used with Liss. 'But he didn't want to interrupt your monster hunt.' There's a question in her tone, but they don't seem to pick up on it.

'And the old shop?' Toady says, taking Sticks' hand in both of hers.

'Gone,' he says, crying and sniffing again. 'But we have a better one now. And none of my animals were hurt. Though Lox turned out to be a crap friend.'

'Not Lox?' Dave says. 'We loved that spiky guy.'

Toady taps at him to be quiet and Sticks shakes his head. 'We did, dad. He was my best mate for a long time.'

'We have a lot of catching up to do,' Toady says, kissing his cheek again, and hugging. 'Ooh, we've missed you, beautiful boy.'

Ettie and Dayne wipe away more tears.

'We'll leave you to it,' Ettie says. 'We're both tired.'

'It was lovely to meet you both,' Dayne says, hugging Toady-loo and Dave. 'You'll be here in the morning?'

Toady looks at Dave and he nods. 'Yeah, we'll be here. For as long as Sticks needs us.'

Sticks beams and sniffles.

'Thanks, Ettie. What a day!'

Ettie and Dayne hold hands, and leave the room, closing the door gently behind them.

Dayne grins. 'That was beautiful,' she says.

'It was. Hey, are you ready to be little yet?'

Dayne shakes her head. 'No. Is that okay? Will something go terribly wrong if I stay big for too long?'

Ettie shakes her head. 'No. No bad side effects.'

'I wanted to fly for a long time and refused to get my wings fixed because it felt like I was admitting I was broken without them, but I like being big, and I'm going to stay big for a day or two. See what I think.'

'Absolutely,' Ettie says with a grin. 'You do whatever you need to do.'

'Right now, I need to sleep.'

'Me too. It's been a good day, though, hasn't it?'

Dayne nods. 'Incredible. The magic, the help, the way it all got done. I can't wait for the open day now. It's going to be great.'

'See you in the morning,' Ettie says, and they head up the stairs.

Dayne squeals, and Ettie joins her at the door to her bedroom – her tiny, pixie-sized bedroom.

They both laugh, and Ettie pats the wall.

Dayne's room is not pixie-sized anymore. It's normal sized.

The swing and the curly wurly slide have been replaced by a huge, sumptuous, pillow covered four poster bed, a dressing table and mirror and a huge wardrobe.

'Look at this,' Dayne says. 'How does this place know exactly what we need, even when we don't?'

Ettie shrugs and laughs. 'I don't know – but I wouldn't have it any other way. I think we're incredibly lucky that we get to call this place home.'

Chapter 82

When Ettie wakes in the morning, she can hear voices chattering away downstairs, and when she follows the happy noise to the kitchen, Toady-loo has already magicked up a spread for them to eat.

Sticks is still beaming from ear to ear, and his mum and dad look so proud.

'Morning,' Ettie says. 'Did you sleep well?'

'We did. Though we didn't join Sticks in the swamp.'

Ettie wrinkles her nose. 'No, as much as we love him, nobody wants to join Sticks in the swamp.'

'And we've seen the custard tap,' Dave says, with a furrowed brow.

Toady laughs. 'Excellent work. Sticks told us how you made a time bubble yesterday and made pixies big and a giant small.'

Ettie gives Sticks a look, but she's secretly pleased. It means a lot to have praise from another witch, especially one as experienced as Toady-loo.

'I've told them all about you and Dayne, and Posey, and Graily, and the fires. Everything.' Sticks rubs his belly. 'Mum's been feeding me for an hour.'

Toady is standing, so she can reach his head to ruffle his hair. He rubs his head against her hand like a cat.

'We miss you so much, baby,' Toady-loo says.

'We do, son,' Dave agrees and Ettie smiles. How lovely – and funny – to see Sticks, who's so huge, getting snuggled and petted and fed by his parents who are so much smaller than him.

'How is the, um, monster hunting going?' Ettie asks, conjuring up a hot cup of tea.

Sticks clears his throat. 'It's good, they've told me all about it, but what if we head over to the shop, I'd love it if mum could help you to magic up some of the things I need.'

'Absolutely,' Ettie says, eyes narrowing slightly. He's up to something. Something shifty. Probably to do with monsters. She sighs, and magicking up a croissant, she follows them out to the shop.

'Morning. Lazy bones,' Dayne says, flying over when she sees them. 'I've been here for ages.'

Posey wanders around the corner, a piece of parchment in her hand. 'Me too,' she says, with a grin.

'I'd have come to help,' Ettie says, feeling like the last one to arrive at a party.

'We didn't want to wake you,' Dayne says. 'We just came to finish a few things off, and make sure everything is ready for you.'

'And it is,' Posey says.

'This is my mum and dad,' Sticks says, introducing Posey to his parents. 'Posey designed this place.'

Dave whistles. 'We saw it last night. Impressive stuff,' he says. 'Makes this little crossroads look much nicer, having the two buildings looking so good.'

'It does,' Ettie says, thinking of the five houses across the road that have been empty since they've been here.

They are all grinning – there is so much good energy here. Everyone is happy, and Sticks couldn't be more chuffed. Having his parents here is the icing on the cake. Or the custard in the doughnut.

'I showed mum and dad the shop last night,' Sticks says. 'And I'm desperate to get the animals in here, so can we...' He wriggles his fat, green fingers, looking eagerly at his mum and Ettie. The two witches laugh, and nod.

Wriggling their fingers, they answer together.

'We absolutely can.'

'I'm just going to go in and get changed,' Posey says. 'I didn't realise how dusty I'd get.'

Chapter 83

Ettie and Toady clean the shop with their magic before they do anything else. They make sure every speck of dust or tiny cobweb is cleared away.

Sticks can't stop crying. With every new object his mum or Ettie magics up, the tears flow afresh. The shelves are stocked with food and toys and blankets, everything and anything a regular pet or magical creature might need for their comfort, care or fun is neatly laid out on the brand new shelves.

His office is decked out with a desk and a chair and more books than he might ever read about animals and their various maladies. The treatment room is kitted out with so many lotions and potions and special ingredients, that Sticks almost wants a sick animal to come along, just so he can tend to it.

The whole place is a triumph. It's exactly what he wanted, but more.

'I don't know what to say,' he says, as his mum conjures up a big jar of sweets to sit on the counter.

'For your customers,' she says. 'And for you.'

He grins and takes a sherbet lemon. 'I don't eat as many sweets now, mum, not now I've got my custard tap.'

Toady-loo grins and hugs him. 'I'm so proud of you. We both are.'

'We are,' Dave says, looking around with wide eyes. 'I've been married to your mother for a long time, and I'm still amazed by the things she can do. It's all so effortless.'

Ettie grins at his words, because he's also describing her magic perfectly. Now she has such ease about her when she performs magic. She doesn't need as much ritual as she used to, she doesn't feel the need to study and revise and work at her craft. Now it's part of her.

'So the grand opening is tomorrow?' Toady-loo asks.

Sticks nods. 'Yeah – we've asked everyone who helped to come, and a few other people too.'

'The King will be here,' Dayne says. 'I want to say thank you for letting my dad and brothers help us yesterday.'

It's still incredible to her and anyone who knows her dad and brothers that the King not only gave them a job, but a place to live too.

Dayne doesn't mention to Sticks' parents about what her dad and her brothers used to get up to. She's hoping the people they hurt will turn up tomorrow, and that they know they'll be safe. She knows her dad and brothers won't let her down. People change and thank goodness they do.

'One last thing,' Dayne says with a grin. 'Actually two.'

She flies out of the shop, and none of them are sure where she's gone.

Amma walks in, laughing. 'Dayne just flew into me. She's fine but she was in a hurry. Look at this place!' She lets out a squeal and runs at Sticks. She grabs him in a hug, even though her arms could never get all the way around him. He smiles and pats her head.

Ettie smiles. He treats her like a buddy, and she thinks Amma wants more than that. Maybe.

'Amma, I want you to meet my parents. They went monster hunting before you came to work at the shop.'

Amma blushes and straightens her hair, holding out a hand.

'Hello. I'm Amma.'

'Toady-loo,' Toady-loo says.

'Dave,' Dave says with a big smile. He's a human and he can never get over meeting all the weird and wonderful creatures that he has since meeting his wife, and still does, especially on their travels.

Dayne flies back, interrupting the introductions.

'Here!' Dayne is holding up two certificates. Sticks' healing certificate and his peddling licence.

'Oh!' He's crying again, and this time most of them join in.

The joy that the shop is finished and ready for all his animals, after the horror and heartbreak of the shop burning down, cannot be underestimated.

'This is just wonderful,' he says, as his mum takes them from Dayne and Sticks them to the wall, right out front where everyone will be able to see them.

'What a day!' Sticks says. 'This place was a wreck yesterday, and now it's ready for the animals. I don't want them cooped up a moment longer. They're going to be so happy here.'

'They will,' Amma says, and touches his arm. 'I'll help you fetch them, if you like.'

'Sure,' Sticks says, holding up his hand for a high five. 'Everyone can help, it'll make it quicker.'

Amma nods. 'Yeah, great.'

They all troop into the alehouse, and Sticks opens the door. The animals slither, strut or pad straight over to him, and Amma, and then sticks tells them the good news.

'Finally,' drawls a purple beaked badger. 'We've been in here forever.'

Sticks grins and ruffles the badger's fur.

'Let's go, whinge bag.'

The badger bristles, but he follows Sticks, Amma and the others back to the shop. Some animals need to be carried, but most of them are happy to walk, slither or fly.

Sticks stands just beaming as he watches them all familiarise themselves with the new space. It's wonderful – much better than what they had before, and while Sticks could never be happy that Hooves and Horns burned down, Hooves and Horns two is pretty spectacular.

He feels a cool rush of air and knows that one of the animals – probably Betty – has found the door to the garden.

He lets out a laugh.

'Best day ever,' he says.

When they finally convince him to leave, they lock up the shop and head inside the alehouse.

Chapter 84

'Hey where's Posey,' Ettie says, suddenly realising that the troll didn't make it back out to the shop. 'She'd love to see it all stocked up and full of animals.'

'I'll knock for her,' Dayne says and the rest head to the den, where the fire is burning low.

Dayne rushes in. 'She's gone.'

'Gone?'

'Gone. Her stuff is there. But she's not. I knocked, but there was no answer, so I went in. She's not in her room and she's not in the bar room or the kitchen.'

'Weird,' Ettie says. 'Did we miss her – maybe she went the back way as we were coming in the front?'

'I don't think so, but I'll look.' Dayne flies out of the room, and Ettie looks at Toady. Toady-loo is an experienced witch.

'What do you think?'

'Can I go in her room?'

Ettie nods and shows her the way.

They all gather outside the door, and Toady goes in. Immediately she doubles over, clutching at her stomach. Dave rushes to her side, arm on her back.

'Darling, what's wrong?'

Sticks takes her hand. 'Mum, what's wrong?'

'She didn't leave,' Toady-loo says, stricken. 'She was taken. By trolls.'

Ettie lets out a deep breath. 'She's a troll. So her family?'

Toady holds up a hand. 'And a goblin. Two trolls. One goblin. Nasty. And angry. They ambushed her, put a hood over her head, and took her.'

'They can't do that!' Sticks says, red with fury.

Dayne flies along the corridor. 'No sign. What?'

'She's been taken,' Ettie says. 'I think it might be her family.'

'No! They wouldn't kidnap their own daughter, surely?' Dave looks horrified.

'Trolls are difficult,' Toady-loo says.

They move through to the den.

'What do we do?' Ettie asks, again looking to Toady-loo and Dave. Sticks' parents have become all of their parents. Dave is pacing the floor.

Toady-loo clasps her hands. 'I need something of hers. We can follow her – like a dog.'

'You can do that?' Ettie's eyes are wide.

'You can too,' Toady says, with a soft smile. 'It's a witch thing.'

'Really? I never knew.'

'It's old magic, but really useful. I used it to cheat during hide and seek when I was little. Nobody could ever figure out how I always won.'

Dayne holds up a t-shirt. 'This is hers.'

Toady takes hold of it and then passes it to Ettie. Ettie copies her, taking a deep breath and then closing her eyes.

'They're not close,' Toady says.

'We were in the shop ages. What if they've hurt her?'

'I'm sure they haven't. I don't think they'd steal her back just to hurt her.'

'Do we know anything about her family?' Dave asks. 'Do they get along?'

Ettie shakes her head. 'She hasn't really shared much, but I don't think it's good – I think she ran away from them and ended up here.'

'We need to go.' Dayne's usual smile has been replaced with a look of utter despair.

'Sticks, stay here with dad and Amma. We don't all need to go. Dayne, come with us, because you can fly. Let's go.'

Out the front of the alehouse, they pause, and Toady-loo conjures up a broomstick for her and one for Ettie.

'We don't know where we're going,' she says. 'So we need transport.'

Ettie bites her lip, and Toady frowns.

'You've never flown before?'

Ettie shakes her head. 'My mum frowned upon them, and then we never learned in the academy, because they assumed all the witches already knew.'

Toady smiles. 'It's easy. Just push down to go, pull up slowly to fly higher. Sharp up to stop, and then bend whichever direction you want to go. Don't lean backwards, stay low and forward. If you fall off, magic yourself a soft landing.'

Ettie clears her throat. 'Sounds easy,' she lies. They have to help Posey, and two witches on the scent must be better than one.

'Ready?' Toady-loo asks, sitting astride her stick like a pro.

Ettie clambers on hers, sure she's going to fall off from a great height, forget to magic a soft landing in the panic and then break her neck. But she nods and smiles.

Dayne flutters close to her. 'You can do this.'

Ettie nods. They have to do this.

'For Posey!' Dayne shouts, and the three of them take off.

Chapter 85

Ettie is happy to stay behind Toady and let her lead the way. She's never heard of tracking magic in witches before, but even though she's hanging back, she can feel that they are going the right way. It's instinctual. She grins – she loves that she still has things to learn.

Dayne flies by the side of her. Ettie smiles; if she falls off, it's more likely that Dayne will catch her than she'll remember to help herself.

'I feel sick,' Dayne shouts, the wind taking her words as she says them.

'Me too,' Ettie says, and it's true. She's gutted that while they were looking at the shop, and filling it with stuff, and getting the animals settled, poor Posey was probably feeling sick and scared and alone. She wishes they'd been there to help her.

'Getting closer,' Toady-loo shouts over her shoulder, taking a sharp right. Ettie turns the broomstick, and almost topples. She took that turn with a little bit too much enthusiasm. She grins; it's scary as heck but also exhilarating. This is what Dayne must feel like with her new wings.

Toady-loo slows, and then drops to the floor. Dayne lands easily beside her. Ettie stumbles but doesn't fall off. Her cheeks are flushed.

'I loved that!' she says with a grin. 'If only I wasn't flying for such a bad reason.'

'Flying is incredible,' Toady-loo says. 'I'm sorry you've never done it before.'

Ettie nods. She'll be doing it again for sure.

'I think they're close,' Toady-loo says, sniffing the air, and then closing her eyes. She cocks her head, and then points. 'That way.' She looks at Ettie. 'You think?'

Ettie nods. Toady-loo is right; they're close.

'What are we going to do?'

'I'll knock them out,' Dayne says. 'Who the hell do they think they are? Kidnapping their own family? A grown woman?' Her cheeks are pink with fury.

'We take her back,' Toady-loo says. 'Trolls don't have any magic, nor do goblins. They might be nasty little things – fighters, scrappy, you know, but they're no match for us.'

Dayne laughs. 'Even without your magic they'd be no match for me. I'm Bugsy's daughter. And with five brothers, I learned how to be handy with my fists at the same time I was learning nursery rhymes.'

Ettie grins. She's so glad that they're friends; she would not want to get on the wrong side of Dayne. She's fearsome enough when she's pixie-sized, but she's the same size as Ettie now, and she doesn't doubt that she could knock anyone out.

Toady-loo magics the broomsticks away, and Ettie feels almost sad. She can't wait to fly again.

'Follow me.'

They wend their way through the trees, and then they see a squat building ahead.

'There.'

Resolute, they walk toward it.

'It's a tavern,' Toady-loo says. 'Let's go in as customers.'

'Good idea. They don't know us, so they won't be on guard if we go in.'

They stroll forwards, just three friends in need of a cold drink.

Toady-loo goes first, and then Dayne. Ettie is happy to hang back. She feels sick, she's so nervous. Her stomach is churning, and flipping, and twisting, and she's sweaty. She hates confrontation so much.

But she owes Posey this; they all do. The way she came to work for them, despite hearing what Sticks said, and the way she came up with the drawings for the shop, and helped to build it, with no fuss or bother. She's a true friend – a good person.

Posey is behind the bar when they walk in, a fresh black eye and split lip.

Her eyes widen when she sees the girls, and she shakes her head, dread and panic clear in her expression. Her eyes dart to a table close to the bar, where a grumpy looking goblin and a dolled up troll are sitting.

Toady smiles at her.

'Three pints of ale please.'

Posey nods, and hands shaking she pours their drinks.

Dayne turns her back on Posey, leaning her elbows on the counter, and watching the customers in the room. She's sure the goblin is the stepdad and the troll is the mum. They look nasty – they're clearly there to watch over Posey so she doesn't think about running away again.

Ettie takes her drink, letting her fingers brush Posey's, mouthing the words, it'll be okay, to her. Posey shakes her head, despondent.

The three of them take sips of their ale.

Toady-loo whispers to Posey. 'I'm Sticks' mum. We're here to help you. How do you want to play it?'

Posey shrugs, and looks down, tears overflowing and spilling down her cheeks.

'You should go,' she whispers, and Ettie's heart nearly breaks.

'We can't leave you here,' she says.

'We're not leaving you here,' Dayne says, voice a little louder than it should be. The goblin looks up sharply.

Posey swallows her panic, and keeping her head down, wipes down the counter top.

'I can't leave. They won't let me. They said they'll keep coming back, keep looking for me, hurt anyone they find trying to help me.'

Toady holds out her hand, and Posey takes it.

'Posey, if you want to leave, they can't stop you. We can do it with a fight. We can do it quietly. I can magic away their memory of you, so they won't even know to come looking for you – it'll be like you never existed to them. But we're not leaving you here.'

Chapter 86

'They hurt you,' Ettie says, bile rising in her throat. 'We can't leave you here.'

'I don't want to hurt them,' Posey says, her voice soft, lost.

'I do,' Dayne says, fury making her cheeks pink and her eyes flash.

'I'd rather just go, quietly, if I can.'

'You can,' Toady-loo says. 'We'll take you back to the alehouse, you can live there, or anywhere you like, but you don't have to stay here. They can't make you.'

Posey steps away to serve another customer.

The goblin comes up to the bar.

'Ladies,' he says, his lip curling.

Ettie's not sure how he's managed to say one word and make it sound so distasteful.

Toady-loo smiles at him, lifts her mug of ale and then takes a sip.

Dayne is staring at him, almost daring him to say something. Ettie can't look at him. He's standing so close to her that she's itchy.

She drinks her drink, hand shaking.

'Goblins aren't the brightest,' the man says, his lip curling into a sneer. He's surprisingly soft spoken – Ettie was expecting him to be loud and nasty.

Dayne laughs. 'You're not the brightest?' she asks him, her voice just dripping with sarcasm.

He tuts. 'What I meant is most goblins aren't the brightest.'

'Right,' Dayne says, and Ettie has a feeling she's enjoying herself. She's usually too small to pick fights. 'So most goblins aren't that bright – but you, you're an exception?'

'That's right,' he says, standing up a little straighter and puffing out his portly chest. 'I can smell a rat when it walks in my pub.'

Dayne shakes her head and takes a step toward him. 'The only rat I smell is you.'

He lifts his hand, and then drops it. Ettie wonders if he was going to swing for Dayne the way he clearly did for Posey.

'I think the rat is a bully too,' Dayne says. 'And I think you know if you swing for me, I'll swing for you straight back.'

He lets out a laugh, a really nasty laugh and curls his chunky hand into a fist.

'I'm not scared of a pixie,' he says. 'Even if she's as big as you.'

Dayne grins. 'You're not scared of a pixie? Not even a pixie called Bugsy?'

The change in Posey's stepdad is almost comical. He visibly pales, and his hands start to shake. 'Bu-Bu-Bugsy?'

Dayne grins. 'Yeah, Bu-Bu-Bugsy is my dad. And d'you know what my dad hates more than anything else?'

The goblin takes a step back.

'My dad hates weaselly, snivelling, ugly bullies, who kidnap and beat women. He hates them so much, that even if I tell him that she came away with us, even if I tell him that you promised to leave her alone and never look for her again, even if I tell him that you were so sorry for what you did you all but peed your pants, he still might come looking for you. Just to make sure, you know?'

Posey's mum stands up.

'Posey. I love you; I only ever did what I was told.'

Dayne turns to her. 'You can shut your mouth, too. The pair of you, before I shut them for you. You make me sick. Posey is an amazing person, and you disgust me. Posey, let's go.'

Posey hesitates only for a second, and then pulls off her pinny.

Dayne holds up a hand. 'You forget about her. Or else.'

Toady-loo grins at Ettie, her hands raised up.

'Guess you don't need magic, when you're a gangster's daughter.'

Outside they all laugh. Dayne chuckles.

'Ex gangster,' she says. She turns to Posey. 'Are you okay?'

Posey nods. 'Scared and hurt.'

Ettie and Toady-loo raise their hands at the same time, and both send their healing magic her way, and then laugh.

'That was actually really easy,' Dayne says, with a shrug.

'Easy for you,' Ettie says. 'I'm still sweating.'

'Join hands, ladies,' Toady says. 'Let's go home.'

'Home,' Posey says, and her eyes fill with tears. 'Thank you.'

As they join hands, her mum comes flying out of the tavern, but Posey nods at Ettie and Toady-loo to magic them away. She will never forgive her mum for taking her stepdad's side and she doesn't want to hear her excuses.

With a whoosh they land back at the alehouse, just outside the front door.

Chapter 87

'Tell me again!' Sticks says, slapping his thighs as the tears of laughter roll down his face.

'We've told you three times!' Dayne says.

'All I would say,' Ettie says. 'Is don't cross this girl. And also, I should make you small again. You're way too scary this size.'

Dayne swats at her but laughs. They are all in good spirits, seated around the kitchen table, which has definitely grown in size to accommodate them all.

Ettie and Toady-loo have conjured up a delicious spread and everyone is happily eating and drinking.

'So, the shop opening tomorrow,' Toady says. 'Is it a big celebration?'

'We've got lots of people coming,' Ettie says. 'We got word out to all of Stick's old customers, and we've got some other people coming too.'

Dayne makes a wry face.

'What?' Toady-loo asks. 'Who's coming?'

Dayne sighs. 'My dad was a pretty bad man.' She holds a hand up. 'He's not anymore. But he was. And he did some bad things to some good people. Him and my brothers. I've invited them to the party, to the shop opening, and I've explained that my dad and my brothers are ready to atone.'

'To atone?' Dave pushes his hair out of his eyes. 'Sounds serious. What are they planning to do?'

'I'll let them explain that tomorrow,' Dayne says. 'If you don't mind?'

'No, I love a bit of suspense,' Toady-loo says. Then she grabs Sticks' hand. 'We're just so proud of you baby boy.'

Sticks blushes through his green skin. 'Thanks mum. Thanks dad. I couldn't have done it without my friends though.'

'Friends are one of life's greatest treasures,' Dave says, sniffling.

Toady-loo puts her arm around him. 'Are you getting sentimental?'

Dave shrugs and Toady laughs. 'Humans!'

Posey clears her throat. 'Can I get sentimental for a sec, too?'

They all nod. She looks wan, exhausted.

'I didn't tell you how bad things were at home when I got here. And it didn't matter. You accepted me anyway.' She takes a sip of her drink then gives Sticks a cheeky look. 'Well, once you'd insulted trolls, at least.'

Toady glares at Sticks. He holds his hands up.

'What! I was just saying it, in general.'

Toady gives him a little swat. 'What do people say about ogres?'

He looks down at his plate, too embarrassed to look his mum in the eyes.

'It's okay,' Posey says, and places a hand on Toady's. 'Trolls are awful, same as ogres.'

'Exceptions prove the rule,' Sticks says, and raises his cup of ale to Posey in a toast. She clinks her glass with hers.

'I never got that,' Dayne says, wrinkling her freckly nose.

'Nobody gets it, dear,' Toady-loo says, grinning.

'So once my son insulted you, and then welcomed you...'

Posey grins. 'You all welcomed me. The alehouse welcomed me. I know magic brought me here, and I know I'm supposed to be here, and I just feel like as bad as everything was before, now it's that good.

I have new friends. I have a new job. And maybe, I'll get to be an architect again, which would be amazing.'

'We're so glad you're here,' Ettie says, raising her cup. 'The alehouse knows what we all need even better than we do.'

'To the alehouse,' Dayne says.

'The enchanted alehouse,' Sticks says.

They all lift their mugs and then the rest of the evening passes with food and conversation, laughter and some tears.

Dayne corners Ettie as they head up to bed. 'Can I stay big for one more day?' she asks. 'I didn't realise how much easier life would be if I was big.'

'You can stay big forever if you want to,' Ettie says, giving her a quick hug. 'Nobody gets to tell you what to do.'

'But a pixie that's not pixie sized?'

'Is still a pixie,' Ettie says, and gives her friend a kiss on the cheek.

Dayne smiles, and slips into her room, which is much smaller now that she's so big. She cuddles into bed, wondering what to do. She's really enjoying being the same size as her friends. Well, not the same as Sticks, he's still massive compared to her and Ettie, but not being tiny has benefits. Though eating food isn't quite as much fun now she can't use it as a seat too.

Chapter 88

When they all wake in the morning, the buzz of excitement is palpable.

The alehouse is shut to customers, but they put a sign on the door, welcoming anyone who turns up for a cold pint to come around to the building next door and join the party.

'I'm so excited,' Sticks says, joining everyone outside the building.

'We're all excited,' Amma says, brushing a bit of mud from his top.

'I'm nervous,' Dayne says, fluttering her wings. 'What if my dad and my brothers screw it up?'

'They won't,' Ettie reassures her, patting her arm. 'They could have said no, when you suggested it. They could have refused. You wouldn't have liked it, but there's no way you could have made them do anything. This is your dad we're talking about, remember?'

Dayne giggles. 'Of course. I could never make any of them do anything I wanted.'

'You made them stop their nonsense,' Sticks says, and holds his hand up for a high five.

'True. Maybe they do listen to me.'

'They're happy to do it,' Ettie says.' And that's all that matters.'

'Ooh, our boy!' Toady-loo says, hugging Sticks, her head resting on his belly.

Ettie and Toady-loo joined forces before Sticks rolled out of his swamp and magicked up some bunting and a brand new sign for the shop. Sticks had burst into happy tears when he saw it.

'We just need to wait for mid-day and then you can cut the ribbon,' Ettie says.

A crowd has gathered, and Ettie keeps everyone topped up with cupcakes and drinks. Toady-loo is too busy fussing over Sticks, including giving him spit washes every time she sees a smudge of dust or dirt on his face.

'Mum,' he says, rubbing at his cheek. 'I'm not five anymore.'

'You're never too old for a spit wash,' Toady-loo says with a laugh.

Dayne sighs, leaning against a tree. Posey grins. 'What's that sigh for?'

'Just a happy sigh,' Dayne says. 'Look, Sticks is so happy, and he's got his parents with him.' She takes a cupcake from Ettie with a smile. 'His customers are so happy for him. He's so happy for himself.'

They all laugh. Sticks is clearly in his element – and it's something none of them have really seen before. He's a natural with his customers, laughing and chatting, pleased as punch to see them all. Some of them have brought their pets with them, and he's even happier to see them.

'Who said ogres were bad?' Posey asks, with a cheeky grin.

'Nowhere near as bad as trolls,' Dayne says, laughing when Posey nudges her. Then she sobers. 'Here's my dad. And my brothers. They look like they're being taken to be hung.'

'Cheer up boys,' she says, crouching down to look at them. They are all back to their normal pixie-sized selves.

'Why are you still pretending to be a giant instead of a pixie, sis?' George asks.

Dayne makes a face. 'I like being bigger. I might stay like it.'

The boys laugh, but her dad looks concerned. She rolls her eyes. 'Dad, Ettie can magic me back to normal in the blink of an eye. It's not a big deal.'

'Fine,' he says. 'Right, when do we say our bit?'

'After Sticks says his,' Dayne says. 'We'll open the shop, cut the ribbon, let him make a speech, and then me and Ettie will gather all your...' She trails off, unsure of what to call the people her father and brothers used to terrorise. Customers seems too friendly. Victims is a better term, but she knows her dad won't like it.

'Anyway, we'll gather everyone in the garden, and then you can tell them.'

'I don't love it,' Bugsy says with a sigh.

Dayne gives him a stern look, then extends the look to her brothers, who all manage to look shame faced – even Frank. 'None of them liked what you did to them. None of them deserved getting a beating, even if they paid you. You guys all crossed the line, and you know it. Hell, you obliterated the line. I don't want to hear another word.'

The fact that she's so big and they're so tiny, makes it funnier, and both Ettie and Posey bite their lips and look the other way, so they don't laugh.

Dayne turns back to them, and then giggles. 'I like being bossy,' she says.

Toady-loo bustles over. 'Is it time?'

Ettie nods her head. It's time.

Chapter 89

Ettie uses magic to make her voice louder, welcoming everyone to the special opening of Hooves and Horns, and then she passes Sticks a knife to cut the ribbon.

There's a huge round of applause, lots of whoops and some growls, barks and fire breathing from the assorted pets and animals, both inside the shop and out.

Sticks wipes the tears from his eyes, and Ettie uses the same magic to make his voice heard.

'I don't know what to say,' Sticks says. 'Seeing you all here. My friends, my parents, my housemates… I love my shop – it's always been part of who I am, and getting a new and improved version, after the fire and the upset of all that.' He takes a deep breath and shakes his head, laughing. 'Anyway, thank you, thank you all. I hope to see many of you here and tell your friends to come too.'

There's more applause, and then Sticks heads into the shop, and lets everyone roam around. He sits at the counter and helps himself to a sweet.

'That was easier than I thought,' he says with a grin.

'We're so happy for you,' Ettie says.

'So happy,' Dayne says, kissing his cheek. 'Do you mind if we leave you here, and do the thing with my dad and my brothers?'

'You carry on,' Sticks says, and they can tell he's in his element.

'I'll stay and help you,' Posey says, grinning at Sticks.

'Me too,' Amma says, standing a little closer to Sticks, and glaring a bit at Posey.

Ettie and Dayne head outside.

'I think Amma likes Sticks,' Ettie says.

'Same!' Dayne says.

'He's oblivious,' Ettie says.

'Absolutely. Typical bloke,' Dayne says with a laugh.

'Ready?'

Dayne nods. 'I'm nervous.'

'Why? This is the perfect outcome. The best way to draw a line under it all and get on with life.'

'You think?'

'I do. it was a great idea.'

'Let's go.'

They easily manage to gather up the people that Dayne spent so long helping, and her dad and brothers spent so long tormenting. They congregate by the river, and Dayne could cry. They all look nervous, and it still sickens her that her family made them all like this. Even Derek, a giant who could squash her dad and brothers like bugs, looks anxious.

Bugsy flies over to her.

'We need that magic thing, for my voice to be heard,' he says, frowning.

'Dad.' Dayne lowers her hand and Bugsy climbs into her palm.

'This is weird,' he says.

She laughs, then lifts him to her face, holding him gently against her cheek. 'Dad I love you, but you all know that you took it too far. This is a really easy way of making up for it. Yeah?'

Bugsy nods, and sighs. 'What goes around comes around. So they say.'

'So they say,' Dayne says, and sets him down on a rock. Her brothers join him, all glad that their dad is the spokesman.

Ettie works her magic, and Bugsy nods his thanks.

'Guys and gals,' he says, unused to feeling like this. Small. Sorry. 'I owe all of you. We owe all of you a lifetime of apologies. What we did was wrong, and it was my daughter.' He points up at Dayne. 'Who made me see the error of my ways. Our ways. We were cruel and wrong. We can't undo it, but we'd like to make up for it.'

Dayne nods at him, so proud now.

'Every Sunday, if you need anything, you'll find us here at the alehouse. You come and ask us for help – with anything. Cooking, cleaning, fixing. We want to make up for what we did. We want to show that we're sorry. You can leave a note for us, if you can't make it, or send someone to fetch us. We're ready to show all of you that we're sorry.'

Dayne looks at her dad, clearly uncomfortable, pulling at the collar of his t-shirt. Her brothers look equally unhappy. Frank is shifting from foot to foot, and the others are looking at their feet.

She clears her throat. She doesn't need to be loud – this group is small enough to hear her big-sized voice.

'I know you were hurt. I know we hurt you.'

'You didn't,' Derek shouts out and then flinches.

'You're right,' Bugsy says. 'I know what Dayne did for all of you and I couldn't be more ashamed of myself and more proud of her. All we can ask for is your forgiveness and all we can beg for is a chance to make it right.'

Dayne nods at him. He's done everything he can, everything she wanted him to. If people choose to take him up on it, that's their choice, not hers.

'I wish I could hug you properly,' Bugsy says. 'You're too big.'

Dayne grins. She really is enjoying towering over everyone.

Chapter 90

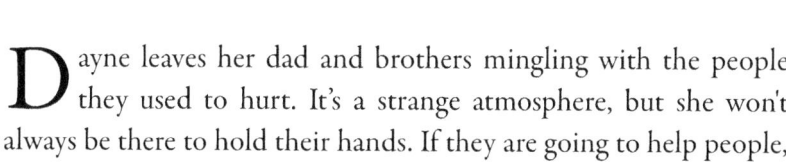

Dayne leaves her dad and brothers mingling with the people they used to hurt. It's a strange atmosphere, but she won't always be there to hold their hands. If they are going to help people, they'll be doing it without Dayne, and so they need to figure out a way to feel comfortable around everyone. Without her.

They head back into Hooves and Horns, and everyone is having a ball. Toady-loo has magicked up more party food, and cakes, and the animals are enjoying being petted by so many people.

'I've made my first sale,' Sticks says, with a grin. 'Sold a frog faced wobble wombat.'

'A what?' Ettie shakes her head and then holds up her hand. 'You know what, it doesn't matter.'

Sticks laughs. 'Lovely creatures they are – all wobbly and friendly.'

'I'm sure,' Dayne says with a laugh.

'How did the thing with your dad and brothers go?' Sticks asks, popping a sweet in his mouth.

'Good,' Dayne says, then cocks her head. 'Awkward, but good. They have to try, right?'

Sticks shrugs. 'It's all any of us can do. I've spent my life bending over backwards to prove I'm the good guy.'

'Oh, and you are Sticks.'

'So good,' Ettie says, helping herself to a cupcake from a tray and popping it in her mouth.

'But they were bad,' he says, quietly, like he's worried one of them might hear him. 'They have some work to do.'

'Well, luckily none of them are afraid of hard work,' Dayne says.

A loud herald interrupts them.

'Ooh, the King?' Dayne says, clapping her hands. 'That'll get people talking about this place, Sticks – the royal seal of approval.'

He straightens up, puffing up his chest.

'Yeah. Let's go out.'

It is the King, in his carriage, and also Briella and Alaysia.

Briella grins at Dayne. 'I love being able to hug you!'

Dayne grins; it's her favourite thing about being big. Proper hugs.

Briella hugs them all, and they bow and curtsey to the King and Alaysia.

He grins. 'Looks good, Sticks,' he says, clapping him on the back.

Sticks grins. 'Would you like to take a look inside, your honour? I've got some cute baby wing bats the Princesses might like.'

The King nods. 'Maybe – it might help cheer Alaysia up.' He shakes his head. 'I really thought that fortune telling thing would help, but it hasn't.'

'But at least she's out and about,' Sticks says. 'Whenever I've got a poo headed giant chicken down in the dumps, I just send it into the fresh air.'

Alaysia glares at him, her ears turning pink at the shame of being compared to a poo headed giant chicken, and Ettie and Dayne cover up their laughter with coughs. Briella snorts and then tries to turn that into a cough. The King glares at her, and she cannot look at him.

Briella clears her throat, and then smiles brightly when her father shoots a look at her, hoping he'll forget that she laughed at her sister. 'Shall we?'

She tucks her arm through his and they head inside the shop.

The customers bow and curtsey as the King passes and a few of the children get super excited to see the Princesses.

'Hey, sir.'

Sticks feels a tug on his tunic and turns to see Theodora, the little goblin who brought him a quack quack at the old shop. Nasty beggars, quack quacks. Luckily the little girl never realised how much danger she was in.

'Hey Theodora, how are you?'

'I'm good. I brought my mum.' She points shyly to a lady who waves at Sticks, and then turns her attention back to the King and the Princesses. 'She's going to buy me a pet,' Theodora says, her eyes wide with excitement.

Her mum comes over. 'Sticks?'

He nods.

'We'd like a pet – something easy to look after, something that won't bite or burn us. Something... simple.'

Sticks grins. 'May I?' He gestures at Theodora, his arms open. She nods, and he scoops her up, and sits her on his shoulders. She claps her hands, and then holds onto his mane of hair so she doesn't fall off.

'She's so cute,' Dayne says.

'So cute,' Ettie agrees. 'I hope he gives them a really sweet and easy to look after pet. And not, you know, something he would have liked.'

They both laugh.

'This is lovely,' Briella says, sidling over to them and leaning on the counter. 'My father is impressed. He's definitely going to buy something for my sister. Sticks is with him now. And a little goblin girl. Alaysia went out for some air by the river. I think Sticks upset her.'

Ettie covers her mouth. 'Don't. He honestly doesn't realise what he's saying.'

Dayne grins. 'I think he thinks being compared to an animal is a compliment.'

'Even if it's a poo headed giant chicken?' Briella asks, her voice high pitched from trying not to laugh.

'Stop!'

They are still giggling when the King comes over, holding Theodora's hand.

Sticks has three fuzzy balls in his hands.

'Dingleflips,' he says, as though that helps any of them.

This sets them off giggling again while the King buys one of them for each of his daughters and one for Theodora.

Her mother blushes and curtesy and bows all at the same time, almost falling over.

Chapter 91

By the end of the afternoon everyone is exhausted. Toady-loo and Dave excuse themselves, and head back to their monster hunt, which still makes Ettie extremely nervous. And suspicious. Very suspicious.

The King, Briella and Alaysia head back to the palace, after they finally found Alaysia out by the river, talking to Frank of all people.

Amma heads home, ready to start work at nine sharp. She already knows that Sticks will still be sleeping in his swamp, but she's more than happy to help, and to step up and assist him in any way she can.

The four of them sit in the den, fire burning and windows open.

'Does the fire ever go out?' Posey asks, and Ettie shakes her head.

'It's a magic fire – it will burn forever.'

'I like it. It smells good and it's comforting,' Dayne says. 'I really hope people ask my dad and brothers to help them. Helping people feels so good – I know it will do them good, not just making up for what they did, but making them better people too.'

'I don't think anything would make my family better people,' Posey says, expression hard to read.

'It must have been awful when they came here,' Sticks says. 'I'm sorry we weren't here to protect you.'

Posey shrugs. 'I don't need protecting, but I know what you mean.'

'I need protecting,' Sticks says with a bashful grin. 'Your family still scare the living daylights out of me,' he says, looking at Dayne.

'Don't upset her,' Ettie says in a mock whisper. 'She's almost as big as you are now.'

They all laugh, because Sticks is still enormous compared to Dayne.

'A good day?' Ettie asks him, and he nods.

'Best day ever. I can't wait to get back to work. Well, you know, a bit of work. I don't want to work too hard.'

They laugh.

Ettie straightens in her seat.

'Puddle Town feels magical,' Ettie says. 'When we were all outside, listening to your speech, waiting for you to open your shop... it felt like a community was coming together. It felt...'

'What?' Dayne asks, watching the smile covering Ettie's face. 'What are you thinking?'

'I'm thinking about Puddle Town,' she says. 'Those empty houses across the road. All the space...'

'What?' Posey asks.

'I don't know,' Ettie says. 'Just thinking, thinking it might be worth talking to the King.'

'About?'

'About Puddle Town, about fixing those houses up, maybe getting shops or people or something going on in them. Maybe building other stuff too.'

'I love that idea,' Dayne says.

'And Posey could plan it, and Dayne could build it,' Sticks says. 'And I could... watch.' He chuckles.

'And Puddle Town would become more than just a crossroads,' Ettie says. 'It would become what it was for a little while today – bustling and busy, a place for people to go and do things.'

'A community,' Dayne says.

'A place where everyone is welcome,' Posey says. 'A safe place.'

'A haven,' Sticks adds, and Ettie points at him. 'Exactly.'

Dayne giggles. 'We don't frown in Puddle Town.'

'We don't. But what if loads of other people didn't either?'

'I think we need to go to visit the King.'

'Tomorrow.'

'Tomorrow.'

'And now?'

'Snackage!' Sticks practically roars the word, making them all jump, but Ettie obliges, conjuring up the food and drink they want as they call it out.

'Are you all happy for me to stay?' Posey asks after a while, when the food platters are almost empty, and they're all stuffed.

'Of course,' Ettie says, straightening in her chair. 'Aren't you happy here?'

'I am,' Posey says. 'Maybe not forever – trolls like their own space. But I also know that trolls are…'

Sticks holds a hand up. 'I know what I said, but that was trolls in general, and not you. You're nothing but loveliness and kindness.'

Posey smiles.

'We want you here,' Dayne says. 'But it's also not up to us. The alehouse brought you here, and only you get to decide when you're ready to leave.'

'Like Graily,' Ettie says. 'Ooh, I wonder when we'll hear back from her.'

'Soon, I hope,' Dayne says.

'You're part of the family now,' Sticks says to Posey.

'That makes me happy,' Posey says with a grin. 'And thank you, all of you. I might get to be an architect because you all had faith in me.'

'You had faith in yourself,' Ettie says.

'My shop is brilliant because of you,' Sticks says, helping himself to the crumbs left on a plate. Ettie conjures up another cupcake for him, and he grins. 'You know what this would be good with?'

'Custard!' they all shout and laugh as he trundles off to cover his cake with custard.

'Take a bowl,' Ettie shouts, but he doesn't listen.

'That's going to be messy,' Dayne says.

Posey covers her hands and lets out a tiny sob. They both rush to her side and put their arms around her.

'I'm fine, I'm fine,' she says, through her tears and sniffles. 'Just happy. Happier than I ever thought I could be.'

Sticks comes back, custard drips all down his chin and t-shirt.

'Are you okay?' he asks, sitting on the chair opposite Posey.

'I am.' She looks up at his custardy face, and smiles. 'I really am.'

Chapter 92

The morning brings rain, and Ettie makes the fire burn a little bit lower. It's a muggy day, and she already feels flustered and sweaty.

'Morning,' Posey says, padding into the room. 'Look at the rain. I guess we'll get to see if our handy work next door holds up.'

Ettie laughs. 'Don't. Everyone worked so hard, imagine if the rain just ruins it all.'

'It's well built,' Posey says, but she looks worried.

'It's really well made and really well designed. You know your stuff. Don't question yourself.'

'It's hard not to,' Poesy says. 'When your family's hard on you, you tend to be hard on you too.'

'Tell me about it,' Ettie says with a laugh. 'Tea?'

Posey nods, and Ettie conjures up a teapot full of tea, and some cups and saucers.

'My family aren't mean to me,' Ettie says. 'They just want nothing to do with me.'

'Why not?'

Ettie shrugs, and sucks on her teeth. 'Because I wasn't good enough for them, I suppose. They had high hopes, and high expectations.'

'And you didn't meet them?'

Ettie shakes her head sadly. 'I don't mind so much now, I get to live here, and I have friends, and I'm a good witch.'

'You are.'

'But for a long time, it hurt me. And when I see Dayne with her family and Sticks with his parents... it hurts all over again.'

'I know what you mean. Shame you can't pick your family.'

'True. I know who I'd pick,' Ettie says.

'Everyone you met here?'

'Everyone I met here. And maybe a few from the academy.'

Ettie's thinking about Liss. But she's not sure where their friendship stands anymore. Were they really best friends if she can't forgive her? Were they really best friends if Liss did what she did?

'Okay?' Posey asks, and Ettie nods. A worry for another day.

'Hungry?'

Posey nods.

'Let's go to the kitchen. I'm going to cook.'

Posey follows her through.

'Morning,' Dayne comes into the kitchen, rubbing her eyes and yawning. 'I could have slept for another whole night.'

'You've been working hard.'

'So have you. Stopping time, changing the sizes of people...'

Ettie smiles. 'The time stopped, but the work you did didn't. I tried to send energy and healing your way, to all of you, but you're bound to ache for a few days.'

'I suppose. It's a good tired though – that tired you feel when you've done a good day's work, honest work, and you feel exhausted but happy.'

'It's been a brilliant few days,' Posey says. 'Do you really think the King might say yes? To Puddle Town?'

Ettie shrugs. 'We don't know him very well, but he's a good King, a sensible man. I think he'd want what was best for the place.'

'We'll go after breakfast?' Dayne asks.

'Yeah. We'll wait for Sticks and all head up together.'

'I bet he's still sleeping in his swamp,' Dayne says, rolling her eyes.

'Not likely,' he says, lumbering into the room, a massive smile on his face. 'I was up with the sun, in the shop, done some sweeping, done some tidying, done some cuddling with snuggly little munchkins.'

They all laugh. 'Sounds perfect,' Dayne says. 'I can't wait to come and help.'

'Me neither.'

'We'll all help,' Ettie says. 'Just tell us what you need and when.'

'But don't give us all the messy jobs,' Dayne says. 'Or I'll...' She holds up her fists.

Sticks grins. 'I'll wait until you're tiny again, and then I'll give you the messy jobs.'

Dayne takes a deep breath. 'I might stay big,' she says, wondering why she's so worried about what they all might think. 'Except on Sundays. When my family visit, I think I'd like to be small, well, the same as them. It's easier for talking and hugging.'

Ettie nods. 'Your call,' she says. 'It's totally up to you.'

'I know. I just... being a giant pixie is weird.'

'No weirder than anything this life has to offer. If you're happy being big, then big you shall stay.'

Ettie grins and conjures up some pastries and fruit.

'I thought you were going to cook?' Posey says, and Ettie shrugs.

'I was, but it seemed too much like hard work.'

They laugh and dig into the hot tea and buttery, flaky pastries. Ettie keeps the food coming, and nobody complains.

As if they ever would.

Chapter 93

'I'm nervous to meet the King,' Posey says, as they stand outside and join hands.

'Didn't you meet him yesterday?'

'Well I curtseyed at him, but I didn't talk to him.'

'He's lovely. So's Briella.'

'How come you know the royal family? That seems real fancy.'

'Sticks helped the King with something.'

'Then Briella ran away from the palace and pretended to be Graily.'

'Graily? The one who went to France?'

'Yeah. She was like all of us – having a bad day, when the alehouse helped her. But she pretended she was Graily.'

'Really?'

'But we think she was supposed to, because if Briella hadn't come to us, there's no way Graily would ever have left.'

'She'd been locked up.'

'In the palace.'

'What?'

'Yeah. But Briella came to us, then we went to the King. It took a minute, but it all got figured out.'

'And now you can pop in to see him?'

'Well, we wouldn't say we could pop in, but I think this is a good idea. We could ask him for help, or offer him help. I don't think any of us would be cheeky enough to ask him for a favour.'

'I might be,' Dayne says, cocking her head as though she's considering what she might ask him for.

They laugh, and with a whoosh they land in the palace grounds.

'This is glorious,' Posey says, eyes wide as she takes in the palace and the grounds and the people.

'It is.'

They're showed to the library, and it's the Princess Briella who comes in first, carrying Flump the fluffy, chubby penguin. As soon as he sees Sticks, he goes wild, flapping his wings and pedalling his little feet.

'Traitor,' she tells him, before kissing his fluffy head, and letting Sticks take him.

'He's adorable,' Posey says, 'does he bite?'

'He would have bitten Dayne when she was little, if I'd given him a chance, but he won't bite you.'

'Even though I'm a...'

Sticks smiles. 'Look at him. Look at him with me. He doesn't have the same prejudices that people have. Ogres, trolls, pixies we're all the same to him.'

Poesy smiles and pets him gently. 'He's so soft.'

'The softest,' Briella says. 'My sister still won't cuddle him because of the whole true love match nonsense.'

Posey makes a confused face, and Ettie pats her arm. 'I'll fill you in later.'

Posey nods, and they all coo at Flump for at least twenty minutes, then Ettie clears her throat.

'We wanted to see your father.'

'The King,' Posey adds, like Briella might not know.

Briella smiles. 'He's here somewhere.'

She sends a servant to find her father and to bring some tea and biscuits.

'Hello again!' the King says, beaming when he comes in. He gives Flump a little tickle under the chin.

'We had an idea,' Ettie says. 'And we wanted to run it by you.'

The King nods and takes a seat, smiling when the tea and biscuits come in. He helps himself to a biscuit, while Dayne plays mother.

'Your ideas have been good so far...' he says. 'Your father is working out wonderfully,' he says to Dayne. 'And your brothers, well I must admit I haven't figured out how to tell them apart yet, but they're definitely good boys.'

Dayne grins, proud as punch.

'Go on,' the King urges her, sipping his tea, and smacking his lips.

'What did you think when you came to the shop yesterday?'

The King frowns. 'Well, I think the shop is wonderful. It was lovely to see all those people. It was very uplifting.'

Ettie grins. 'Well, Posey here,'

Posey chokes on her tea, coughing and then wiping her mouth, and then standing up to dip into a curtsey. 'Sorry, your majesty.'

The King shakes his head. 'Nothing to be sorry for.'

'Posey here,' Ettie continues, 'designed the shop for Sticks. She's an architect.'

'Well, that's very clever,' the King says, nabbing another biscuit.

'Thank you,' Posey says, blushing and unable to look him in the eye.

'We thought yesterday was wonderful too,' Ettie says. 'A real sense of community.'

The King nods, and Briella is leaning forward in her seat, biscuit in hand, waiting to see what Ettie has to say.

'We wondered if you might think it's a good idea to develop the houses opposite the alehouse and the shop. To make Puddle Town more than just a crossroads. To make it a community, a place where people can shop or gather or make friends...'

The King closes his eyes, mulling it over. Briella silently claps her hands. Great idea, she mouths.

The King opens his eyes. 'I find that idea very pleasing,' he says. 'Tell me more.'

'Well, Posey would design the place – all to be approved by you of course. Dayne would help to build or renovate the place, along with my magic, like we did with the shop.'

'I wanted to help build the shop,' Sticks says, feeding a bit of biscuit to Flump. 'I felt it was important that I built it up after what happened to the last shop.'

'Of course,' the King says, steepling his fingers.

'But with my magic, Dayne's skills and Posey's vision – it would be quick, cost effective and really, really lovely.'

Dayne grins. 'Imagine having what we had yesterday, every day. A real gathering place for all the people to meet.'

'North, South, East, West, they can all come together in Puddle Town.'

They all look at him, expectantly, and he nods.

'I love it.' He lifts his cup of tea. 'To Puddle Town.'

They all repeat the phrase, happy and excited and nervous too.

Chapter 94

They stay for more than an hour, chatting with Briella, while the King has other work to do. They eventually pull Sticks away from Flump and they head back to the alehouse with a quick whoosh.

'I'll go and open the bar,' Posey says, and the others gather in the den.

'That went well,' Dayne says. 'I'm really excited. What do you think we need here? What shops?'

'I don't know,' Ettie says. 'A book shop would be nice.'

'A sweet shop,' Sticks says, licking his lips.

'What would you like, Dayne?'

She shrugs. 'I don't know. Well, I used to go to these little shops with my mum. I don't know what you'd call them, but they had all sorts of weird and wonderful things in them – old things, new things, weird things.'

'A curiosity shop?' Ettie asks, not sure if she's right.

'Maybe,' Dayne says, with another shrug. 'I'm more excited about helping than I am about what actually ends up there.'

'I think it could be really wonderful. Like you said, Sticks, it could be a haven. A safe place for everyone and anyone.'

'I love it. I'm so excited,' Dayne says, clapping her hands and fluttering her wings.

'I'd like a custard shop,' Sticks says, with a grin.

'A shop full of custard?' Ettie looks doubtful.

He shrugs. 'No custard flavour things... sweet, cakes, doughnuts, soup.'

'Custard soup. Wouldn't that just pretty much be custard?' Dayne says, laughing. 'You're a custard fiend.'

'I might go and get a bit now,' he says. 'Be a nice snack.'

'Be lovely,' Ettie says, sharing a look with Dayne. They both hold in their giggles.

Then there's a knock at the door.

'Shall we see who's there first? Before you get all custardy?'

Sticks nods and they all head to the front door and when they open it, Dayne squeals.

'Graily!'

Graily grins and shakes her head. 'Look at you! How did you get so big?'

Dayne grins. 'Ettie.'

'I love it.'

'We've missed you. Come in, come in. Who's with you?'

Graily steps aside and a tall red woman, who would look almost human if it wasn't for the antenna coming off her head, and the black spots covering her body.

Ettie shakes her head. It can't be. Surely?

'Smudge?'

The woman nods, and Dayne squeals again.

'Come in, come in, we have so much to catch up on.'

THE END

WANT MORE FROM GEMMA PERFECT?

.

Visit her website, www.gemmaperfect.com

.

Notes on the book...

This book was so hard to finish, and not because it was hard to write, but because of HEALTH.

The first three months of the year battered me with eye infections, ear infections, tooth ache – and a tooth out, skin breakouts, a burn on my wrist from soup of all things which stopped me writing for weeks, it was so painful. I had five lots of antibiotics over a three and a half week period, and I could barely remember what day of the week it was, never mind write a book!

I cancelled the pre order for this book twice, which usually puts you in Amazon pre order jail for a year, but luckily, they have stopped this for the time being, so I was able to get the pre order for book three up at the same time as publishing this.

I had a ball writing about Ettie, Sticks and Dayne again – and I hope you're happy that Graily came back! I love these guys so much, and I have so many plans for them – I hope you stick around for a long time, just to keep up with all their shenanigans.

Again, I hope you'll excuse the modern-day food in what I otherwise envisage as a medieval setting – I can't not put all the good food in. Imagine Sticks without his custard tap – you can't, can you? It would be cruel.

Thank you!
Gemma

.

Other books by Gemma Perfect
YA fantasy
The Kingmaker Series
The Kingmaker

Seize the Crown
Born to Rule
The first Queen
The Accidental Witch Trilogy
The Accidental Witch
The Accidental Invitation
The Accidental End
The Fairy Queen Trilogy
The Rise of the Fairy Queen
The Fall of the Fairy Queen
The Triumph of the Fairy Queen
The Unbitten Duology
Unbitten
Unbroken
.

Romance
Learn to Love Again
Love Song
Love Fool
Addicted to Love
It Must be Love
.

Thrillers
Bloody Justice
Deadly Justice

Printed in Dunstable, United Kingdom